Amelia Edith Huddleston Barr

Winter Evening Tales

Amelia Edith Huddleston Barr

Winter Evening Tales

ISBN/EAN: 9783337088675

Printed in Europe, USA, Canada, Australia, Japan

Cover: Foto ©Andreas Hilbeck / pixelio.de

More available books at **www.hansebooks.com**

WINTER EVENING TALES.

BY

AMELIA E. BARR,

Author of "A Bow of Orange Ribbon," "Jan Vedder's Wife,"
"Friend Olivia," etc., etc.

———

PUBLISHED BY

THE CHRISTIAN HERALD,

Louis Klopsch, Proprietor,

BIBLE HOUSE, NEW YORK.

Press and Bindery of
HISTORICAL PUBLISHING CO.,
PHILADELPHIA.

PREFACE.

In these "Winter Evening Tales," Mrs. Barr has spread before her readers a feast that will afford the rarest enjoyment for many a leisure hour. There are few writers of the present day whose genius has such a luminous quality, and the spell of whose fancy carries us along so delightfully on its magic current. In these "Tales"—each a perfect gem of romance, in an artistic setting—the author has touched many phases of human nature. Some of the stories in the collection sparkle with the spirit of mirth; others give glimpses of the sadder side of life. Throughout all, there are found that broad sympathy and intense humanity that characterize every page that comes from her pen. Her men and women are creatures of real flesh and blood, not deftly-handled puppets; they move, act and speak spontaneously, with the full vigor of life and the strong purpose of persons who are participating in a real drama, and not a make-believe.

Mrs. Barr has the rare gift of writing from heart to heart. She unconsciously infuses into her readers a liberal share of the enthusiasm that moves the people of her creative imagination. One cannot read any of her books without feeling more than a spectator's interest; we are, for the moment, actual sharers in the joys and the sorrows, the misfortunes and the triumphs of the men and women to whom she introduces us. Our sympathy, our love, our admiration, are kindled by their noble and attractive qualities; our mirth is excited by the absurd and incongruous aspects of some characters, and our hearts are thrilled by the frequent revelation of such goodness and true human feeling as can only come from pure and noble souls.

In these "Tales," as in many of her other works, humble life has held a strong attraction for Mrs. Barr's pen. Her mind and heart naturally turn in this direction; and although her wonderful talent, within its wide range, deals with all stations and conditions of life, she has but little relish for the gilded artificialities of society, and a strong love for those whose condition makes life for them something real and earnest and definite of purpose. For this reason, among many others, the Christian people of America have a hearty admiration for Mrs. Barr and her work, knowing it to be not only of surpassing human interest, but spiritually helpful and inspiring, with an influence that makes for morality and good living, in the highest sense in which a Christain understands the term.

G. H. SANDISON.

New York, 1896.

CONTENTS.

Winter Evening Tales.

CASH.

A PROBLEM OF PROFIT AND LOSS, WORKED BY DAVID LOCKERBY.

PART I.

"Gold may be dear bought."

A narrow street with dreadful "wynds" and "vennels" running back from it was the High street of Glasgow at the time my story opens. And yet, though dirty, noisy and overcrowded with sin and suffering, a flavor of old time royalty and romance lingered amid its vulgar surroundings; and midway of its squalid length a quaint brown frontage kept behind it noble halls of learning, and pleasant old courts full of the "air of still delightful studies."

From this building came out two young men in academic costume. One of them set his face dourly against the clammy fog and drizzling rain, breathing it boldly, as if it was the balmiest oxygen; the other, shuddering, drew his scarlet toga around him and said, mournfully, ''Ech, Davie, the High street is an ill furlong on the de'il's road! I never tread it, but I think o' the weary, weary miles atween it and Eden.''

''There is no road without its bad league, Willie, and the High street has its compensations; its prison for ill-doers, its learned college, and its holy High Kirk. I am one of St. Mungo's bairns, and I'm not above preaching for my saint.''

''And St. Mungo will be proud of your birthday yet, Davie. With such a head and such a tongue, with knowledge behind, and wit to the fore, there is a broad road and an open door for David Lockerby. You may come even to be the Lord Rector o' Glasgow College yet.''

''Wisdom is praised and starves; I am thinking it would set me better to be Lord Provost of Glasgow city.''

''The man who buried his one talent did not go scatheless, Davie; and what now if he had had ten?''

''You are aye preaching, Willie, and whiles it is very untimeous. Are you going to Mary Moir's to-night?''

''Why should I? The only victory over love is through running away.''

David looked sharply at his companion but as they were at the Trongate there was no time for further remark. Willie Caird turned eastward toward Glasgow Green, David hailed a passing omnibus and was soon set down before a handsome house on the Sauchiehall Road. He went in by the back door, winning from old Janet, in spite of herself, the grimmest shadow of a smile.

''Are my father and mother at home, Janet?''

''Deed are they, the mair by token that they hae been quarreling anent you till the peacefu' folks like mysel' could hae wished them mair sense, or further away.''

''Why should they quarrel about me?''

''Why, indeed, since they'll no win past your ain makin' or marring? But the mistress is some kin to Zebedee's wife, I'm thinking, and she wad fain set you up in a pu'pit and gie you the keys o' St. Peter; while maister is for haeing you it a bank or twa in your pouch, and add Ellenmount to Lockerby, and—''

''And if I could, Janet?''

''Tut, tut, lad! If it werna for 'if' you might put auld Scotland in a bottle.''

''But what was the upshot, Janet?''

''I canna tell. God alone understan's quarreling folk.''

Then David went upstairs to his own room, and when he came down again his face was set as dourly against the coming interview as it had been against the mist and rain. The point at issue was quite familiar to him; his mother wished him to continue his studies and prepare for the ministry. In her opinion the greatest of all men were the servants of the King, and a part of the spiritual power and social influence which they enjoyed in St. Mungo's ancient city she earnestly coveted for her son. "Didn't the Bailies and the Lord Provost wait for them? And were not even the landed gentry and nobles obligated to walk behind a minister in his gown and bands?"

Old Andrew Lockerby thought the honor good enough, but money was better. All the twenty years that his wife had been dreaming of David ruling his flock from the very throne of a pulpit, Andrew had been dreaming of him becoming a great merchant or banker, and winning back the fair lands of Ellenmount, once the patrimonial estate of the house of Lockerby. During these twenty years both husband and wife had clung tenaciously to their several intentions.

Now David's teachers—without any knowledge of these diverse influences—had urged on him the duty of cultivating the unusual talents confided to him, and of consecrating them to some noble service of God and humanity. But David was ruled by many opposite feelings, and had with all his book-learning the very smallest

intimate acquaintance with himself. He
knew neither his strong points nor his
weak ones, and had not even a suspicion of
the mighty potency of that mysterious love
for gold which really was the ruling passion
in his breast.

The argument so long pending he knew
was now to be finally settled, and he was
by no means unprepared for the discussion.
He came slowly down stairs, counting the
points he wished to make on his fingers,
and quite resolved neither to be coaxed nor
bullied out of his own individual opinion.
He was a handsome, stalwart fellow, as
Scotchmen of two-and-twenty go, for it
takes about thirty-five years to fill up and
perfect the massive frames of ''the men of
old Gaul.'' About his thirty-fifth year
David would doubtless be a man of noble
presence; but even now there was a sense
of youth and power about him that was
very attractive, as with a grave smile he
lifted a book, and comfortably disposed
himself in an easy chair by the window.
For David knew better than begin the conversation; any advantages the defendant
might have he determined to retain.

After a few minutes' silence his father
said, ''What are you reading, Davie? It
ought to be a guid book that puts guid
company in the background.''

David leisurely turned to the title

page. '''Selections from the Latin Poets,' father.''

''A fool is never a great fool until he kens Latin. Adam Smith or some book o' commercial economics wad set ye better, Davie.''

''Adam Smith is good company for them that are going his way, father: but there is no way a man may take and not find the humanities good road-fellows.''

''Dinna beat around the bush, guidman; tell Davie at once that you want him to go 'prentice to Mammon. He kens well enough whether he can serve him or no.''

''I want Davie to go 'prentice to your ain brither, guid wife—it's nane o' my doing if you ca' your ain kin ill names—and, Davie, your uncle maks you a fair offer, an' you'll just be a born fool to refuse it.''

''What is it, father?''

''Twa years you are to serve him for £200 a year; and at the end, if both are satisfied, he will gie you sich a share in the business as I can buy you—and, Davie, I'se no be scrimping for such an end. It's the auldest bank in Soho, an' there's nane atween you and the head o' it. Dinna fling awa' good fortune—dinna do it, Davie, my dear lad. I hae lookit to you for twenty years to finish what I hae begun—for twenty years I hae been telling mysel' 'my

Davie will win again the bonnie braes o' Ellenmount.'"

There were tears in old Andrew's eyes, and David's heart thrilled and warmed to the old man's words; in that one flash of sympathy they came nearer to each other than they had ever done before.

And then spoke his mother: "Davie, my son, you'll no listen to ony sich temptation. My brither is my brither, and there are few folk o' the Gordon line a'thegither wrang, but Alexander Gordon is a dour man, and I trow weel you'll serve hard for ony share in his money bags. You'll just gang your ways back to college and tak' up your Greek and Hebrew and serve in the Lord's temple instead of Alexander Gordon's Soho Bank; and, Davie, if you'll do right in this matter you'll win my blessing and every plack and bawbee o' my money." Then, seeing no change in David's face, she made her last, great concession—"And, Davie, you may marry Mary Moir, an' it please you, and I'll like the lassie as weel as may be."

"Your mither, like a' women, has sought you wi' a bribe in her hand, Davie. You ken whether she has bid your price or not. When you hae served your twa years I'se buy you a £20,000 share in the Gordon Bank, and a man wi' £20,000 can pick and choose the wife he likes best. But i'm aboon bribing you—a fair offer isna a bribe."

The concession as to Mary Moir was the one which Davie had resolved to make his turning point, and now both father and mother had virtually granted it. He had told himself that no lot in life would be worth having without Mary, and that with her any lot would be happy. Now that he had been left free in this matter he knew his own mind as little as ever.

"The first step binds to the next," he answered, thoughtfully. "Mary may have something to say. Night brings counsel. I will e'en think over things until the morn."

A little later he was talking both offers over with Mary Moir, and though it took four hours to discuss them they did not find the subject tedious. It was very late when he returned home, but he knew by the light in the house-place that Janet was waiting up for him. Coming out of the wet, dark night, it was pleasant to see the blazing ingle, the white-sanded floor, and the little round table holding some cold moor-cock and the pastry that he particularly liked.

"Love is but cauldrife cheer, my lad," said Janet, "an' the breast o' a bird an' a raspberry tartlet will be nane out o' the way." David was of the same opinion. He was very willing to enjoy Janet's good things and the pleasant light and warmth. Besides, Janet was his oldest confidant and friend—a friend that had never failed him in any of his boyish troubles or youthful scrapes.

It gave her pleasure enough for a while to watch him eat, but when he pushed aside the bird and stretched out his hand for the raspberry dainties, she said, "Now talk a bit, my lad. If others hae wared money on you, I hae wared love, an' I want to ken whether you are going to college, or whether you are going to Lunnon amang the proud, fause Englishers?"

"I am going to London, Janet."

"Whatna for?"

"I am not sure that I have any call to be a minister, Janet—it is a solemn charge."

"Then why not ask for a sure call? There is nae key to God's council chamber that I ken of."

"Mary wants me to go to London."

"Ech, sirs! Sets Deacon Moir's dochter to send a lad a wrang road. I wouldna hae thocht wi' her bringing up she could hae swithered for a moment—but it's the auld, auld story; where the deil canna go by himsel' he sends a woman. And David Lockerby will tyne his inheritance for a pair o' blue e'en and a handfu' o' gowden curls. Waly! waly! but the children o' Esau live for ever."

"Mary said,"—

"I dinna want to hear what Mary said.

It would hae been nae loss if she'd ne'er spoken on the matter; but if you think makin' money, an' hoarding money is the measure o' your capacity you ken yousel', sir, dootless. Howsomever you'll go to your ain room now; I'm no going to keep my auld e'en waking just for a common business body.''

Thus in spite of his father's support, David did not find his road to London as fair and straight as he could have wished. Janet was deeply offended at him, and she made him feel it in a score of little ways very annoying to a man fond of creature comforts and human sympathy. His mother went about the necessary preparations in a tearful mood that was a constant reproach, and his friend Willie did not scruple to tell him that "he was clean out o' the way o' duty.''

''God has given you a measure o' St. Paul's power o' argument, Davie, and the verra tongue o' Apollos—weapons wherewith to reason against all unrighteousness and to win the souls o' men.''

''Special pleading, Willie.''

''Not at all. Every man's life bears its inscription if he will take the trouble to read it. There was James Grahame, born, as you may say, wi' a sword in his hand, and Bauldy Strang wi' a spade, and Andrew Semple took to the balances and the 'rithmetic as a duck takes to the water. Do you not mind the day you spoke anent the African missions to the young men in St. Andrews' Ha'? Your words flew like arrows—every ane o' them to its mark; and your heart burned and your e'en glowed, till we were a' on fire with you, and there wasna a lad there that wouldna hae followed you to the vera Equator. I wouldna dare to bury such a power for good, Davie, no, not though I buried it fathoms deep in gold."

From such interviews as these Davie went home very miserable. If it had not been for Mary Moir he would certainly have gone back to his old seat by Willie Caird in the Theological Hall. But Mary had such splendid dreams of their life in London, and she looked in her hope and beauty so bewitching, that he could not bear to hint a disappointment to her. Besides, he doubted whether she was really fit for a minister's wife, even if he should take up the cross laid down before him—and as for giving up Mary, he would not admit to himself that there could be a possible duty in such a contingency.

But that even his father had doubts and hesitations was proven to David by the contradictory nature of his advice and charges. Thus on the morning he left Glasgow, and as they were riding together

2

to the Caledonian station, the old man said, "Your uncle has given you a seat in his bank, Davie, and you'll mak' room for yoursel' to lie down, I'se warrant. But you'll no forget that when a guid man thrives a' should thrive i' him; and giving for God's sake never lessens the purse."

"I am but one in a world full, father. I hope I shall never forget to give according to my prosperings."

"Tak the world as it is, my lad, and no' as it ought to be; and never forget that money is money's brither—an' you put two pennies in a purse they'll creep thegither.

"But then Davie, I am free to say gold won't buy everything, and though rich men hae long hands, they won't reach to heaven. So, though you'll tak guid care o' yoursel', you will also gie to God the things that are God's."

"I have been brought up in the fear of God and the love of mankind, father. It would be an ill thing for me to slink out of life and leave the world no better for my living."

"God bless you, lad; and the £20,000 will be to the fore when it is called for, and you shall make it £60,000, and I'll see again Ellenmount in the Lockerby's keeping. But you'll walk in the ways o' your fathers, and gie without grudging of your increase."

David nodded rather impatiently. He could hardly understand the struggle going on in his father's heart—the wish to say something that might quiet his own conscience, and yet not make David's unnecessarily tender. It is hard serving God and Mammon, and Andrew Lockerby was miserable and ashamed that morning in the service.

And yet he was not selfish in the matter —that much in his favor must be admitted. He would rather have had the fine, handsome lad he loved so dearly going in and out his own house. He could have taken great interest in all his further studies, and very great pride in seeing him a successful "placed minister;" but there are few Scotsmen in whom pride of lineage and the good of the family does not strike deeper than individual pleasure. Andrew really believed that David's first duty was to the house of Lockerby.

He had sacrificed a great deal toward this end all his own life, nor were his sacrifices complete with the resignation of his only child to the same purpose. To a man of more than sixty years of age it is a great trial to have an unusual and unhappy atmosphere in his home; and though Mrs. Lockerby was now tearful and patient under her disappointment, everyone knows that tears and patience may be a miserable kind of comfort. Then, though Janet had as yet preserved a dour and angry silence, he knew that sooner or later she would begin a guerilla warfare of sharp words, which he feared he would have mainly to bear, for Janet, though his housekeeper, was also "a far-awa cousin," had been forty years in his house, and was not accustomed to withhold her opinions on any subject.

Fortunately for Andrew Lockerby, Janet finally selected Mary Moir as the Eve specially to blame in this transgression. "A proud up-head lassie," she asserted, "that cam o' a family wha would sell their share o' the sunshine for pounds sterling!'

From such texts as this the two women in the Lockerby house preached little daily sermons to each other, until comfort grew out of the very stem of their sorrow, and they began to congratulate each other that "puir Davie was at ony rate outside the glamour o' Mary Moir's temptations."

"For she just bewitched the laddie," said Janet, angrily; and, doubtless, if the old laws regarding witches had been in Janet's administration it would have gone hardly with pretty Mary Moir.

PART II.

"God's work is soon done."

It is a weary day when the youth first discovers that after all he will only become a man; and this discovery came with a depressing weight one morning to David, after he had been counting bank notes for three hours. It was noon, but the gas was lit, and in the heavy air a dozen men sat silent as statues, adding up figures and making entries. He thought of the college courts, and the college green, of the crowded halls, and the symposia, where both mind and body had equal refection. There had been days when he had a part in these things, and when to "strive with things impossible," or "to pluck honor from the pale-faced moon," had not been unreasonable or rash; but now it almost seemed as if Mr. Buckle's dreary gospel was a reality, and men were machines, and life was an affair to be tabulated in averages.

He had just had a letter from Willie Caird, too, and it had irritated him. The wounds of a friend may be faithful, but they are not always welcome. David determined to drop the correspondence. Willie was going one way and he another. They might never see each other again; and—

If they should meet one day,
If *both* should not forget
They could clasp hands the accustomed way.

For by simply going with the current in which in great measure, subject yet to early influences, he found himself, David Lockerby had drifted in one twelve months far enough away from the traditions and feelings of his home and native land. Not that he had broken loose into any flagrant sin, or in any manner cast a shadow on the perfect respectability of his name. The set in which Alexander Gordon and his nephew lived sanctioned nothing of the kind. They belonged to the best society, and were of those well-dressed, well-behaved people whom Canon Kingsley described as "the sitters in pews."

In their very proper company David had gone to ball and party, to opera and theatre. On wet Sundays they sat together in St. George's Church; on fine Sundays they had sailed quietly down the Thames, and eaten their dinner at Richmond. Now, sin is sin beyond all controversy, but there were none of David's companions to whom these things were sins in the same degree as they were to David.

To none of them had the holy Sabbath ever been the day it had been to him; to none of them was it so richly freighted with memories of wonderful sermons and solemn sacraments that were foretastes of heaven. Coming with a party of gentlemanly fellows slowly rowing up the Thames and humming some passionate recitative from an opera, he alone could recall the charmful stillness of a Scotch Sabbath, the worshiping crowds, and the evening psalm ascending from so many thousand hearthstones:

O God of Bethel, by whose hand
Thy people still are led.

He alone, as the oars kept time to "aria" or "chorus," heard above the witching melody the solemn minor of "St. Mary's," or the tearful tenderness of "Communion."

To most of his companions opera and theatre had come as a matter of course, as a part of their daily life and education. David had been obliged to stifle conscience, to disobey his father's counsels and his mother's pleadings, before he could enjoy them. He had had, in fact, to cultivate a taste for the sin before the sin was pleasant to him; and he frankly told himself that night, in thinking it all over, that it was harder work getting to hell than to heaven.

But then in another year he would become a partner, marry Mary, and begin a new life. Suddenly it struck him with a new force that he had not heard from Mary for nearly three weeks. A fear seized him that while he had been dancing and making merry Mary had been ill and suffering. He was amazed at his own heartlessness, for surely nothing but sickness would have made Mary forget him.

The next morning as he went to the bank he posted a long letter to her, full of affection and contrition and rose-colored pictures of their future life. He had risen an hour earlier to write it, and he did not fail to notice what a healthy natural pleasure even this small effort of self-denial gave him. He determined that he would that very night write long letters to his mother and Janet, and even to his father. "There was a good deal he wanted to say to him about money matters, and his marriage, and fore-talk always saved after-talk. Besides it would keep the influence of the old and better life around him to be in closer communion with it."

Thus thinking, he opened the door of his uncle's private room, and said cheerily, "Good morning, uncle."

"Good morning, Davie. Your father is here."

Then Andrew Lockerby came forward, and his son met him with outstretched hands and paling cheeks. "What is it, father? Mother? Mary? Is she dead?"

"'Deed, no, my lad. There's naething

wrang but will turn to right. Mary Moir was married three days syne, and I thocht you wad rather hear the news from ane that loved you. That's a', Davie; and indeed it's a loss that's a great gain."

"Who did she marry?"

"Just a bit wizened body frae the East Indies, a'most as yellow as his gold, an' as auld as her father. But the Deacon is greatly set up wi' the match—or the settlements—and Mary comes o' a gripping kind. There's her brother Gavin, he'd sell the ears aff his head, an' they werena fastened on."

Then David went away with his father, and after half-an-hour's talk on the subject together it was never mentioned more between them. But it was a blow that killed effectually all David's eager yearnings for a loftier and purer life. And it not only did this, but it also caused to spring up into active existence a passion which was to rule him absolutely—a passion for gold. Love had failed him, friendship had proved an annoyance, company, music, feasting, amusements of all kinds were a weariness now to think of. There seemed nothing better for him than to become a rich man.

"I'll buy so many acres of old Scotland and call them by the Lockerby's name; and I'll have nobles and great men come bowing and becking to David Lockerby as they do to Alexander Gordon. Love is refused, and wisdom is scorned, but everybody is glad to take money; then money is best of all things."

Thus David reasoned, and his father said nothing against his arguments. Indeed, they had never understood one another so well. David, for the first time, asked all about the lands of Ellenmount, and pledged himself, if he lived and prospered, to fulfill his father's hope. Indeed, Andrew was altogether so pleased with his son that he told his brother-in-law that the £20,000 would be forthcoming as soon as ever he choose to advance David in the firm.

"I was only waiting, Lockerby, till Davie got through wi' his playtime. The lad's myself o'er again, an' I ken weel he'll ne'er be contented until he settles cannily doon to his interest tables."

So before Andrew Lockerby went back to Glasgow David was one of the firm of Gordon & Co., sat in the directors' room, and began to feel some of the pleasant power of having money to lend. After this he was rarely seen among men of his own age—women he never mingled with. He removed to his uncle's stately house in Baker street, and assimilated his life very much to that of the older money maker. Occasionally he took a run northward to Glasgow, or a month's vacation on the

Continent, but nearly all such journeys were associated with some profitable loan or investment. People began to speak of him as a most admirable young man, and indeed in some respects he merited the praise. No son ever more affectionately honored his father and mother, and Janet had been made an independent woman by his grateful consideration.

He was so admirable that he ceased to interest people, and every time he visited Glasgow fewer and fewer of his old acquaintances came to see him. A little more than ten years after his admission to the firm of Gordon & Co. he came home at the new year, and presented his father with the title-deeds of Ellenmount and Netherby. The next day old Andrew was welcomed on the City Exchange as "Lockerby of Ellenmount, gentleman." "I hae lived lang enough to hae seen this day," he said, with happy tears; and David felt a joy in his father's joy that he did not know again for many years. For while a man works for another there is an ennobling element in his labor, but when he works simply for himself he has become the greatest of all slaves. This slavery David now willingly assumed; the accumulation of money became his business, his pleasure, the sum of his daily life.

Ten years later both his uncle and father

were dead, and both had left David every shilling they possessed. Then he went on working more eagerly than ever, turning his tens of thousands into hundreds of thousands and adding acre to acre, and farm to farm, until Lockerby was the richest estate in Annandale. When he was forty-five years of age fortune seemed to have given him every good gift except wife and children, and his mother, who had nothing else to fret about, worried Janet continually on this subject.

"Wife an' bairns, indeed!" said Janet; "vera uncertain comforts, ma'am, an' vera certain cares. Our Master Davie likes aye to be sure o' his bargains."

"Weel, Janet, it's a great cross to me—an' him sae honored, an' guid an' rich, wi' no a shilling ill-saved to shame him."

"Tut, tut, ma'am! The river doesna swell wi' clean water. Naebody's charged him wi' wrangdoing—that's enough. There's nae need to set him up for a saint."

"An' you wanted him to be a minister, Janet."

"I was that blind—ance."

"We are blind creatures, Janet."

"Wi' *excepts*, ma'am; but they'll ne'er be found amang mithers. "

This conversation took place one lovely Sabbath evening, and just at the same time

David was standing thoughtfully on Princes
street, Edinburgh, wondering to which
church he had better turn his steps. For a
sudden crisis in the affairs of a bank in
that city had brought him hurriedly to
Scotland, and he was not only a prudent
man who considered public opinion, but
was also in a mood to conciliate that
opinion so long as the outward conditions
were favorable. Whatever he might do in
London, in Scotland he always went to
morning and evening service.

He was also one of those self-dependent
men who dislike to ask questions or advice
from anyone. Though a comparative
stranger he would not have allowed himself to think that anyone could direct him
better than he could choose for himself.
He looked up and down the street, and
finally followed a company which increased
continually until they entered an old church
in the Canongate.

Its plain wooden pews and old-fashioned
elevated pulpit rather pleased than offended
David, and the air of antiquity about the
place consecrated it in his eyes. Men like
whatever reminds them of their purest and
best days, and David had been once in the
old Relief Church on the Doo Hill in Glasgow—just such a large, bare, solemn-looking
house of worship. The still, earnest men
and women, the droning of the precentor,

the antiquated singing pleased and soothed him.   He did not notice much the thin little fair man who conducted the services; for he was holding a session with his own soul.

A peculiar movement among the congregation announced that the sermon was beginning, and David, looking up, saw that the officiating minister had been changed. This man was swarthy and tall, and looked like some old Jewish prophet, as he lifted his rapt face and cried, like one crying in the wilderness, "Friends! I have a question to ask you to-night: '*What shall it profit a man if he gain the whole world and lose his own soul?*'"

For   twenty-three   years David   had silenced that voice, but it had found him out again—it was Willie Caird's.   At first interested and curious, David soon became profoundly   moved   as   Willie,   in   clear, solemn, thrilling sentences, reasoned of life and death and judgment to come.   Not that he followed his arguments, or was more than dimly conscious of the moving eloquence that stirred the crowd as a mighty wind stirs the trees in the forest: for that dreadful question smote, and smote, and smote upon his heart as if determined to have an answer.

What   shall   it   profit?   What   shall   it profit?   What shall it profit?   David was quick enough at counting material loss and profit, but here was a question beyond his computation. He went silently out of the church, and wandered away by Holyrood Palace and St. Anthony's Chapel to the pathless, lonely beauty of Salisbury Crags. There was no answer in nature for him. The stars were silent above, the earth silent beneath. Weariness brought him no rest; if he slept, he woke with the start of a hunted soul, and found him asking that same dreadful question. When he looked in the mirror his own face queried of him, "What profit?" and he was compelled to make a decided effort to prevent his tongue uttering the ever present thought.

But at noon he would meet the defaulting bank committee, "and doubtless his lawful business would take its proper share of his thought!" He told himself that it was the voice and face of his old friend that had affected him so vividly, and that if he went and chatted over old times with Willie, he would get rid of the disagreeable influence.

The influence, however, went with him into the creditors' committee room. The embarrassed officials had dreaded greatly the interview. No one hoped for more than bare justice from David Lockerby. "Clemency, help, sympathy! You'll get blood out o' a stane first, gentlemen," said the old cashier, with a dour, hopeless face.

And yet that morning David Lockerby amazed no one so much as himself. He went to the meeting quite determined to have his own—only his own—but something asked him, "*What shall it profit?*" and he gave up his lawful increase and even offered help. He went determined to speak his mind very plainly about mismanagement and the folly of having losses; and something asked him, "*What shall it profit?*" and he gave such sympathy with his help that the money came with a blessing in its hand.

The feeling of satisfaction was so new to him that it embarrassed and almost made him ashamed. He slipped ungraciously away from the thanks that ought to have been pleasant, and found himself, almost unconsciously, looking up Willie's name in the clerical directory, "Dr. William Caird, 22 Moray place." David knew enough of Edinburgh to know that Moray place contained the handsomest residences in the city, and therefore he was not astonished at the richness and splendor of Willie's library; but he was astonished to see him surrounded by five beautiful boys and girls, and evidently as much interested in their lessons and sports as if he was one of them.

"Ech! Davie man! but I'm glad to see you!" That was all of Willie's greeting, but his eyes filled, and as the friends held each other's hands Davie came very near touching for a moment a David Lockerby no one had seen for many long years. But he said nothing during his visit of Willie's sermon, nor indeed in several subsequent ones. Scotsmen are reticent on all matters, and especially reticent about spiritual experience; and though Davie lingered in Edinburgh a week, he was neither able to speak to Willie about his soul, nor yet in all their conversations get rid of that haunting, uncomfortable influence Willie had raised.

But as they stood before the Queen's Hotel at midnight bidding each other an affectionate farewell, David suddenly turned Willie round and opened up his whole heart to him. And as he talked he found himself able to define what had been only hitherto a vague, restless sense of want.

"I am the poorest rich man and the most miserable failure, Willie Caird, that ever you asked yon fearsome question of—and I know it. I have achieved millions, and I am a conscious bankrupt to my own soul. I have wasted my youth, neglected my talents and opportunities, and whatever the world may call me I am a wretched breakdown. I have made money—plenty of it—and it does not pay me. What am I to do?"

"You ken, Davie, my dear, dear lad, what

3

advice the Lord Jesus gave to the rich man
—'distribute unto the poor—and come, follow me!'''

Then up and down Princes street, and
away under the shadow of the Castle Hill,
Willie and David walked and talked, till
the first sunbeams touched St. Leonard's
Crags. If it was a long walk a grand work
was laid out in it.

"You shall be more blessed than your
namesake," said Willie, "for though
David gathered the gold, and the wood,
and the stone, Solomon builded therewith.
Now, an' it please God, you shall do your
ain work, and see the topstone brought on
with rejoicing."

Then at David's command, workmen
gathered in companies, and some of the
worst "vennels" in old Glasgow were
torn down; and the sunshine flooded
"wynds" it had scarcely touched for centuries, and a noble building arose that was
to be a home for children that had no
home. And the farms of Ellenmount fed
them, and the fleeces of Lockerby clothed
them, and into every young hand was put
a trade that would win it honest bread.

In a short time even this undertaking
began to be too small for David's energies
and resources, and he joined hands with
Willie in many other good works, and gave
not only freely of his gold, but also of his

time and labor. The old eloquence that
stirred his classmates in St. Andrew's Hall
"till they would have followed him to the
equator" began to stir the cautious Glasgow traders to the bottom of their hearts
and their pocketbooks; and men who didn't
want to help in a crusade against drunken-
ness, or in a crusade for the spread of the
Gospel, stopped away from Glasgow City
Hall when David Lockerby filled the chair
at a public meeting and started a subscrip-
tion list with £1000 down on the table.

But there were two old ladies that never
stopped away, though one of them always
declared "Master Davie had fleeched her
last bawbee out o' her pouch;" and the
other generally had her little whimper
about Davie "waring his substance upon
ither folks' bairns."

"There's bonnie Bessie Lamont, Janet;
an' he would marry her we might live to
see his ain sons and daughters in the old
house."

"'Deed, then, ma'am, our Davie has
gotten him a name better than that o' sons
an' dochters; and though I am sair disappointed in him—"

"You shouldn't say that, Janet; he made
a gran' speech the day."

"A speech isna a sermon, ma'am; though
I'll ne'er belittle a speech wi' a £1000
argument."

"And there was Deacon Moir, Janet, who didna approve o' the scheme, and who would therefore gie nothing at a'."

"The Deacon is sae godly that God doesna get a chance to improve his condition, ma'am. But for a' o' Deacon Moir's disapproval I'se count on the good work going on."

" 'Deed yes, Janet, and though our Davie should ne'er marry at a'—"

"There'll be generations o' lads an' lasses, ma'am, that will rise up in auld Scotland an' go up an' down through a' the warld a' ca' David Lockerby 'blessed.' "

FRANZ MÜLLER'S WIFE.

"Franz, good morning. Whose philosophy is it now? Hegel, Spinosa, Kant or Dugald Stewart?"

"None of them. I am reading *Faust.*"

"Worse and worse. Better wrestle with philosophies than lose yourself in the clouds. At any rate, if the poets are to send the philosophers to the right about, stick to Shakespeare."

"He is too material. He can't get rid of men and women."

"They are a little better, I should think, than Mephisto. Come, Franz, condescend to cravats and kid gloves, and let us go and see my cousin Christine Stromberg."

"I do not know the young lady."

"Of course not. She has just returned from a Munich school. Her brother Max was at the Lyndons' great party, you remember?"

"I don't remember, Louis. In white cravats and black coats all men look alike."

"But you will go?"

"If you wish it, yes. There are some uncut reviews on the table: amuse yourself while I dress."

"Thanks, I have my cigar case. I will take a smoke and think of Christine."

For some reason quite beyond analysis, Franz did not like this speech. He had never seen Christine Stromberg, but yet he half resented the careless use of her name. It fell upon some soul consciousness like a familiar and personal name, and yet he vainly recalled every phase of his life for any clew to this familiarity.

He was a handsome fellow, with large, clearly-cut features and gray, thoughtful eyes. In a conversation that interested him his face lighted up with a singularly beautiful animation, but usually it was as still and passionless as if the soul was away on a dream or a visit. Even the regulation cravat and coat could not destroy his individuality, and Louis looked admiringly at him, and said, "You are still Franz Müller. No one is just like you. I should think Cousin Christine will fall in love with you."

Again Franz's heart resented this speech. It had been waiting for love for many a year, but he could not jest or speculate about it. No one but the thoughtless, favored Louis ever dared to do it before Franz, and no one ever spoke lightly of women before him, for the worst of men are sensitive to the presence of a pure and lofty nature, and are generally willing to respect it.

Franz dreamed of women, but only of noble women, and even for those who fell below his ideal he had a thousand apologies and a world of pity. It was strange that such a man should have lived thirty years, and never have really loved any mortal woman. But his hour had come at last. As soon as he saw Christine Stromberg he loved her. A strange exaltation possessed him; his face was radiant; he talked and sung with a brilliancy that amazed even those most familiar with his rare exhibitions of such moods. And Christine seemed fascinated by his beauty and wit. The hours passed like moments; and when the girl stood watching him down the moon-lit avenue, she almost trembled to remember what questions Franz's eyes had asked her and how strangely familiar the clasp of his hand and the sound of his voice had seemed to her.

"I wonder where I have seen him before," she murmured—"I wonder where it was?" and to this thought she slowly took off one by one her jewels, and brushed out her long black hair; nay, when she fell asleep, it was only to take it up again in dreams.

As for Franz, he was in far too ecstatic a mood to think of sleep. "One has too few of such godlike moments to steep them in unconsciousness," he said to himself. And so he sat smoking and thinking and watching the waning moon sink lower and lower, until it was no longer night, but dawning day.

"In a few hours now I can go and see Christine." At this point in his love he had no other thought. He was too happy to speculate on any probability as yet. It was sufficient at present to know that he had found his love, that she lived at a definite number on a definite avenue, and that in six or seven hours more he might see her again.

He chose the earlier number. It was just eleven o'clock when he rung Mr. Stromberg's bell. Mrs. Stromberg passed through the hall as he entered, and greeted him pleasantly. "Christine and I are just going to have breakfast," she said, in her jolly, hearty way. "Come in Mr. Müller, and have a cup of coffee with us."

Nothing could have delighted Franz so much. Christine was pouring it out as he entered the pretty breakfast parlor. How beautiful she looked in her long loose morning dress! How bewitching were its numerous bows of pale ribbon! He had a sense of hunger immediately, and he knew that he made an excellent breakfast; but of what he ate or what he drank he had not the slightest conception.

A cup of coffee passing through Christine's hands necessarily suffered some wonderful change. It could not, and it did not, taste like ordinary coffee. In the same mysterious way chicken, eggs and rolls became sublimated. So they ate and laughed and chatted, and I am quite sure that Milton never imagined a meal in Eden half so delightful as that breakfast on the avenue.

When it was over, it came into Franz's heart to offer Christine a ride. They were standing together among the flowers in the bay window, and the trees outside were in their first tender green, and the spring skies and the spring airs were full of happiness and hope. Christine was arranging and watering her lilies and pansies, and somehow in helping her Franz's hands and hers had lingered happily together. So now love gave to this mortal an immortal's confidence. He never thought of sighing and fearing and trembling. His soul had claimed Christine, and he firmly believed that sooner or later she would hear and understand what he had to say to her.

"Shall we ride?" he said, just touching her fingers, and looking at her with eyes and face glowing with a wonderful happiness.

Alas, Christine could think of mamma, and of morning calls and of what people would say. But Franz overruled every scruple; he conquered mamma, and laughed at society; and before Christine had

decided which of her costumes was most
becoming, Franz was waiting at the door.

How they rattled up the avenue and
through the park! How the green
branches waved in triumph, and how the
birds sang and gossiped about them! By
the time they arrived at Mount St. Vincent
they had forgotten they were mortal. Then
the rest in the shady gallery, and the sub-
sidence of love's exaltation into love's
silent tender melancholy, were just as bliss-
ful.

They came slowly home, speaking only
in glances and monosyllables, but just before they parted Franz said, ''I have been
waiting thirty years for you, Christine;
to-day my life has blossomed.''

And though Christine did not make any
audible answer, he thought her blush sufficient; besides, she took the lilies from her
throat and gave them to him.

Such a dream of love is given only to the
few whom the gods favor. Franz must
have stood high in their grace, for it lasted
through many sweet weeks and months for
him. He followed the Strombergs to
Newport, and laid his whole life down at
Christine's feet. There was no definite
engagement between them, but every one
understood that would come as surely as
the end of the season.

Money matters and housekeeping must

eventually intrude themselves, but the romance and charm of this one summer of life should be untouched. And Franz was not anxious at all on this score. His father, a shrewd business man, had early seen that his son was a poet and a dreamer. "It is not the boy's fault," he said to his partner, "he gets it from his grandfather, who was always more out of this world than in it."

So he wisely allowed Franz to follow his natural tastes, and contented himself with carefully investing his fortune in such real estate and securities as he believed would insure a safe, if a slow increase. He had bought wisely, and Franz's income was a certain and handsome one, with a tendency rather to increase than decrease, and quite sufficient to maintain Christine in all the luxury to which she had been accustomed.

So when he returned to the city he intended to speak to Mr. Stromberg. All he had should be Christine's and her father should settle the matter just as he thought best for his daughter. In a general way this was understood by all parties, and everyone seemed inclined to sympathize with the happy feeling which led the lovers to deprecate during these enchanted days any allusion which tended to dispel the exquisite charm of their young lives' idyl.

Perhaps it would have been better if they

had remembered the ancient superstition and themselves done something to mar their perfect happiness. Polycrates offered his ring to avert the calamity sure to follow unmitigated pleasure or success, and Franz ought, perhaps, to have also made an effort to propitiate his envious Fate.

But he did not, and toward the very end of the season, when the October days had thrown a kind of still melancholy over the world that had been so green and gay, Franz's dream was rudely broken—broken by a Mr. James Barker Clarke, a blustering, vulgar man of fifty, worth *three millions*. In some way or other he seemed to have a great deal of influence over Mr. Stromberg, who paid him unqualified respect, and over Mrs. Stromberg, who seemed to fear him.

Mr. Stromberg's "private ledger" alone knew the whole secret; for of course money was at the foundation. Indeed, in these days, in all public and private troubles, it is proper to ask, not "Who is she?" but "How much is it?" Franz Müller and James Barker Clarke hated each other on sight. Still Franz had no idea at first that this ugly, uncouth man could ever be a rival to his own handsome person and passionate affection.

In a few days, however, he was compelled to actually consider the possibility of

such a thing. Mr. Stromberg had assumed
an attitude of such extreme politeness, and
Mrs. Stromberg avoided him if possible,
and if not possible, was constrained and
unhappy in the familiar relations that she
had accepted so happily all summer. As
for Christine, she had constant headaches,
and her eyes were often swollen and red
with weeping.

At length, without notice, the family left
Newport, and went to stay a month with
some relative near Boston. A pitiful little
note from Christine informed him of this
fact; but as he received no information as
to the locality of her relative's house, and
no invitation to call, he was compelled for
the present to do as Christine asked him—
wait patiently for their return.

At first he got a few short tender notes,
but they were evidently written in such
sorrow that he was almost beside himself
with grief and anger. When these ceased
he went to Boston, and without difficulty
found the house where Christine was staying. He was received at first very shyly
by Mrs. Stromberg, but when Franz poured
out his love and misery, the poor old lady
wept bitterly, and moaned out that she
could not help it, and Christine could not
help it, and that they were all very miserable.

Finally she was persuaded to let him see

Christine, "just for five minutes." The poor girl came to him, a shadow of her gay self, and, weeping in his arms, told him he must bid her good-by forever. The five minutes were lengthened into a long, terrible hour, and Franz went back to New York with the knowledge that in that hour his life had been broken in two for this life.

One night toward the close of November his friend Louis called. "Franz," he said, "have you heard that Christine Stromberg is to marry old Clarke?"

"Yes."

"No one can trust a woman. It is a shame of Christine."

"Louis, speak of what you know. Christine is an angel. If a woman appears to do wrong, there is probably some brute of a man behind her forcing her to do it."

"I thought she was to be your wife."

"She is my wife in soul and feeling. No one, thank God, can help that. If I was Clarke, I would as willingly marry a corpse as Christine Stromberg. Do not speak of her again, Louis. The poor innocent child! God bless her!" And he burst into a passion of weeping that alarmed his friend for his reason, but which was probably its salvation.

In a week Franz had left for Europe, and the next Christmas, Christine and James Barker Clarke were married, and began housekeeping in a style of extravagant splendor. People wondered and exclaimed at Christine's reckless expenditure, her parents advised, her husband scolded; but though she never disputed them, she quietly ignored all their suggestions. She went to Paris, and lived like a princess; Rome, Vienna and London wondered over her beauty and her splendor; and wherever she went Franz followed her quietly, haunting her magnificent salons like a wretched spectre.

They rarely or never spoke. Beyond a grave inclination of the head, or a look whose profound misery he only understood, she gave him no recognition. The world held her name above reproach, and considered that she had done very well to herself.

Ten years passed away, but the changes they brought were such as the world regards as natural and inevitable. Christine's mother died and her father married again; and Christine had a son and a daughter. Franz watched anxiously to see if this new love would break up the icy coldness of her manners. Sometimes he was conscious of feeling angrily jealous of the children, but he always crushed down the wretched passion. "If Christine loved a flower, would I not love it also?" he asked himself; "and these little ones, what have they done?'' So at last he got to separate them entirely from every one but Christine, and to regard them as part and portion of his love.

But at the end of ten years a change came, neither natural nor expected. Franz was walking moodily about his library one night, when Louis came to tell him of it. Louis was no longer young, and was married now, for he had found out that the beaten track is the safest.

''Franz,'' he said, ''have you heard about Clarke? His affairs are frightfully wrong, and he shot himself an hour ago.''

''And Christine? Does she know? Who has gone to her?''

''My wife is with her. Clarke shot himself in his own room. Christine was the first to reach him. He left a letter saying he was absolutely ruined.''

''Where will Christine and the children go?''

''I suppose to her father's. Not a pleasant place for her now. Christine's stepmother dislikes both her and the children.''

Franz said no more, and Louis went away with a feeling of disappointment. ''I thought he would have done something for her,'' he said to his wife. ''Poor Christine will be very poor and dependent.''

Ten days after he came home with a different story. ''There never was a woman as lucky about money as Cousin Christine,'' he said. ''Hardy & Hall sent her notice to-day that the property at Ryebeach settled on her before her marriage by Mr. Clarke was now at her disposal. It seems the old gentleman anticipated the result of his wild speculations, and in order to provide for his wife, quietly bought and placed in Hardy's charge two beautifully furnished cottages. There is something like an accumulation of sixteen thousand dollars of rentage; and as one is luckily empty, Christine and the children are going there at once. I always thought the property was Hardy's own before. Very thoughtful in Clarke.''

''It is not Clarke one bit. I don't believe he ever did it. It is some arrangement of Franz Müller's.''

''For goodness' sake don't hint such a thing, Lizzie! Christine would not go, and we should have her here very soon. Besides, I don't believe it. Franz took the news very coolly, and he has kept out of my way since.''

The next day Louis was more than ever of his wife's opinion. ''What do you think, Lizzie?'' he said. ''Franz came to me to-day and asked if Clarke did not once loan me two thousand dollars. I told him Clarke gave me two thousand about the time we were married.''

4

" 'Say *loaned*, Louis,' he answered, 'to oblige me. Here is two thousand and the interest for six years. Go and pay it to Christine; she must need money.' So I went.''

"Is she settled comfortably?''

"Oh, very. Go and see her often. Franz is sure to marry her, and he is growing richer every day.''

It seemed as if Louis's prediction would come true. Franz began to drive out every afternoon to Ryebeach. At first he contented himself with just passing Christine's gate. But he soon began to stop for the children, and having taken them a drive, to rest a while on the lawn, or in the parlor, while Christine made him a cup of tea.

For Franz tired very easily now, and Christine saw what few others noticed: he had become pale and emaciated, and the least exertion left him weary and breathless. She knew in her heart that it was the last summer he would be with her. Alas! what a pitiful shadow of their first one! It was hard to contrast the ardent, handsome lover of ten years ago with the white, silently happy man who, when October came, had only strength to sit and hold her hand, and gaze with eager, loving eyes into her face.

One day his physician met Louis on Broadway. "Mr. Curtin,'' he said, "your

friend Müller is very ill. I consider his
life measured by days, perhaps hours. He
has long had organic disease of the heart.
It is near the last.''

''Does he know it?''

''Yes, he has known it long. Better see
him at once.''

So Louis went at once. He found Franz
calmly making his last preparations for the
great event. ''I am glad you are come,
Louis,'' he said; ''I was going to send for
you. See this cabinet full of letters. I
have not strength left to destroy them;
burn them for me when—when I am gone.

''This small packet is Christine's dear
little notes: bury them with me: there are
ten of them, every one ten years old.''

''Is that all, dear Franz?''

''Yes; my will has long been made. Except a legacy to yourself, all goes to Christine—dear, dear Christine!''

''You love her yet, then, Franz?''

''What do you mean? I have loved her for
ages. I shall love her forever. She is the
other half of my soul. In some lives I have
missed her altogether let me be thankful
that she has come so near me in this one.''

''Do you know what you are saying,
Franz?''

''Very clearly, Louis. I have always
believed with the oldest philosophers that
souls were created in pairs, and that it is

permitted them in their toilsome journey
back to purity and heaven sometimes to
meet and comfort each other. Do you
think I saw Christine for the first time in
your uncle's parlor? Louis, I have fairer
and grander memories of her than any
linked to this life. I must leave her now
for a little. God knows when and where
we meet again; but *He does know;* that is
my hope and consolation.''

Whatever were Louis's private opinions
about Franz's theology it was impossible to
dissent at that hour, and he took his
friend's last instructions and farewell with
such gentle, solemn feelings as had long
been strange to his heart.

In the afternoon Franz was driven out to
Christine's. It was the last physical effort
he was capable of. No one saw the parting of those two souls. He went with
Christine's arms around him, and her lips
whispering tender, hopeful farewells. It
was noticed however, that after Franz's
death a strange change came over Christine
--a beautiful nobility and calmness of character, and a gentle setting of her life to the
loftiest aims.

Louis said she had been wonderfully
moved by the papers Franz left. The ten
letters she had written during the spring-
time of their love went to the grave with
him, but the rest were of such an

extraordinary nature that Louis could not refrain from showing them to his cousin, and then at her request leaving them for her to dispose of. They were indeed letters written to herself under every circumstance of her life, and directed to every place in which she had sojourned. In all of them she was addressed as "Beloved Wife of my Soul," and in this way the poor fellow had consoled his breaking, longing heart.

To some of them he had written imaginary answers, but as these all referred to a financial secret known only to the parties concerned in Christine's and his own sacrifice, it was proof positive that he had written only for his own comfort. But it was perhaps well they fell into Christine's hands: she could not but be a better woman for reading the simple records of a strife which set perfect unselfishness and childlike submission as the goal of its duties.

Seven years after Franz's death Christine and her daughter died together of the Roman fever, and James Barker Clarke, junior, was left sole inheritor of Franz's wealth.

"A German dreamer!"

Ah, well, there are dreamers and dreamers. And perchance he that seeks fame, and he that seeks gold, and he that seeks power, may all alike, when this shadowy existence is over, look back upon life "as a dream when one awaketh."

THE VOICE AT MIDNIGHT.

"It is the King's highway that we are in; and know this, His messengers are on it. They who have ears to hear will hear; and He opens the eyes of some, and they see things not to be lightly spoken of."

It was John Balmuto who said these words to me. John was a Shetlander, and for forty years he had gone to the Arctic seas with the whale boats. Then there had come to him a wonderful experience. He had been four days and nights alone with God upon the sea, among mountains of ice reeling together in perilous madness, and with little light but the angry flush of the aurora. Then, undoubtedly, was born that strong faith in the Unseen which made him an active character in the facts I am going to relate.

After his marvelous salvation, he devoted his life to the service of God by entering that remarkable body of lay evangelists attached to the Presbyterian Church in Highland parishes, called "The Men," and he became noted throughout the Hebrides for his labors, and for his knowledge of the Scriptures.

Circumstances, that summer, had thrown

us together; I, a young woman, just entering an apparently fortunate life; he, an
aged saint, standing on the borderland of
eternity. And we were sitting together, in
the gray summer gloaming, when he said
to me, "Thou art silent to-night. What
hast thou, then, on thy mind?"

"I had a strange dream. I cannot shake
off its influence. Of course it is folly, and
I don't believe in dreams at all." And it
was then he said to me, "It is the King's
highway that we are in, and know this,
His messengers are on it."

"But it was only a dream."

"Well, God speaks to His children 'in
dreams, and by the oracles that come in
darkness.'"

"He used to do so."

"Wilt thou then say that He has ceased
so to speak to men? Now, I will tell thee
a thing that happened; I will tell thee just
the bare facts; I will put nothing to, nor
take anything away from them.

"'Tis five years ago the first day of last
June. I was in Stornoway in the Lews,
and I was going to the Gairloch Preachings. It was rough, cheerless weather, and
all the fishing fleet were at anchor for the
night, with no prospect of a fishing. The
fishers were sitting together talking over
the bad weather, but, indeed, without that
bitterness that I have heard from landsmen

when it would be the same trouble with them. So I gathered them into Donald Brae's cottage, and we had a very good hour. I noticed a stranger in the corner of the room, and some one told me he was one of those men who paint pictures, and I saw that he was busy with a pencil and paper even while we were at the service. But the next day I left for the Preachings, and I thought no more of him, good or bad.

"On the first of September I was in Oban. I had walked far and was very tired, but I went to John MacNab's cottage, and, after I had eat my kippered herring and drank my tea, I felt better. Then I talked with John about the resurrection of the body, for he was in a tribulation of thoughts and doubts as to whether our Lord had a permanent humanity or not.

"And I said to him, John, Christ redeemed our whole nature, and it is this way: the body being ransomed, as well as the spirit, by no less a price than the body of Christ, shall be equally cleansed and glorified. Now, then, after I had gone to my room, I was sitting thinking of these things, and of no other things whatever. There was not a sound but that of the waves breaking among the rocks, and drawing the tinkling pebbles down the beach after them. Then the ears of my spiritual body were opened, and I heard

these words, '*I will go with thee to Glasgow!*'
Instead of saying to the heavenly message,
'I am ready!' I began to argue with myself
thus: 'Whatever for should I go to Glasgow? I know not anyone there. No one
knows me. I have duties at Portsee not to
be left. I have no money for such a journey—'

"I fell asleep to such thoughts. Then
I dreamed of—or I saw—a woman fair as
the daughters of God, and she said, '*I will
go with thee to Glasgow!*' With a strange
feeling of being hurried and pressed I
awoke—wide awake, and without any conscious will of my own, I answered, 'I am
ready. I am ready now.'

"As I left the cottage it was striking
twelve, and I wondered what means of
reaching Glasgow I should find at midnight. But I walked straight to the pier,
and there was a small steamer with her
steam up. She was blowing her whistle
impatiently, and when the skipper saw me
coming, he called to me, in a passion,
'Well, then, is it all night I shall wait for
thee?'

"I soon perceived that there was a mistake, and that it was not John Balmuto he
had been instructed to wait for. But I
heeded not that: I was under orders I durst
not disobey. She was a trading steamer,
with a perishable cargo of game and lobsters,

and so she touched at no place whatever till we reached Glasgow. One of her passengers was David MacPherson of Harris, a very good man, who had known me in my visitations. He was going to Glasgow as a witness in a case to be tried between the Harris fishers and their commission house in Glasgow.

"As we walked together from the steamer, he said to me, 'Let us go round by the court house, John, and I'll find out when I'll be required.' That was to my mind; I did not feel as if I could go astray, whatever road was taken, and I turned with him the way he desired to go. He found the lawyer who needed him in the court house, and while they talked together I went forward and listened to the case that was in hand.

"It was a trial for murder, and I could not keep my eyes off the young man who was charged with the crime. He seemed to be quite broken down with shame and sorrow. Before MacPherson called me the court closed and the constables took him away. As he passed me our eyes met, and my heart dirled and burned, and I could not make out whatever would be the matter with me. All night his face haunted me. I was sure I had seen it some place; and besides it would blend itself with the dream which had brought me to Glasgow.

"In the morning I was early at the court house and I saw the prisoner brought in. There was the most marvelous change in his looks. He walked like a man who has lost fear, and his face was quite calm. But now it troubled me more than ever. Whatever had I to do with the young man? Yet I could not bear to leave him.

"I listened and found out that he was accused of murdering his uncle. They had been traveling together and were known to have been at Ullapool on the thirtieth of May. On the first of June the elder man was found in a lonely place near Oban, dead, and, without doubt, from violence. The chain of circumstantial evidence against his nephew was very strong. To judge by it I would have said myself to him, 'Thou art certainly guilty.'

"On the other side the young man declared that he had quarreled with his uncle at Ullapool and left him clandestinely. He had then taken passage in a Manx fishing smack which was going to the Lews, but he had forgotten the name of the smack. He was not even certain if the boat was Manx. The landlord of the inn, at which he said he stayed when in the Lews, did not remember him. 'A thing not to be expected,' he told the jury, 'for in the summer months, what with visitors, and what with the fishers, a face in Stornoway was

like a face on a crowded street. The young
man might have been there'—

"The word *Stornoway* made the whole
thing clear to me. The prisoner was the
man I had noticed with a pencil and paper
among the fishers in Donald Brae's cottage.
Yes, indeed he was! I knew then why I
had been sent to Glasgow. I walked
quickly to the bar, and lifting my bonnet
from my head, I said to the judge, 'My
lord, the prisoner *was* in Stornoway on the
first of June. I saw him there !'

" He gave a great cry of joy and turned
to me ; and in a moment he called out :
' You are the man who read the Bible to the
fishers. I remember you. I have your
likeness among my drawings.' And I
said, ' I am the man.'

"Then my lord, the judge, made them
swear me, and he said they would hear my
evidence. For one moment I was a coward.
I thought I would hide God's share in the
deliverance, lest men should doubt my
whole testimony. The next, I was telling
the true story: how I had been called at
midnight—twice called; how I had found
Evan Conochie's boat waiting for me; how
on the boat I had met David MacPherson,
and been brought to the court house by
him, having no intention or plan of my
own in the matter.

"And there was a great awe in the room

as I spoke. Every one believed what I said, and my lord asked for the names of the fishers who were present in Donald Brae's cottage on the night of the first of June. Very well, then, I could give many of them, and they were sent for, and the lad was saved, thank God Almighty!"

"How do you explain it, John?"

"No, I will not try to explain it; for it is not to be hoped that anyone can explain by human reason the things surpassing human reason."

"Do you know what became of the young man?"

"I will tell thee about him. He is a very rich young man, and the only child of a widow, known like Dorcas of old for her great goodness to the Lord's poor. But when his mother died it did not go well and peaceably between him and his uncle; and it is true that he left him at Ullapool without a word. Well, then, he fell into this sore strait, and it seemed as if all hope of proving his innocence was over.

"But that very night on which I saw him first, he dreamed that his mother came to him in his cell and she comforted him and told him, 'To-morrow, surely, thy deliverer shall speak for thee.' He never doubted the heavenly vision. 'How could I?' he asked me. 'My mother never deceived me in life; would she come to me, even in a dream, to tell me a lie? Ah, no!'"

"Is he still alive?"

"God preserve him for many a year yet! I'll only require to speak his name"— and when he had done so, I knew the secret spring of thankfulness that fed the never-ceasing charity of one great, good man.

"And yet, John," I urged, "how can spirit speak with spirit?"

"'*How?*' I will tell thee, that word 'how' has no business in the mouth of a child of God. When I was a boy, who had dreamed 'how' men in London might speak with men in Edinburgh through the air, invisible and unheard? That is a matter of trade now. Can thou imagine what subtle secret lines there may be between the spiritual world and this world?"

"But dreams, John?"

"Well, then, dreams. Take the dream life out of thy Bible and, oh, how much thou wilt lose! All through it this side of the spiritual world presses close on the human side. I thank God for it. Yes, indeed! Many things I hear and see which say to me that Christians now have a kind of shame in what is mystical or super-natural. But thou be sure of this—the supernaturalism of the Bible, and of every Christian life is not one of the difficulties of our faith, *it is the foundation of our faith.* The Bible is a supernatural book, the law of a supernatural religion; and to part with this element is to lose out of it the flavor of heaven, and the hope of immortality. Yes, indeed!''

This conversation occurred thirty years ago. Two years since, I met the man who had experienced such a deliverance, and he told me again the wonderful story, and showed me the pencil sketch which he had made of John Balmuto in Donald Brae's cottage. He had painted from it a grand picture of his deliverer, wearing the long black camlet cloak and head-kerchief of the order of evangelists to which he belonged. I stood reverently before the commanding figure, with its inspired eyes and rapt expression; for, during those thirty years, I also had learned that it was only those

> Who ne'er the mournful midnight hours
> Weeping upon their bed have sate,
> Who know you not, Ye Heavenly Powers.

SIX, AND HALF-A-DOZEN.

Slain in the battle of life. Wounded and
fallen, trampled in the mire and mud of the
conflict, then the ranks closed again and
left no place for her. So she crawled aside
to die. With a past whose black despair
was as the shadow of a starless night, a
future which her early religious training
lit up with the lurid light of hell, and the
strong bands of a pitiless death dragging
her to the grave—still she craved, as the
awful hour drew near, to see once more the
home of her innocent childhood. Not that
she thought to die in its shelter—any one
who knew David Todd knew also that was
a hopeless dream; but if, IF her father
should say one pardoning word, then she
thought it would help her to understand
the love of God, and give her some strength
to trust in it.

Early in the evening, just as the sun was
setting and the cows were coming lowing
up the little lane, scented with the bursting
lilac bushes, she stood humbly at the gate
her father must pass in order to go to the
hillside fold to shelter the ewes and lambs.
Very soon she saw him coming, his Scotch
bonnet pulled over his brows, his steps

steadied by his shepherd's staff. His lips
were firmly closed, and his eyes looked far
over the hills; for David was a mystic in
his own way, and they were to him temples
not made with hands in which he had seen
and heard wonderful things. Here the
storehouses of hail and lightning had been
opened in his sight, and he had watched in
the sunshine the tempest bursting beneath
his feet. He had trod upon rainbows and
been waited upon by spectral mists. The
voices of winds and waters were in his
heart, and he passionately believed in God.
But it was the God of his own creed—jealous, just and awful in that inconceivable
holiness which charges his angels with folly
and detects impurity in the sinless heavens.
So, when he approached the gate he saw,
but would not see, the dying girl who
leaned against it. Whatever he felt he
made no sign. He closed it without hurry,
and then passed on the other side.

"Father! O, father! speak one word to
me."

Then he turned and looked at her,
sternly and awfully.

"Thou art nane o' my bairn. I ken
naught o' thee."

Without another glance at the white,
despairing face, he walked rapidly on; for
the spring nights were chilly, and he must
gather his lambs into the fold, though this

5

poor sheep of his own household was left
to perish.

But, if her father knew her no more, the
large sheep-dog at his side was not so cruel.
No theological dogmas measured Rover's
love; the stain on the spotless name of his
master's house, which hurt the old man
like a wound, had not shadowed his memory. He licked her hands and face, and
tried with a hospitality and pity which
made him so much nearer the angels than
his master to pull her toward her home.
But she shook her head and moaned pitifully; then throwing her arms round the
poor brute she kissed him with those passionate kisses of repentance and love which
should have fallen on her father's neck.
The dog (dumb to all but God) pleaded
with sorrowful eyes and half-frantic ges-
tures; but she turned wearily away toward
a great circle of immense rocks—relics of a
religion scarcely more cruel than that which
had neither pity nor forgiveness at the
mouth of the grave. Within their shadow
she could die unseen; and there next morning a wagoner, attracted by the plaintive
howling of a dog, found her on the ground,
dead.

There are set awful hours between every
soul and heaven. Who knows what passed
between Lettice Todd and her God in that
dim forsaken temple of a buried faith?

Death closes tenderly even the eyes full of tears, and her face was beautiful with a strange peace, though its loveliness was marred and its youth "seared with the autumn of strange suffering."

At the inquest which followed, her stern old father neither blamed nor excused himself. He accepted without apology the verdict of society against him; only remarking that its reproof was "a guid example o' Satan correcting sin."

Scant pity and less ceremony was given to her burial. Death, which draws under the mantle of Charity the pride, cruelty and ambition of men, covering them with those two narrow words *Hic jacet!* gives also to the woman who has been a sinner all she asks—oblivion. In no other way can she obtain from man toleration. The example of the whitest, purest soul that ever breathed on earth, in this respect, is ignored in the church He founded. The tenderest of human hearts, "when lovely woman stooped to folly," found no way of escape for her but to "die;" and those closet moralists, with filthy fancies and soiled souls, who abound in every community, regard her with that sort of scorn which a Turk expresses when he says "Dog of a Christian." Poor Lettice! She had procured this doom—first by sacrificing herself to a blind and cruel love, and then

to the importunate demands of hunger,
"oldest and strongest of passions." Ah! if
there was no pity in Heaven, no justice
beyond the grave, what a cruel irony this
life would be! For, while the sexton
shoveled hastily over the rude coffin the
obliterating earth, there passed the grave-
yard another woman equally fallen from all
the apostle calls "lovely and of good report." One whose youth and hopes and
marvelous beauty had been sold for houses
and lands and a few thousand pounds a
year. But, though her life was a living
lie, the world praised her, because she "had
done well unto herself." Yet, at the last
end, the same seed brought forth the same
fruit, and the Lady of Hawksworth Hall
learned, with bitter rapidity, that riches
are too poor to buy love. Scarcely had she
taken possession of her splendid home before she longed for the placid happiness of
her mother's cottage, and those evening
walks under the beech-trees, whose very
memory was now a sin. Over her beautiful face there crept a pathetic shadow,
which irritated the rude and noisy squire
like a reproach. He had always had what
he wanted. Not even the beauty of all the
border counties had been beyond his means
to buy but somehow he felt as if in this
bargain he had been overreached. Her
better part eluded his possession, and he

felt dissatisfied and angry. Expostulations grew into cruel words; cruel words came to crueler blows. *Yes, blows.* English gentlemen thirty years ago knew their privileges; and that was one of them. She was as much and as lawfully his as the horses in his stables or the hounds in his kennels. He beat them, too, when they did not obey him. Her beauty had betrayed her into the hands of misery. She had wedded it, and there was no escape for her. One day, when her despair and suffering was very great, some tempting devil brought her a glass of brandy, and she drank it. It gave her back for a few hours her departed sceptre; but at what a price! Her slave soon became her master. Stimulus and stupefaction, physical exhaustion and mental horrors, the abandonment of friends and the brutality of a coarse and cruel husband, brought her at last to the day of reckoning. She died, seven years after her marriage, in the delirium of opium. There were physicians and servants around her, and an unloving husband waiting for the news of his release. I think I would rather have died where Lettice did—under the sky, with the solemn mountains lifting their heads in a perpetual prayer around me, and that faithful dog licking my hands and mourning my wasted life.

Now, wherein did these two women

differ? One sinned through an intense and
self-sacrificing love, and in obedience to the
strongest calls of want. Her sin, though
it was beyond the pale of the world's toleration, was yet one *according to Nature.*
The other, in a cold spirit of barter, vol-
untarily and deliberately exchanged her
youth and beauty, the hopes of her own
and another's life, for carriages, jewels,
fine clothing and a luxurious table. She
loathed the price she had to pay, and her
sin was an unnatural one. For this kind
of prostitution, which religion blesses and
society praises, there seems to be no re-
dress; but for that which results as the
almost inevitable sequence of one lapse of
chastity *we*, the pious, the virtuous, the
irreproachable, are all to blame. Who or
what make it impossible for them to retrace
their steps? Do they ever have reason to
hope that the family hearth will be open to
them if they go back? Prodigal sons may
return, and are welcomed with tears of joy
and clasped by helping hands; but alas!
how few parents would go to meet a sin-
ning daughter. Forgetting our Master's
precepts, forgetting our human frailty,
forgetting our own weakness, we turn
scornfully from the weeping Magdalen,
and leave her "alone with the irreparable."
Marriage is a holy and a necessary rite.
We would deprecate *any* loosening of this

great house-band of society; but we do say
that where it is the *only distinction* between
two women, one of whom is an honored ma-
tron, and the other a Pariah and an outcast, there is "something in the world
amiss"—something beyond the cure of law
or legislation, and that they can only be
reached by the authority of a Christian
press and the influence of Christian example.

THE STORY OF DAVID MORRISON.

I think it is very likely that many New Yorkers were familiar with the face of David Morrison. It was a peculiarly guileless, kind face for a man of sixty years of age; a face that looked into the world's face with something of the confidence of a child. It had round it a little fringe of soft, light hair, and above that a big blue Scotch bonnet of the Rob Roryson fashion.

The bonnet had come with him from the little Highland clachan, where he and his brother Sandy had scrambled through a hard, happy boyhood together. It had sometimes been laid aside for a more pretentious headgear, but it had never been lost; and in his old age and poverty had been cheerfully—almost affectionately—resumed.

"Sandy had one just like it," he would say. "We bought them thegither in Aberdeen. Twa braw lads were we then. I'm wonderin' where poor Sandy is the day!"

So, if anybody remembers the little spare man, with the child-like, candid face and the big blue bonnet, let them recall him kindly. It is his true history I am telling to-day.

Davie had, as I said before, a hard boyhood. He knew what cold, hunger and long hours meant as soon as he knew anything; but it was glorified in his memory by the two central figures in it—a good mother, for whom he toiled and suffered cheerfully, and a big brother who helped him bravely over all the bits of life that were too hard for his young feet.

When the mother died, the lads sailed together for America. They had a "far-awa' cousin in New York, who, report said, had done well in the plastering business, and Sandy never doubted but that one Morrison would help another Morrison the wide world over. With this faith in their hearts and a few shillings in their pockets, the two lads landed. The American Morrison had not degenerated. He took kindly to his kith and kin, and offered to teach them his own craft.

For some time the brothers were well content; but Sandy was of an ambitious, adventurous temper, and was really only waiting until he felt sure that wee Davie could take care of himself. Nothing but the Great West could satisfy Sandy's hopes; but he never dreamt of exposing his brother to its dangers and privations.

"You're nothing stronger than a bit lassie, Davie," he said, "and you're no to fret if I don't take you wi' me. I'm going to make a big fortune, and when I have gotten the gold safe, I'se come back to you, and we'll spend it thegither dollar for dollar, my wee lad."

"Sure as death! You'll come back to me?"

"Sure as death, I'll come back to you, Davie!" and Sandy thought it no shame to cry on his little brother's neck, and to look back, with a loving, hopeful smile at Davie's sad, wistful face, just as long as he could see it.

It was Davie's nature to believe and to trust. With a pitiful confidence and constancy he looked for the redemption of his brother's promise. After twenty years of absolute silence, he used to sit in the evenings after his work was over, and wonder "how Sandy and he had lost each other." For the possibility of Sandy forgetting him never once entered his loyal heart.

He could find plenty of excuses for Sandy's silence. In the long years of their separation many changes had occurred even in a life so humble as Davie's. First, his cousin Morrison died, and the old business was scattered and forgotten. Then Davie had to move his residence very frequently; had even to follow lengthy jobs into various country places, so that his old address soon became a very blind clew to him.

Then seven years after Sandy's departure

the very house in which they had dwelt
was pulled down; an iron factory was built
on its site, and probably a few months
afterward no one in the neighborhood
could have told anything at all about Davie
Morrison. Thus, unless Sandy should come
himself to find his brother, every year made
the probability of a letter reaching him less
and less likely.

Perhaps, as the years went by, the prospect of a reunion became more of a dream
than an expectation. Davie had married
very happily, a simple little body, not un-
like himself, both in person and disposition.
They had one son, who, of course, had been
called Alexander, and in whom Davie
fondly insisted, the lost Sandy's beauty
and merits were faithfully reproduced.

It is needless to say the boy was extravagantly loved and spoiled. Whatever
Davie's youth had missed, he strove to
procure for "Little Sandy." Many an
extra hour he worked for this unselfish
end. Life itself became to him only an
implement with which to toil for his boy's
pleasure and advantage. It was a common-
place existence enough, and yet through it
ran one golden thread of romance.

In the summer evenings, when they
walked together on the Battery, and in
winter nights, when they sat together by
the stove, Davie talked to his wife and

child of that wonderful brother, who had gone to look for fortune in the great West. The simplicity of the elder two and the enthusiasm of the youth equally accepted the tale.

Somehow, through many a year, a belief in his return invested life with a glorious possibility. Any night they might come home and find Uncle Sandy sitting by the fire, with his pockets full of gold eagles, and no end of them in some safe bank, besides.

But when the youth had finished his schooldays, had learned a trade and began to go sweethearting, more tangible hopes and dreams agitated all their hearts; for young Sandy Morrison opened a carpenter's shop in his own name, and began to talk of taking a wife and furnishing a home.

He did not take just the wife that pleased his father and mother. There was nothing, indeed, about Sallie Barker of which they could complain. She was bright and capable, but they *felt* a want they were not able to analyze; the want was that pure unselfishness which was the ruling spirit of their own lives.

This want never could be supplied in Sallie's nature. She did right because it was her duty to do right, not because it gave her pleasure to do it. When they had been married three years the war broke out, and soon afterward Alexander Morrison was drafted for the army. Sallie, who was daily expecting her second child, refused all consolation; and, indeed, their case looked hard enough.

At first the possibility of a substitute had suggested itself; but a family consultation soon showed that this was impossible without hopelessly straitening both houses. Everyone knows that dreary silence which follows a long discussion, that has only confirmed the fear of an irremediable misfortune. Davie broke it in this case in a very unexpected manner.

"Let me go in your place, Sandy. I'd like to do it, my lad. Maybe I'd find your uncle. Who knows? What do you say, old wife? We've had more than twenty years together. It is pretty hard for Sandy and Sallie, now, isn't it?"

He spoke with a bright face and in a cheerful voice, as if he really was asking a favor for himself; and, though he did not try to put his offer into fine, heroic words, nothing could have been finer or more heroic than the perfect self-abnegation of his manner.

The poor old wife shed a few bitter tears; but she also had been practicing self-denial for a lifetime, and the end of it was that Davie went to weary marches and lonely watches, and Sandy staid at home.

This was the break-up of Davie's life.

His wife went to live with Sandy and Sallie, and the furniture was mostly sold.

Few people could have taken these events as Davie did. He even affected to be rather smitten with the military fever, and, when the parting came, left wife and son and home with a cheerful bravery that was sad enough to the one old heart who had counted its cost.

In Davie's loving, simple nature there was doubtless a strong vein of romance. He was really in hopes that he might come across his long-lost brother. He had no very clear idea as to localities and distances, and he had read so many marvelous war stories that all things seemed possible in its atmosphere. But reality and romance are wide enough apart.

Davie's military experience was a very dull and weary one. He grew poorer and poorer, lost heart and hope, and could only find comfort for all his sacrifices in the thought that "at least he had spared poor Sandy."

Neither was his home-coming what he had pictured it in many a reverie. There was no wife to meet him—she had been three months in the grave when he got back to New York—and going to his daughter-in-law's home was not—well, it was not like going to his own house.

Sallie was not cross or cruel, and she

was grateful to Davie, but she did not *love* the old man.

He soon found that the attempt to take up again his trade was hopeless. He had grown very old with three years' exposure and hard duty. Other men could do twice the work he could, and do it better. He must step out from the ranks of skilled mechanics and take such humble positions as his failing strength permitted him to fill.

Sandy objected strongly to this at first. "He could work for both," he said, "and he thought father had deserved his rest."

But Davie shook his head—"he must earn his own loaf, and he must earn it now, just as he could. Any honest way was honorable enough." He was still cheerful and hopeful, but it was noticeable that he never spoke of his brother Sandy now; he had buried that golden expectation with many others. Then began for Davie Morrison the darkest period of his life. I am not going to write its history.

It is not pleasant to tell of a family sinking lower and lower in spite of its brave and almost desperate efforts to keep its place—not pleasant to tell of the steps that gradually brought it to that pass, when the struggle was despairingly abandoned, and the conflict narrowed down to a fight with actual cold and hunger.

It is not pleasant, mainly, because in

such a struggle many a lonely claim is piti-
lessly set aside. In the daily shifts of bare
life, the tender words that bring tender acts
are forgotten. Gaunt looks, threadbare
clothes, hard day-labor, sharp endurance of
their children's wants, made Sandy and
Sallie Morrison often very hard to those to
whom they once were very tender.

David had noticed it for many months.
He could see that Sallie counted grudgingly
the few pennies he occasionally required.
His little newspaper business had been de-
clining for some years; people took fewer
papers, and some did not pay for those they
did take. He made little losses that were
great ones to him, and Sallie had long been
saying it would "be far better for father to
give up the business to Jamie; he is now sixteen and bright enough to look after his own."

This alternative David could not bear to
think of; and yet all through the summer
the fear had constantly been before him.
He knew how Sallie's plans always ended;
Sandy was sure to give into them sooner
or later, and he wondered if into their
minds had ever come the terrible thought
which haunted his own—*would they commit
him, then, to the care of public charities?*

"We have no time to love each other,"
he muttered, sadly, "and my bite and sup
is hard to spare when there is not enough
to go round. I'll speak to Sandy myself

about it—poor lad! It will come hard on him to say the first word.''

The thought once realized began to take shape in his mind, and that night, contrary to his usual custom, he could not go to sleep. Sandy came in early, and the children went wearily off to bed. Then Sallie began to talk on the very subject which lay so heavy on his own heart, and he could tell from the tone of the conversation that it was one that had been discussed many times before.

''He only made bare expenses last week and there's a loss of seventy cents this week already. Oh, Sandy, Sandy! there is no use putting off what is sure to come. Little Davie had to do without a drink of coffee to-night, and *his* bread, you know, comes off theirs at every meal. It is very hard on us all!''

''I don't think the children mind it, Sallie. Every one of them loves the old man—God bless him! He was a good father to me.''

''I would love him, too, Sandy, if I did not see him eating my children's bread. And neither he nor they get enough. Sandy, do take him down to-morrow, and tell him as you go the strait we are in. He will be better off; he will get better food and every other comfort. You must do it, Sandy; I can bear this no longer.''

6

"It's getting near Christmas, Sallie. Maybe he'll get New Year's presents enough to put things straight. Last year they were nearly eighteen dollars, you know."

"Don't you see that Jamie could get that just as well? Jamie can take the business and make something of it. Father is letting it get worse and worse every week. We should have one less to feed, and Jamie's earnings besides. Sandy, *it has got to be!* Do it while we can make something by the step."

"It is a mean, dastardly step, Sallie. God will never forgive me if I take it," and David could hear that his son's voice trembled.

In fact, great tears were silently dropping from Sandy's eyes, and his father knew it, and pitied him, and thanked God that the lad's heart was yet so tender. And after this he felt strangely calm, and dropped into a happy sleep.

In the morning he remembered all. He had not heard the end of the argument, but he knew that Sallie would succeed; and he was neither astonished nor dismayed when Sandy came home in the middle of the day and asked him to "go down the avenue a bit."

He had determined to speak first and spare Sandy the shame and the sorrow of it; but something would not let him do it.

In the first place, a singular lightness of heart came over him; he noticed all the gay preparations for Christmas, and the cries and bustle of the streets gave him a new sense of exhilaration. Sandy fell almost unconsciously into his humor. He had a few cents in his pocket, and he suddenly determined to go into a cheap restaurant and have a good warm meal with his father.

Davie was delighted at the proposal and gay as a child; old memories of days long past crowded into both men's minds, and they ate and drank, and then wandered on almost happily. Davie knew very well where they were going, but he determined now to put off saying a word until the last moment. He had Sandy all to himself for this hour; they might never have such another; Davie was determined to take all the sweetness of it.

As they got lower dòwn the avenue, Sandy became more and more silent; his eyes looked straight before him, but they were brimful of tears, and the smile with which he answered Davie's pleasant prattle was almost more pitiful than tears.

At length they came in sight of a certain building, and Sandy gave a start and shook himself like a man waking out of a sleep. His words were sharp, his voice almost like that of a man in mortal danger, as he turned Davie quickly round, and said:

"We must go back now, father. I will not go another step this road—no, by heaven! though I die for it!"

"Just a little further, Sandy."

And Davie's thin, childlike face had an inquiry in it that Sandy very well understood.

"No, no, father, no further on this road, please God!"

Then he hailed a passing car, and put the old man tenderly in it, and resolutely turned his back upon the hated point to which he had been going.

Of course he thought of Sallie as they rode home, and the children and the trouble there was likely to be. But somehow it seemed a light thing to him. He could not helping nodding cheerfully now and then to the father whom he had so nearly lost; and, perhaps, never in all their lives had they been so precious to each other as when, hand-in-hand, they climbed the dark tenement stair together.

Before they reached the door they heard Sallie push a chair aside hastily, and come to meet them. She had been crying, too, and her very first words were, "Oh, father! I am so glad!—so glad!"

She did not say what for, but Davie took her words very gratefully, and he made no remark, though he knew she went into debt at the grocery for the little extras with which she celebrated his return at supper. He understood, however, that the danger was passed, and he went to sleep that night thanking God for the love that had stood so hard a trial and come out conqueror.

The next day life took up its dreary tasks again, but in Davie's heart there was a strange presentiment of change, and it almost angered the poor, troubled, taxed wife to see him so thoughtlessly playing with the children. But the memory of the wrong she had nursed against him still softened and humbled her, and when he came home after carrying round his papers, she made room for him at the stove, and brought him a cup of coffee and a bit of bread and bacon.

Davie's eyes filled, and Sallie went away to avoid seeing them. So then he took out a paper that he had left and began to read it as he ate and drank.

In a few minutes a sudden sharp cry escaped him. He put the paper in his pocket, and, hastily resuming his old army cloak and Scotch bonnet, went out without a word to anyone.

The truth was that he had read a personal notice which greatly disturbed him. It was to the effect that, "If David Morrison, who left Aberdeen in 18—, was still alive, and would apply to Messrs. Morgan & Black, Wall street, he would hear of something to his advantage."

His long-lost brother was the one thought in his heart. He was going now to hear something about Sandy.

"He said 'sure as death,' and he would mind that promise at the last hour, if he forgot it before; so, if he could not come, he'd doubtless send, and this will be his message. Poor Sandy! there was never a lad like him!"

When he reached Messrs. Morgan & Black's, he was allowed to stand unnoticed by the stove a few minutes, and during them his spirits sank to their usual placid level. At length some one said:

"Well, old man, what do *you* want?"

"I am David Morrison, and I just came to see what *you* wanted."

"Oh, you are David Morrison! Good! Go forward—I think you will find out, then, what we want."

He was not frightened, but the man's manner displeased him, and, without answering, he walked toward the door indicated, and quietly opened it.

An old gentleman was standing with his back to the door, looking into the fire, and one rather younger, was writing steadily away at a desk. The former never moved; the latter simply raised his head with an annoyed look, and motioned to Davie to close the door.

"I am David Morrison, sir."

"Oh, Davie! Davie! And the old blue bonnet, too! Oh, Davie! Davie, lad!"

As for Davie, he was quite overcome. With a cry of joy so keen that it was like a sob of pain, he fell fainting to the floor. When he became conscious again he knew that he had been very ill, for there were two physicians by his side, and Sandy's face was full of anguish and anxiety.

"He will do now, sir. It was only the effect of a severe shock on a system too impoverished to bear it. Give him a good meal and a glass of wine."

Sandy was not long in following out this prescription, and during it what a confiding session these two hearts held! Davie told his sad history in his own unselfish way, making little of all his sacrifices, and saying a great deal about his son Sandy, and Sandy's girls and boys.

But the light in his brother's eyes, and the tender glow of admiration with which he regarded the unconscious hero, showed that he understood pretty clearly the part that Davie had always taken.

"However, I am o'erpaid for every grief I ever had, Sandy," said Davie, in conclusion, "since I have seen your face again, and you're just handsomer than ever, and you eight years older than me, too."

Yes, it was undeniable that Alexander

Morrison was still a very handsome, hale old gentleman; but yet there was many a trace of labor and sorrow on his face; and he had known both.

For many years after he had left Davie, life had been a very hard battle to him. During the first twenty years of their separation, indeed, Davie had perhaps been the better off, and the happier of the two.

When the war broke out, Sandy had enlisted early, and, like Davie, carried through all its chances and changes the hope of finding his brother. Both of them had returned to their homes after the struggle equally hopeless and poor.

But during the last eleven years fortune had smiled on Sandy. Some call of friendship for a dead comrade led him to a little Pennsylvania village, and while there he made a small speculation in oil, which was successful. He resolved to stay there, rented his little Western farm, and went into the oil business.

"And I have saved thirty thousand dollars, hard cash, Davie. Half of it is yours, and half mine. See! Fifteen thousand has been entered from time to time in your name. I told you, Davie, that when I came back we would share dollar for dollar, and I would not touch a cent of your share no more than I would rob the United States Treasury."

It was a part of Davie's simple nature that he accepted it without any further protestation. Instinctively he felt that it was the highest compliment he could pay his brother. It was as if he said: "I firmly believed the promise you made me more than forty years ago, and I firmly believe in the love and sincerity which this day redeems it." So Davie looked with a curious joyfulness at the vouchers which testified to fifteen thousand dollars lying in the Chemical Bank, New York, to the credit of David Morrison; and then he said, with almost the delight of a schoolboy:

"And what will you do wi' yours, Sandy?"

"I am going to buy a farm in New Jersey, Davie. I was talking with Mr. Black about it this morning. It will cost twelve thousand dollars, but the gentleman says it will be worth double that in a very few years. I think that myself, Davie, for I went yesterday to take a good look at it. It is never well to trust to other folks' eyes, you know."

"Then, Sandy, I'll go shares wi' you. We'll buy the farm together and we'll live together—that is, if you would like it."

"What would I like better?"

"Maybe you have a wife, and then—"

"No, I have no wife, Davie. She died

nearly thirty years ago. I have no one but you.''

''And we will grow small fruits, and raise chickens and have the finest dairy in the State, Sandy.''

''That is just my idea, Davie.''

Thus they talked until the winter evening began to close in upon them, and then Davie recollected that his boy, Sandy, would be more than uneasy about him.

''I'll not ask you there to-night, brother; I want them all to myself to-night. 'Deed, I've been selfish enough to keep this good news from them so long.''

So, with a hand-shake that said what no words could say, the brothers parted, and Davie made haste to catch the next up-town car. He thought they never had traveled so slowly; he was half inclined several times to get out and run home.

When he arrived there the little kitchen was dark, but there was a fire in the stove and wee Davie—his namesake—was sitting, half crying, before it.

The child lifted his little sorrowful face to his grandfather's, and tried to smile as he made room for him in the warmest place.

''What's the matter, Davie?''

''I have had a bad day, grandfather. I did not sell my papers, and Jack Dacey gave me a beating besides; and—and I really do think my toes are frozen off.''

Then Davie pulled the lad on to his knee, and whispered

"Oh, my wee man, you shall sell no more papers. You shall have braw new clothes, and go to school every day of your life. Whist! yonder comes mammy."

Sallie came in with a worried look, which changed to one of reproach when she saw Davie.

"Oh, father, how could you stay abroad this way? Sandy is fair daft about you, and is gone to the police stations, and I don't know where—"

Then she stopped, for Davie had come toward her, and there was such a new, strange look on his face that it terrified her, and she could only say: "Father! father! what is it?"

"It is good news, Sallie. My brother Sandy is come, and he has just given me fifteen thousand dollars; and there is a ten-dollar bill, dear lass, for we'll have a grand supper to-night, please God."

By and by they heard poor Sandy's weary footsteps on the stair, and Sallie said:

"Not a word, children. Let grandfather tell your father."

Davie went to meet him, and, before he spoke, Sandy saw, as Sallie had seen, that his father's countenance was changed, and that something wonderful had happened.

"What is the matter, father?"

"Fifteen thousand dollars is the matter, my boy; and peace and comfort and plenty, and decent clothes and school for the children, and a happy home for us all in some nice country place."

When Sandy heard this he kissed his father, and then covering his face with his hands, sobbed out:

"Thank God! thank God!"

It was late that night before either the children or the elders could go to sleep. Davie told them first of the farm that Sandy and he were going to buy together, and then he said to his son:

"Now, my dear lad, what think you is best for Sallie and the children?"

"You say, father, that the village where you are going is likely to grow fast."

"It is sure to grow. Two lines of railroad will pass through it in a month."

"Then I would like to open a carpenter's shop there. There will soon be work enough; and we will rent some nice little cottage, and the children can go to school, and it will be a new life for us all. I have often dreamed of such a chance, but I never believed it would come true."

But the dream came more than true. In a few weeks Davie and his brother were settled in their new home, and in the adjoining village Alexander Morrison, junior, had opened a good carpenter and builder's shop, and had begun to do very well.

Not far from it was the coziest of old stone houses, and over it Sallie presided. It stood among great trees, and was surrounded by a fine fruit garden, and was prettily furnished throughout; besides which, and best of all, *it was their own*—a New Year's gift from the kindest of grandfathers and uncles. People now have got well used to seeing the Brothers Morrison.

They are rarely met apart. They go to market and to the city together. What they buy they buy in unison, and every bill of sale they give bears both their names. Sandy is the ruling spirit, but Davie never suspects, for Sandy invariably says to all propositions, "If my brother David agrees, I do," or, "If brother David is satisfied, I have no more to say," etc.

Some of the villagers have tried to persuade them that they must be lonely, but they know better than that. Old men love a great deal of quiet and of gentle meandering retrospection; and David and Sandy have each of them forty years' history to tell the other. Then they are both very fond of young Sandy and the children.

Sandy's projects and plans and building contracts are always well talked over at the farm before they are signed, and the children's lessons and holidays, and even their new clothes, interest the two old men almost as much as they do Sallie.

As for Sallie, you would scarcely know her. She is no longer cross with care and quarrelsome with hunger. I always did believe that prosperity was good for the human soul, and Sallie Morrison proves the theory. She has grown sweet tempered in its sunshine, is gentle and forbearing to her children, loving and grateful to her father-in-law, and her husband's heart trusts in her.

Therefore let all those fortunate ones who are in prosperity give cheerfully to those who ask of them. It will bring a ten-fold blessing on what remains, and the piece of silver sent out on its pleasant errand may happily touch the hand that shall bring the giver good fortune through all the years of life.

TOM DUFFAN'S DAUGHTER.

Tom Duffan's cabinet-pictures are charming bits of painting; but you would cease to wonder how he caught such delicate home touches if you saw the room he painted in; for Tom has a habit of turning his wife's parlor into a studio, and both parlor and pictures are the better for the habit.

One bright morning in the winter of 1872 he had got his easel into a comfortable light between the blazing fire and the window, and was busily painting. His cheery little wife—pretty enough in spite of her thirty-seven years—was reading the interesting items in the morning papers to him, and between them he sung softly to himself the favorite tenor song of his favorite opera. But the singing always stopped when the reading began; and so politics and personals, murders and music, dramas and divorces kept continually interrupting the musical despair of "Ah! che la morte ognora."

But even a morning paper is not universally interesting, and in the very middle of an elaborate criticism on tragedy and Edwin Booth, the parlor door partially

opened, and a lovelier picture than ever
Tom Duffan painted stood in the aperture
—a piquant, brown-eyed girl, in a morning
gown of scarlet opera flannel, and a perfect
cloud of wavy black hair falling around her.

"Mamma, if anything on earth can interest you that is not in a newspaper, I
should like to know whether crimps or curls
are most becoming with my new seal-skin
set."

"Ask papa."

"If I was a picture, of course papa would
know; but seeing I am only a poor live
girl, it does not interest him."

"Because, Kitty, you never will dress
artistically."

"Because, papa, I must dress fashion-
ably. It is not my fault if artists don't
know the fashions. Can't I have mamma
for about half an hour?"

"When she has finished this criticism of
Edwin Booth. Come in, Kitty; it will do
you good to hear it."

"Thank you, no, papa; I am going to
Booth's myself to-night, and I prefer to do
my own criticism." Then Kitty disappeared, Mrs. Duffan skipped a good deal of
criticism, and Tom got back to his "Ah!
che la morte ognora" much quicker than
the column of printed matter warranted.

"Well, Kitty child, what do you want?"

"See here."

"Tickets for Booth's?"

"Parquette seats, middle aisle; I know them. Jack always does get just about the same numbers."

"Jack? You don't mean to say that Jack Warner sent them?"

Kitty nodded and laughed in a way that implied half a dozen different things.

"But I thought that you had positively refused him, Kitty?"

"Of course I did mamma—I told him in the nicest kind of way that we must only be dear friends, and so on."

"Then why did he send these tickets?"

"Why do moths fly round a candle? It is my opinion both moths and men enjoy burning."

"Well, Kitty, I don't pretend to understand this new-fashioned way of being 'off' and 'on' with a lover at the same time. Did you take me from papa simply to tell me this?"

"No; I thought perhaps you might like to devote a few moments to papa's daughter. Papa has no hair to crimp and no braids to make. Here are all the hair-pins ready, mamma, and I will tell you about Sarah Cooper's engagement and the ridiculous new dress she is getting."

It is to be supposed the bribe proved attractive enough, for Mrs. Duffan took in hand the long tresses, and Kitty rattled

7

away about wedding dresses and traveling suits and bridal gifts with as much interest as if they were the genuine news of life, and newspaper intelligence a kind of grown-up fairy lore.

But anyone who saw the hair taken out of crimps would have said it was worth the trouble of putting it in; and the face was worth the hair, and the hair was worth the exquisite hat and the rich seal-skins and the tantalizing effects of glancing silk and beautiful colors. Depend upon it, Kitty Duffan was just as bright and bewitching a life-sized picture as anyone could desire to see; and Tom Duffan thought so, as she tripped up to the great chair in which he was smoking and planning subjects, for a "good-by" kiss.

"I declare, Kitty! Turn round, will you? Yes, I declare you are dressed in excellent taste. All the effects are good. I wouldn't have believed it."

"Complimentary, papa. But 'I told you so.' You just quit the antique, and take to studying *Harper's Bazar* for effects; then your women will look a little more natural."

"Natural? Jehoshaphat! Go way, you little fraud!"

"I appeal to Jack. Jack, just look at the women in that picture of papa's, with the white sheets draped about them. What do they look like?"

"Frights, Miss Kitty."

"Of course they do. Now, papa."

"You two young barbarians!" shouted Tom, in a fit of laughter; for Jack and Kitty were out in the clear frosty air by this time, with the fresh wind at their backs, and their faces steadily set toward the busy bustle and light of Broadway. They had not gone far when Jack said, anxiously, "You haven't thought any better of your decision last Friday night, Kitty, I am afraid."

"Why, no, Jack. I don't see how I can, unless you could become an Indian Commissioner or a clerk of the Treasury, or something of that kind. You know I won't marry a literary man under any possible circumstances. I'm clear on that subject, Jack."

"I know all about farming, Kitty, if that would do."

"But I suppose if you were a farmer, we should have to live in the country. I am sure that would not do."

Jack did not see how the city and farm could be brought to terms; so he sighed, and was silent.

Kitty answered the sigh. "No use in bothering about me, Jack. You ought to be very glad I have been so honest. Some girls would have 'risked' you, and in a week you'd have been just as miserable!"

"You don't dislike me, Kitty?"

"Not at all. I think you are first-rate."

"It is my profession, then?"

"Exactly."

"Now, what has it ever done to offend you?"

"Nothing yet, and I don't mean it ever shall. You see, I know Will Hutton's wife: and what that woman endures! It's just dreadful."

"Now, Kitty!"

"It is, Jack. Will reads all his fine articles to her, wakes her up at nights to listen to some new poem, rushes away from the dinner table to jot down what he calls 'an idea,' is always pointing out 'splendid passages' to her, and keeps her working just like a slave copying his manuscripts and cutting newspapers to pieces. Oh, it is just dreadful!"

"But she thoroughly enjoys it."

"Yes, that is such a shame. Will has quite spoiled her. Lucy used to be real nice, a jolly, stylish girl. Before she was married she was splendid company; now, you might just as well mope round with a book."

"Kitty, I'd promise upon my honor—at the altar, if you like—never to bother you with anything I write; never to say a word about my profession."

"No, no, sir! Then you would soon be

finding some one else to bother, perhaps some blonde, sentimental, intellectual 'friend.' What is the use of turning a good-natured little thing like me into a hateful dog in the manger? I am not naturally able to appreciate you, but if you were *mine*, I should snarl and bark and bite at any other woman who was.''

Jack liked this unchristian sentiment very much indeed. He squeezed Kitty's hand and looked so gratefully into her bright face that she was forced to pretend he had ruined her glove.

''I'll buy you boxes full, Kitty; and, darling, I am not very poor; I am quite sure I could make plenty of money for you.''

''Jack, I did not want to speak about money; because, if a girl does not go into raptures about being willing to live on crusts and dress in calicos for love, people say she's mercenary. Well, then, I am mercenary. I want silk dresses and decent dinners and matinees, and I'm fond of having things regular; it's a habit of mine to like them all the time. Now I know literary people have spasms of riches, and then spasms of poverty. Artists are just the same. I have tried poverty occasionally, and found its uses less desirable than some people tell us they are.''

''Have you decided yet whom and what you will marry, Kitty?''

"No sarcasm, Jack. I shall marry the first good honest fellow that loves me and has a steady business, and who will not take me every summer to see views."

"To see views?"

"Yes. I am sick to death of fine scenery and mountains, 'scarped and jagged and rifted,' and all other kinds. I've seen so many grand landscapes, I never want to see another. I want to stay at the Branch or the Springs, and have nice dresses and a hop every night. And you know papa *will* go to some lonely place, where all my toilettes are thrown away, and where there is not a soul to speak to but famous men of one kind or another."

Jack couldn't help laughing; but they were now among the little crush that generally gathers in the vestibule of a theatre, and whatever he meant to say was cut in two by a downright hearty salutation from some third party.

"Why, Max, when did you get home?"

"To-day's steamer." Then there were introductions and a jingle of merry words and smiles that blended in Kitty's ears with the dreamy music, the rustle of dresses, and perfume of flowers, and the new-comer was gone.

But that three minutes' interview was a wonderful event to Kitty Duffan, though she did not yet realize it. The stranger had touched her as she had never been touched before. His magnetic voice called something into being that was altogether new to her; his keen, searching gray eyes claimed what she could neither understand nor withhold. She became suddenly silent and thoughtful; and Jack, who was learned in love lore, saw in a moment that Kitty had fallen in love with his friend Max Raymond.

It gave him a moment's bitter pang; but if Kitty was not for him, then he sincerely hoped Max might win her. Yet he could not have told whether he was most pleased or angry when he saw Max Raymond coolly negotiate a change of seats with the gentleman on Kitty's right hand, and take possession of Kitty's eyes and ears and heart. But there is a great deal of human nature in man, and Jack behaved, upon the whole, better than might have been expected.

For once Kitty did not do all the talking. Max talked, and she listened; Max gave opinions, and she indorsed them; Max decided, and she submitted. It was not Jack's Kitty at all. He was quite relieved when she turned round in her old piquant way and snubbed him.

But to Kitty it was a wonderful evening —those grand old Romans walking on and off the stage, the music playing, the people applauding and the calm, stately man on her right hand explaining this and that, and looking into her eyes in such a delicious, perplexing way that past and present were all mingled like the waving shadows of a wonderful dream.

She was in love's land for about three hours; then she had to come back into the cold frosty air, the veritable streets, and the unmistakable stone houses. But it was hardest of all to come back and be the old radiant, careless Kitty.

"Well, pussy, what of the play?" asked Tom Duffan; "you cut ·——'s criticism short this morning. Now, what is yours?"

"Oh, I don't know, papa. The play was Shakespeare's, and Booth and Barrett backed him up handsomely."

"Very fine criticism indeed, Kitty. I wish Booth and Barrett could hear it."

"I wish they could; but I am tired to death now. Good night, papa; good night, mamma. I'll talk for twenty in the morning."

"What's the matter with Kitty, mother?"

"Jack Warner, I expect."

"Hum! I don't think so."

"Men don't know everything, Tom."

"They don't know anything about women; their best efforts in that line are only guesses at truth."

"Go to bed, Tom Duffan; you are getting prosy and ridiculous. Kitty will explain herself in the morning."

But Kitty did not explain herself, and she daily grew more and more inexplicable. She began to read: Max brought the books, and she read them. She began to practice: Max liked music, and wanted to sing with her. She stopped crimping her hair: Max said it was unnatural and inartistic. She went to scientific lectures and astronomical lectures and literary societies: Max took her.

Tom Duffan did not quite like the change, for Tom was of that order of men who love to put their hearts and necks under a pretty woman's foot. He had been so long used to Kitty dominant, to Kitty sarcastic, to Kitty willful, to Kitty absolute, that he could not understand the new Kitty.

"I do not think our little girl is quite well, mother," he said one day, after studying his daughter reading the *Endymion* without a yawn.

"Tom, if you can't 'think' to better purpose, you had better go on painting. Kitty is in love."

"First time I ever saw love make a woman studious and sensible."

"They are uncommon symptoms; nevertheless, Kitty's in love. Poor child!"

"With whom?"

"Max Raymond;" and the mother dropped her eyes upon the ruffle she was

pleating for Kitty's dress, while Tom
Duffau accompanied the new-born thought
with his favorite melody.

Thus the winter passed quickly and happily away. Greatly to Kitty's delight, before its close Jack found the "blonde,
sentimental, intellectual friend," who could
appreciate both him and his writings; and
the two went to housekeeping in what Kitty
called "a large dry-goods box." The
merry little wedding was the last event of a
late spring, and when it was over the summer quarters were an imperative question.

"I really don't know what to do,
mother," said Tom. "Kitty vowed she
would not go to the Peak this year, and I
scarcely know how to get along without it."

"Oh, Kitty will go. Max Raymond has
quarters at the hotel lower down."

"Oh, oh! I'll tease the little puss."

"You will do nothing of the kind, Tom,
unless you want to go to Cape May or the
Branch. They both imagine their motives
undiscovered; but you just let Kitty know
that you even suspect them, and she won't
stir a step in your direction."

Here Kitty, entering the room, stopped
the conversation. She had a pretty lawn
suit on, and a Japanese fan in her hand.
"Lawn and fans, Kitty," said Tom: "time
to leave the city. Shall we go to the
Branch, or Saratoga?"

"Now, papa, you know you are joking; you always go to the Peak."

"But I am going with you to the seaside this summer, Kitty. I wish my little daughter to have her whim for once."

"You are better than there is any occasion for, papa. I don't want either the Branch or Saratoga this year. Sarah Cooper is at the Branch with her snobby little husband and her extravagant toilettes; I'm not going to be patronized by her. And Jack and his learned lady are at Saratoga. I don't want to make Mrs. Warner jealous, but I'm afraid I couldn't help it. I think you had better keep me out of temptation."

"Where must we go, then?"

"Well, I suppose we might as well go to the Peak. I shall not want many new dresses there; and then, papa, you are so good to me all the time, you deserve your own way about your holiday."

And Tom Duffan said, "*Thank you, Kitty*," in such a peculiar way that Kitty lost all her wits, blushed crimson, dropped her fan, and finally left the room with the lamest of excuses. And then Mrs. Duffan said, "Tom, you ought to be ashamed of yourself! If men know a thing past ordinary, they must blab it, either with a look or a word or a letter; I shouldn't wonder if Kitty told you to-night she was going to

the Branch, and asked you for a $500 check
—serve you right, too.''

But if Kitty had any such intentions,
Max Raymond changed them. Kitty went
very sweetly to the Peak, and two days
afterward Max Raymond, straying up the
hills with his fishing rod, strayed upon
Tom Duffan, sketching. Max did a great
deal of fishing that summer, and at the end
of it Tom Duffan's pretty daughter was in-
extricably caught. She had no will but
Max's will, and no way but his way. She
had promised him never to marry any one
but him; she had vowed she would love
him, and only him, to the end of her life.

All these obligations without a shadow
or a doubt from the prudent little body.
Yet she knew nothing of Max's family or
antecedents; she had taken his appearance
and manners, and her father's and mother's
respectful admission of his friendship, as
guarantee sufficient. She remembered that
Jack, that first night in the theatre, had
said something about studying law together; and with these items, and the satisfactory fact that he always had plenty of
money, Kitty had given her whole heart,
without conditions and without hostages.

Nor would she mar the placid measure of
her content by questioning; it was enough
that her father and mother were satisfied
with her choice. When they returned to

the city, congratulations, presents and preparations filled every hour. Kitty's importance gave her back a great deal of her
old dictatorial way. In the matter of
toilettes she would not suffer even Max to
interfere. "Results were all men had to
do with," she said; "everything was inartistic to them but a few yards of linen
and a straight petticoat."

Max sighed over the flounces and flutings
and lace and ribbons, and talked about
"unadorned beauty;" and then, when Kitty
exhibited results, went into rhapsodies of
wonder and admiration. Kitty was very
triumphant in those days, but a little drop
of mortification was in store for her. She
was exhibiting all her pretty things one
day to a friend, whose congratulations
found their climax in the following statement:

"Really, Kitty, a most beautiful ward-
robe! and such an extraordinary piece of
luck for such a little scatter-brain as you!
Why, they do say that Mr. Raymond's last
book is just wonderful."

"*Mr. Raymond's last book!*" And Kitty
let the satin-lined morocco case, with all its
ruby treasures, fall from her hand.

"Why, haven't you read it, dear? So
clever, and all that, dear."

Kitty had tact enough to turn the conversation; but just as soon as her visitor

had gone, she faced her mother, with blazing eyes and cheeks, and said, ''What is Max's business—a lawyer?''

''Gracious, Kitty! What's the matter? He is a scientist, a professor, and a great—''

''*Writer?*''

''Yes.''

''Writes books and magazine articles and things?''

''Yes.''

Kitty thought profoundly for a few moments, and then said, ''*I thought so.* I wish Jack Warner was at home.''

''What for?'

''Only a little matter I should like to have out with him; but it will keep.''

Jack, however, went South without visiting New York, and when he returned, pretty Kitty Duffan had been Mrs. Max Raymond for two years. His first visit was to Tom Duffan's parlor-studio. He was painting and singing and chatting to his wife as usual. It was so like old times that Jack's eyes filled at the memory when he asked where and how was Mrs. Raymond.

''Oh, the professor had bought a beautiful place eight miles from the city. Kitty and he preferred the country. Would he go and see them?''

Certainly Jack would go. To tell the truth, he was curious to see what other miracles matrimony had wrought upon

Kitty. So he went, and came back wondering.

"Really, dear," says Mrs. Jack Warner, the next day, "how does the professor get along with that foolish, ignorant little wife of his?"

"Get along with her? Why, he couldn't get along without her! She sorts his papers, makes his notes and quotations, answers his letters, copies his manuscripts, swears by all he thinks and says and does, through thick and thin, by day and night. It's wonderful, by Jove! I felt spiteful enough to remind her that she had once vowed that nothing on earth should ever induce her to marry a writer."

"What did she say?"

"She turned round in her old saucy manner, and answered, 'Jack Warner, you are as dark as ever. I did not marry the writer, I married *the man*.' Then I said, 'I suppose all this study and reading and writing is your offering toward the advancement of science and social regeneration?'"

"What then?"

"She laughed in a very provoking way, and said, 'Dark again, Jack; *it is a labor of love*.'"

"Well I never!"

"Nor I either."

THE HARVEST OF THE WIND.

CHAPTER I.

"As a city broken down and without walls, so is
he that hath no rule over his own spirit."

> "My soul! Master Jesus, my soul!
> My soul!
> Dar's a little thing lays in my heart,
> An' de more I dig him de better he spring:
> My soul!
> Dar's a little thing lays in my heart
> An' he sets my soul on fire:
> My soul!
> Master Jesus, my soul! my soul!"

The singer was a negro man, with a very
black but very kindly face; and he was
hoeing corn in the rich bottom lands of the
San Gabriel river as he chanted his joyful
little melody. It was early in the morning,
yet he rested on his hoe and looked anxiously toward the cypress swamp on his left
hand.

"I'se mighty weary 'bout Massa Davie;
he'll get himself into trouble ef he stay dar
much longer. Ole massa might be 'long
most any time now." He communed with
himself in this strain for about five minutes, and then threw his hoe across his

shoulder, and picked a road among the hills of growing corn until he passed out of the white dazzling light of the field into the grey-green shadows of the swamp. Threading his way among the still black bayous, he soon came to a little clearing in the cypress.

Here a young man was standing in an attitude of expectancy—a very handsome man clothed in the picturesque costume of a ranchero. He leaned upon his rifle, but betrayed both anger and impatience in the rapid switching to and fro of his riding-whip. "Plato, she has not come!" He said it reproachfully, as if the negro was to blame.

"I done tole you, Massa Davie, dat Miss Lulu neber do noffing ob dat kind; ole massa 'ticlarly objects to Miss Lulu seeing you at de present time."

"My father objects to every one I like."

"Ef Massa Davie jist 'lieve it, ole massa want ebery thing for his good."

"You oversize that statement considerably, Plato. Tell my father, if he asks you, that I am going with Jim Whaley, and give Miss Lulu this letter."

"I done promise ole massa neber to gib Miss Lulu any letter or message from you, Massa Davie."

In a moment the youth's handsome face was flaming with ungovernable passion, and he lifted his riding-whip to strike.

8

"For de Lord Jesus' sake don't strike, Massa Davie! Dese arms done carry you when you was de littlest little chile. Don't strike me!"

"I should be a brute if I did, Plato;" but the blow descended upon the trunk of the tree against which he had been leaning, with terrible force. Then David Lorimer went striding through the swamp, his great bell spurs chiming to his uneven, crashing tread.

Plato looked sorrowfully after him. "Poor Massa Davie! He's got de drefful temper; got it each side ob de house— father and mother, bofe. I hope de good Massa above will make 'lowances for de young man—got it bofe ways, he did." And he went thoughtfully back to his work, murmuring hopes and apologies for the man he loved, with all the forgiving unselfishness of a prayer in them.

In some respects Plato was right. David Lorimer had inherited, both from father and mother, an unruly temper. His father was a Scot, dour and self-willed; his mother had been a Spanish woman, of San Antonio —a daughter of the grandee family of Yturris. Their marriage had not been a happy one, and the fiery emotional Southern woman had fretted her life away against the rugged strength of the will which opposed hers. David remembered his mother well, and idolized her memory; right or wrong, he had always espoused her quarrel, and when she died she left, between father and son, a great gulf.

He had been hard to manage then, but at twenty-two he was beyond all control, excepting such as his cousin, Lulu Yturri, exercised over him. But this love, the most pure and powerful influence he acknowledged, had been positively forbidden. The elder Lorimer declared that there had been too much Spanish blood in the family; and it is likely his motives commended themselves to his own conscience. It was certain that the mere exertion of his will in the matter gave him a pleasure he would not forego. Yet he was theoretically a religious man, devoted to the special creed he approved, and rigidly observing such forms of worship as made any part of it. But the law of love had never yet been revealed to him; he had feared and trembled at the fiery Mount of Sinai, but he had not yet drawn near to the tenderer influences of Calvary.

He was a rich man also. Broad acres waved with his corn and cotton, and he counted his cattle on the prairies by tens of thousands; but nothing in his mode of life indicated wealth. The log-house, stretching itself out under gigantic trees, was of the usual style of Texan architecture—

broad passages between every room, sweep-
ing from front to rear; and low piazzas,
festooned with flowery vines, shading it on
every side. All around it, under the live
oaks, were scattered the negro cabins, their
staring whitewash looking picturesque
enough under the hanging moss and dark
green foliage. But, simple as the house
was, it was approached by lordly avenues,
shaded with black-jack and sweet gum and
chincapin, interwoven with superb magnolias and gorgeous tulip trees.

The Scot in a foreign country, too, often
steadily cultivates his national peculiarities.
James Lorimer was a Scot of this type. As
far as it was possible to do so in that sunshiny climate, he introduced the grey,
sombre influence of the land of mists and
east winds. His household was ruled with
stern gravity; his ranch was a model of
good management; and though few affected
his society, he was generally relied upon
and esteemed; for, though opinionated,
egotistical, and austere, there was about
him a grand honesty and a sense of
strength that would rise to every occasion.

And so great is the influence of any
genuine nature, that David loved his father
in a certain fashion. The creed he held
was a hard one; but when he called his
family and servants together, and unflinch-
ingly taught it, David, even in his worst

moods, was impressed with his sincerity and solemnity. There was between them plenty of ground on which they could have stood hand in hand, and learned to love one another; but a passionate authority on the one hand, and a passionate independence on the other, kept them far apart.

Shortly before my story opens there had been a more stubborn quarrel than usual, and James Lorimer had forbidden his son to enter his house until he chose to humble himself to his father's authority. Then David joined Jim Whaley, a great cattle drover, and in a week they were on the road to New Mexico with a herd of eight thousand.

This news greatly distressed James Lorimer. He loved his son better than he was aware of. There was a thousand deaths upon such a road; there was a moral danger in the companionship attending such a business, which he regarded with positive horror. The drove had left two days when he heard of its departure; but such droves travel slowly, and he could overtake it if he wished to do so. As he sat in the moonlight that night, smoking, he thought the thing over until he convinced himself that he ought to overtake it. Even if Davie would not return with him, he could tell him of his danger, and urge him to his duty and thus, at any rate, relieve his own conscience of a burden.

Arriving at this conclusion, he looked up and saw his niece Lulu leaning against one of the white pilasters supporting the piazza. He regarded her a moment curiously, as one may look at a lovely picture. The pale, sensitive face, the swaying, graceful figure, the flowing white robe, the roses at her girdle, were all sharply revealed by the bright moonlight, and nothing beautiful in them escaped his notice. He was just enough to admit that the temptation to love so fair a woman must have been a great one to David. He had himself fallen into just such a bewitching snare, and he believed it to be his duty to prevent a recurrence of his own married life at any sacrifice.

"Lulu!"

"Yes, uncle."

"Have you spoken with or written to Davie lately?"

"Not since you forbid me."

He said no more. He began wondering if, after all, the girl would not have been better than Jim Whaley. In a dim way it struck him that people for ever interfering with destiny do not always succeed in their intentions. It was an unusual and unpractical vein of thought for James Lorimer, and he put it uneasily away. Still over and over came back the question, "What if Lulu's influence would have been

sufficient to have kept David from the wild
reckless men with whom he was now con-
sorting?'' For the first time in his life he
consciously admitted to himself that he
might have made a mistake.

The next morning he was early in the saddle. The sky was blue and clear, the air full
of the fresh odor of earth and clover and
wild flowers. The swallows were making
a jubilant twitter, the larks singing on the
edge of the prairie—the glorious prairie,
which the giants of the unflooded world
had cleared off and leveled for the dwelling-
place of Liberty. In his own way he enjoyed the scene; but he could not, as he
usually did, let the peace of it sink into his
heart. He had suddenly become aware
that he had an unpleasant duty to perform,
and to shirk a duty was a thing impossible
to him. Until he had obeyed the voice of
Conscience, all other voices would fail to
arrest his interest or attention.

He rode on at a steady pace, keeping the
track very easily, and thinking of Lulu in
a persistent way that was annoying to him.
Hitherto he had given her very little
thought. Half reluctantly he had taken
her into his household when she was four
years of age, and she had grown up there
with almost as little care as the vines which
year by year clambered higher over the
piazzas. As for her beauty he had thought

no more of it than he did of the beauty of
the magnolias which sheltered his door-
step. Mrs. Lorimer had loved her niece,
and he had not interfered with the affection. They were both Yturris; it was
natural that they should understand one
another.

But his son was of a different race, and
the inheritor of his own traditions and prejudices. A Scot from his own countryside
had recently settled in the neighborhood,
and at the Sabbath gathering he had seen
and approved his daughter. To marry his
son David to Jessie Kennedy appeared to
him a most desirable thing, and he had
considered its advantages until he could
not bear to relinquish the idea. But when
both fathers had settled the matter, David
had met the question squarely, and declared
he would marry no woman but his cousin
Lulu. It was on this subject father and
son had quarrelled and parted; but for all
that, James Lorimer could not see his only
son taking a high road to ruin, and not
make an effort to save him.

At sundown he rested a little, but the
trail was so fresh he determined to ride on.
He might reach David while they were
camping, and then he could talk matters
over with more ease and freedom. Near
midnight the great white Texas moon
flooded everything with a light wondrously

soft, but clear as day, and he easily found
Whaley's camp—a ten-acre patch of grass
on the summit of some low hills.

The cattle had all settled for the night,
and the "watch" of eight men were slowly
riding in a circle around them. Lorimer
was immediately challenged; and he gave
his name and asked to see the captain.
Whaley rose at once, and confronted him
with a cool, civil movement of his hand to
his hat. Then Lorimer observed the man
as he had never done before. He was evidently not a person to be trifled with.
There was a fixed look about him, and a
deliberate coolness, sufficiently indicating
a determined character; and a belt around
his waist supported a six-shooter and revealed the glittering hilt of a bowie knife.

"Captain, good night. I wish to speak
with my son, David Lorimer."

"Wall, sir, you can't do it, not by no
manner of means, just yet. David Lorimer
is on watch till midnight."

He was perfectly civil, but there was
something particularly irritating in the way
Whaley named David Lorimer. So the
two men sat almost silent before the camp
fire until midnight. Then Whaley said,
"Mr. Lorimer, your son is at liberty now.
You'll excuse me saying that the shorter
you make your palaver the better it will
suit me."

Lorimer turned angrily, but Whaley was walking carelessly away; and the retort that rose to his lips was not one to be shouted after a man of Whaley's desperate character with safety. As his son approached him he was conscious of a thrill of pleasure in the young man's appearance.

Physically, he was all he could desire. No Lorimer that ever galloped through Eskdale had the national peculiarities more distinctively. He was the tall, fair Scot, and his father complacently compared his yellow hair and blue eyes with the "dark, deil-like beauty" of Whaley.

"Davie," and he held out his hand frankly, "I hae come to tak ye back to your ain hame. Let byganes be byganes, and we'll start a new chapter o' life, my lad. Ye'll try to be a gude son, and I'll aye be a gude father to ye."

It was a great deal for James Lorimer to say; and David quite appreciated the concession, but he answered—

"Lulu, father? I cannot give her up."

"Weel, weel, if ye are daft to marry a strange woman, ye must e'en do sae. It is an auld sin, and there have aye been daughters o' Heth to plague honest houses wi'. But sit down, my lad; I came to talk wi' ye anent some decenter way of life than this."

The talk was not altogether a pleasant

one; but both yielded something, and it was finally agreed that as soon as Whaley could pick up a man to fill Davie's place Davie should return home. Lorimer did not linger after this decision. Whaley's behavior had offended him and without the ceremony of a "good-bye," he turned his horse's head eastward again.

Picking up a man was not easy; they certainly had several offers from emigrants going west, and from Mexicans on the route, but Whaley seemed determined not to be pleased. He disliked Lorimer and was deeply offended at him interfering with his arrangements. Every day that he kept David was a kind of triumph to him. "He might as well have asked me how I'd like my drivers decoyed away. I like a man to be on the square," he grumbled. And he said these and similar things so often, that David began to feel it impossible to restrain his temper.

Anger, fed constantly by spiteful remarks and small injustices, grows rapidly; and as they approached the Apache mountains, the men began to notice a fixed tightening of the lips, and a stern blaze in the young Scot's eyes, which Whaley appeared to delight in intensifying.

"Thar'll be mischief atween them two afore long," remarked an old drover; "Lorimer is gittin' to hate the captain with such a vim that he's no appetite for his food left.''

''It'll be a fair fight, and one or both'll get upped; that's about it.''

At length they met a party of returning drovers, and half a dozen men among them were willing to take David's place. Whaley had no longer any pretence for detaining him. They were at the time between two long, low spurs of hills, enclosing a rich narrow valley, deep with ripened grass, gilded into flickering gold by the sun and the dewless summer days. All the lower ridges were savagely bald and hot—a glen paved with gold and walled with iron. Oh, how the sun did beat and shiver, and shake down into the breathless valley!

The cattle were restless, and the men had had a hard day. David was weary; his heart was not in the work; he was glad it was his last watch. It began at ten o'clock, and would end at midnight. The weather was gloomy, and the few stars which shone between the rifts of driving clouds just served to outline the mass of sleeping cattle.

The air also was surcharged with electricity, though there had been no lightning.

''I wouldn't wonder ef we have a 'run' to-night,'' said one of the men. ''I've seen a good many stampedes, and they allays happens on such nights as this one.''

''Nonsense!'' replied David. ''If a

cayote frightens one in a drove the panic spreads to all. Any night would do for a 'run.' ''

" 'Taint so, Lorimer. Ef you've a drove of one thousand or of ten thousand it's all the same; the panic strikes every beast at the same moment. It's somethin' in the air; 'taint my business to know what. But you look like a 'run' yourself, restless and hot, and as ef somethin' was gitting 'the mad' up in you. I noticed Whaley is 'bout the same. I'd keep clear of him, ef I was you.''

"No, I won't. He owes me money, and I'll make him pay me!''

"Don't! Thar, I've warned you, David Lorimer, and that let's me out. Take your own way now.''

For half an hour David pondered this caution, and something in his own heart seconded it. But when the trial of his temper came he turned a deaf ear to every monition. Whaley went swaggering by him, and as he passed issued an unnecessary order in a very insolent manner. David asked pointedly, "Were you speaking to me, Captain?''

"I was.''

"Then don't you dare to do it again, sir; never, as long as you live!''

Before the words were out of his mouth, every one of the drove of eight thousand were on their feet like a flash of lightning; every one of them exactly at the same instant. With a rush like a whirlwind leveling a forest, they were off in the darkness.

The wild clatter, the crackling of a river of horns, and the thundering of hoofs, was deafening. Whaley, seeing eighty thousand dollars' worth of cattle running away from him, turned with a fierce imprecation, and gave David a passionate order "to ride up to the leaders," and then he sprang for his own mule.

David's time was now fully out, and he drew his horse's rein tight and stood still.

"Coward!" screamed Whaley; "try and forget for an hour that you have Spanish blood in you."

A pistol shot answered the taunt. Whaley staggered a second, then fell without a word. The whole scene had not occupied a minute; but it was a minute that branded itself on the soul of David Lorimer. He gazed one instant on the upturned face of his slain enemy, and then gave himself up to the wild passion of the pursuit.

By the spectral starlight he could see the cattle outlined as a black, clattering, thundering stream, rushing wildly on, and every instant becoming wilder. But David's horse had been trained in the business; he knew what the matter was, and scarce needed any guiding. Dashing along by the side of the stampede, they soon overtook the leaders and joined the men, who were gradually pushing against the foremost cattle on the left so as to turn them to the right. When once the leaders were turned the rest blindly followed and thus, by constantly turning them to the right, the leaders were finally swung clear around, and overtook the fag end of the line.

Then they rushed around in a circle, the centre of which soon closed up, and they were "milling;" that is, they had formed a solid wheel, and were going round and round themselves in the same space of ground. Men who had noticed how very little David's heart had been in his work were amazed to see the reckless courage he displayed. Round and round the mill he flew, keeping the outside stock from flying off at a tangent, and soothing and quieting the beasts nearest to him with his voice. The "run" was over as suddenly as it commenced, and the men, breathless and exhausted, stood around the circle of panting cattle.

"Whar's the Captain?" said one; "he gin'rally soop'rintends a job like this himself."

"And likes to do it. Who's seen the Captain? Hev you, Lorimer?"

"He was in camp when I started. My time was up just as the 'run' commenced."

No more was said; indeed, there was little opportunity for conversation. The cattle were to watch; it was still dark; the men were weary with the hard riding and the unnatural pitch to which their voices had been raised. David felt that he must get away at once; any moment a messenger from the camp might bring the news of Whaley's murder; and he knew well that suspicion would at once rest upon him.

He offered to return to camp and report "all right," and the offer was accepted; but, at the first turn, he rode away into the darkness of a belt of timber. The cayotes howled in the distance; there was a rush of unclean night birds above him, and the growling of panther cats in the underwood. But in his soul there was a terror and a darkness that made all natural terrors of small account. His own hands were hateful to him. He moaned out loudly like a man in an agony. He measured in every moment's space the height from which he had fallen; the blessings from which he must be an outcast, if by any means he might escape the shameful punishment of his deed. He remembered at that hour his father's love, the love that had so finely asserted itself when the occasion for it came. Lulu's tenderness and beauty, the hope of home and children, the respect of his fellow-men, all sacrificed for a moment's passionate revenge. He stood face to face with himself, and, dropping the reins, cowered down full of terror and grief at the future which he had evoked. Within hopeless sight of Hope and Love and Home, he was silent for hours gazing despairingly after the life which had sailed by him, and not daring—

> "——to search through what sad maze,
> Thenceforth his incommunicable ways
> Follow the feet of death."

CHAPTER II.

"——and sin, when it is finished, bringeth forth death." James i. 15.

Blessed are they who have seen Nature in those rare, ineffable moments when she appears to be asleep—when the stars, large and white, bend stilly over the dreaming earth, and not a breath of wind stirs leaf or flower. On such a night James Lorimer sat upon his south verandah smoking; and his niece Lulu, white and motionless as the magnolia flowers above her, mused the hour away beside him. There were little ebony squads of negroes huddled together around the doors of their quarters, but they also were singularly quiet. An angel of silence had passed by no one was inclined to

9

disturb the tranquil calm of the dreaming earth.

There is nothing good in this life which Time does not improve. In ten days the better feelings which had led James Lorimer to seek his son in the path of moral and physical danger had grown as Divine seed does grow. This very night, in the scented breathless quiet, he was longing for David's return, and forming plans through which the future might atone for the past. Gradually the weary negroes went into the cabins, rolled themselves in their blankets and fell into that sound, dreamless sleep which is the compensation of hard labor. Only Lulu watched and thought with him.

Suddenly she stood up and listened. There was a footstep in the avenue, and she knew it. But why did it linger, and what dreary echo of sorrow was there in it?

"That is David's step, uncle; but what is the matter? Is he sick?"

Then they both saw the young man coming slowly through the gloom, and the shadow of some calamity came steadily on before him. Lulu went to the top of the long flight of white steps, and put out her hands to greet him. He motioned her away with a woeful and positive gesture, and stood with hopeless yet half defiant attitude before his father.

In a moment all the new tenderness was gone.

In a voice stern and scornful he asked, "Well, sir, what is the matter? What hae ye been doing now?"

"I have shot Whaley!"

The words were rather breathed than spoken, but they were distinctly audible. The father rose and faced his wretched son.

Lulu drew close to him, and asked, in a shocked whisper, "Dead?"

"Dead!"

"But you had a good reason, David; I know you had. He would have shot you? —it was in self-defence?—it was an accident? Speak, dear!"

"He called me a coward, and—"

"You shot him! Then you are a coward, sir!" said Lorimer, sternly; "and having made yourself fit for the gallows, you are a double coward to come here and force upon me the duty of arresting you. Put down your rifle, sir!"

Lulu uttered a long low wail. "Oh, David, my love! why did you come here? Did you hope for pity or help in his heart? And what can I do Davie, but suffer with you?" But she drew his face down and kissed it with a solemn tenderness that taught the wretched man, in one moment, all the blessedness of a woman's devotion, and all the misery that the indulgence of his ungovernable temper had caused him.

"We will hae no more heroics, Lulu. As a magistrate and a citizen it is my duty to arrest a murderer on his ain confession."

"Your duty!" she answered, in a passion of scorn. "Had you done your duty to David in the past years, this duty would not have been to do. Your duty or anything belonging to yourself, has always been your sole care. Wrong Davie, wrong me, slay love outright, but do your duty, and stand well with the world and yourself! Uncle, you are a dreadful Christian!"

"How dare you judge me, Lulu? Go to your own room at once!"

"David, dearest, farewell! Fly!—you will get no pity here. Fly!"

"Sit down, sir, and do not attempt to move!"

"I am hungry, thirsty, weary and wretched, and at your mercy, father. Do as you will with me." And he laid his rifle upon the table.

Lorimer looked at the hopeless figure that almost fell into the chair beside him, and his first feeling was one of mingled scorn and pity.

"How did it happen? Tell me the truth. I want neither excuses nor deceptions."

"I have no desire to make them. There was a 'run,' just as my time was out.

Whaley, in an insolent manner, ordered me to help turn the leaders. I did not move. He called me a coward, and taunted me with my Spanish blood—it was my dear mother's.''

"That is it," answered Lorimer, with an anger all the more terrible for its restraint; "it is the Spanish blood wi' its gasconade and foolish pride.''

"Father! You have a right to give me up to the hangman; but you have no right to insult me.''

The next moment he fell senseless at his father's feet. It was the collapse of consciousness under excessive physical exhaustion and mental anguish; but Lorimer, who had never seen a man in such extremity, believed it to be death. A tumult of emotions rushed over him, but assistance was evidently the first duty, and he hastened for it. First he sent the housekeeper Cassie to her young master, then he went to the quarters to arouse Plato.

When he returned, Lulu and Cassie were kneeling beside the unconscious youth. "You have murdered him!" said Lulu, bitterly; and for a moment he felt something of the remorseful agony which had driven the criminal at his feet into a short oblivion. But very soon there was a slight reaction, and the father was the first to see it. "He has only fainted; bring some wine here!"

Then he remembered the weakness of the voice which had said, "I am hungry, and thirsty, and weary and wretched."

When David opened his eyes again his first glance was at his father. There was something in that look that smote the angry man to his heart of hearts. He turned away, motioning Plato to follow him. But even when he had reached his own room and shut his door, he could not free himself from the influence evoked by that look of sorrowful reproach.

Plato stood just within the door, nervously dangling his straw hat. He was evidently balancing some question in his own mind, and the uncertainty gave a queer restlessness to every part of his body.

"Plato, you are to watch the young man down-stairs; he is not to be allowed to leave the house."

"Yes, sar."

"He has committed a great crime, and he must abide the consequences."

No answer.

"You understand that, Plato?"

"Dunno, sar. I mighty sinful ole man myself. Dunno bout de consequences."

"Go, and do as I bid you!"

When he was alone he rose slowly and locked his door. He wanted to do right, but he was like a man in the fury and darkness of a great tempest: he could not

see any road at all. There was a Bible on
his dressing-table, and he opened it; but
the verses mingled together, and the sense
of everything seemed to escape him. The
hand of the Great Father was stretched out
to him in the dark, but he could not find it.
He knew that at the bottom of his heart lay
a wish that David would escape from justice. He knew that a selfish shame about
his own fair character mingled with his
father's love; his motives and feelings were
so mixed that he did not dare to bring
them, in their pure truthfulness, to the feet
of God; for as yet he did not understand
that ''like as a father pitieth his children,
so the Lord pitieth them that fear Him;''
he thought of the Divine Being as, one so
jealous for His own rights and honor that
He would have the human heart a void,
so that he might reign there supremely.
So all that terrible night he stood smitten
and astonished on a threshold he could not
pass.

In another room the question was being
in a measure solved for him. Cassie
brought in meat and bread and wine, and
David ate, and felt refreshed. Then the
love of life returned, and the terror of a
shameful death; and he laid his hand upon
his rifle and looked round to see what
chance of escape his father had left him.
Plato stood at the door, Lulu sat by his

side, holding his hand. On her face there was an expression of suffering, at once defiant and despairing—a barren suffering, without hope. They had come to that turn on their unhappy road when they had to bid each other "Farewell!" It was done very sadly, and with few words.

"You must go now, beloved."

He held her close to his heart and kissed her solemnly and silently. The next moment she turned on him from the open door a white, anguished face. Then he was alone with Plato.

"Plato, I must go now. Will you saddle the brown mare for me?"

"She am waiting, Massa David. I tole Cassie to get her ready, and some bread and meat, and *dis*, Massa Davie, if you'll 'blige ole Plato." Then he laid down a rude bag of buckskin, holding the savings of his lifetime.

"How much is there, Plato?"

"Four hundred dollars, sar. Sorry it am so little."

"It was for your freedom, Plato."

"I done gib dat up, Massa Davie. I'se too ole now to git de rest. Ef you git free, dat is all I want."

They went quietly out together. It was not long after midnight. The brown mare stood ready saddled in the shadow, and Cassie stood beside her with a small bag holding a change of linen and some cooked food. The young man mounted quickly, grasped the kind hands held out to him, and then rode away into the darkness. He went softly at first, but when he reached the end of the avenue at a speed which indicated his terror and his mental suffering.

Cassie and Plato watched him until he became an indistinguishable black spot upon the prairie; then they turned wearily towards the cabins. They had seen and shared the long sorrow and discontent of the household; they hardly expected anything but trouble in some form or other. Both were also thinking of the punishment they were likely to receive; for James Lorimer never failed to make an example of evil-doers; he would hardly be disposed to pass over their disobedience.

Early in the morning Plato was called by his master. There was little trace of the night of mental agony the latter had passed. He was one of those complete characters who join to perfect physical health a mind whose fibres do not easily show the severest strain.

"Tell Master David to come here."

"Massa David, sar! Massa David done gone, sar!" The old man's lips were trembling, but otherwise his nervous restlessness was over. He looked his master calmly in the face.

"Did I not tell you to stop him?"

"Ef de Lord in heaven want him stopped, Massa James, He'll send the messenger—Plato could not do it!"

"How did he go?"

"On de little brown mare—his own horse done broke all up."

"How much money did you give him?"

"Money, sar?"

"How much? Tell the truth."

"Four hundred dollars."

"That will do. Tell Cassie I want **my** breakfast."

At breakfast he glanced at Lulu's empty chair, but said nothing. In the house all was as if no great sin and sorrow had darkened its threshold and left a stain upon its hearthstone. The churning and cleaning was going on as usual. Only Cassie was quieter, and Lulu lay, white and motionless, in the little vine-shaded room that looked too cool and pretty for grief to enter. The unhappy father sat still all day, pondering many things that he had not before thought of. Every footfall made his heart turn sick, but the night came, and there was no further bad news.

On the second day he went into Lulu's room, hoping to say a word of comfort to her. She listened apathetically, and turned her face to the wall with a great sob. He began to feel some irritation in

the atmosphere of misery which surrounded
him. It was very hard to be made so
wretched for another's sin. The thought
in an instant became a reproach. Was he
altogether innocent? The second and third
days passed; he began to be sure then that
David must have reached a point beyond
the probability of pursuit.

On the fourth day he went to the cotton
field. He visited the overseer's house, he
spent the day in going over accounts and
making estimates. He tried to forget that
something had happened which made life
appear a different thing. In the grey,
chill, misty evening he returned home.
The negroes were filing down the long lane
before him, each bearing their last basket
of cotton—all of them silent, depressed
with their weariness, and intensely sensitive to the melancholy influence of the
autumn twilight.

Lorimer did not care to pass them. He
saw them, one by one, leave their cotton at
the ginhouse, and trail despondingly off to
their cabins. Then he rode slowly up to
his own door. A man sat on the verandah
smoking. At the sight of him his heart
fell fathoms deep.

"Good evening." He tried to give his
voice a cheerful welcoming sound, but he
could not do it; and the visitor's attitude
was not encouraging.

"Good evening, Lorimer. I'm right sorry to tell you that you will be wanted on some unpleasant business very early to-morrow morning."

He tried to answer, but utterly failed; his tongue was as dumb as his soul was heavy. He only drew a chair forward and sat down.

"Fact is your son is in a tighter place than any man would care for. I brought him up to Sheriff Gillelands' this afternoon. Perhaps he can make it out a case of 'justifiable homicide'—hope he can. He's about as likely a young man as I ever saw."

Still no answer.

"Well, Lorimer, I think you're right. Talking won't help things, and may make them a sight worse. You'll be over to Judge Lepperts' in the morning?—say about ten o'clock."

"Yes. Will you have some supper?"

"No; this is not hungry work. My pipe is more satisfactory under the circumstances. I'll have to saddle up, too. There's others to see yet. Is there any one particular you'd like on the jury?"

"No. You must do your duty, Sheriff."

He heard him gallop away, and stood still, clasping and unclasping his hands in a maze of anguish. David at Sheriff Gillelands'! David to be tried for murder in the morning! What could he do? If David had not confessed to the shooting of Whaley, would he be compelled to give his evidence? Surely, conscience would not require so hard a duty of him.

At length he determined to go and see David before he decided upon the course he ought to take. The sheriff's was only about three miles distant. He rode over there at once. His son, with travel-stained clothes and blood-shot hopeless eyes, looked up to see him enter. His heart was full of a great love, but it was wronged, even at that hour, by an irritation that would first and foremost assert itself. Instead of saying, "My dear, dear lad!" the lament which was in his heart, he said, "So this is the end of it, David?"

"Yes. It is the end."

"You ought not to have run away."

"No. I ought to have let you surrender me to justice; that would have put you all right."

"I wasna thinking o' that. A man flying from justice is condemned by the act."

"It would have made no matter. There is only one verdict and one end possible."

"Have you then confessed the murder?"

He awaited the answer in an agony. It came with a terrible distinctness. "Whaley lived thirty hours. He told. His brother-in-law has gone on with the cattle. Four of the drivers are come back as witnesses. They are in the house.''

''But you have not yourself confessed?''

''Yes. I told Sheriff Gillelands I shot the man. If I had not done so you would; I knew that. I have at least spared you the pain and shame of denouncing your own son!''

''Oh, David, David! I would not. My dear lad, I would not! I would hae gane to the end o' the world first. Why didna you trust me?''

''How could I, father?''

He let the words drop wearily, and covered his face with his hands. After a pause, he said, ''Poor Lulu! Don't tell her if you can help it, until—all is over. How glad I am this day that my mother is dead!''

The wretched father could endure the scene no longer. He went into the outer room to find out what hope of escape remained for his son. The sheriff was full of pity, and entered readily into a discussion of David's chances. But he was obliged to point out that they were extremely small. The jury and the judge were all alike cattle men; their sympathies were positively against everything likely to weaken the discipline necessary in carrying large herds of cattle safely across the continent. In the moment of extremest

danger, David had not only refused assistance, but had shot his employer.

"He called him a coward, and you'll
admit that's a vera aggravating name."

The sheriff readily admitted that under
any ordinary circumstances in Texas that
epithet would justify a murder; "but," he
added, "most any Texan would say he was
a coward to stand still and see eight thousand head of cattle on the stampede. You'll
excuse me, Lorimer, I'd say so myself."

He went home again and shut himself in
his room to think. But after many hours,
he was just as far as ever from any coherent
decision. Justice! Justice! Justice! The
whole current of his spiritual and mental
constitution ran that road. Blood for blood;
a life for a life; it was meet and right, and
he acknowledged it with bleeding heart
and streaming eyes. But, clear and dis-
tinct above the tumult of this current, he
heard something which made him cry out
with an equally unhappy father of old,
"Oh, Absalom! My son, my son Absalom!"

Then came the accuser and boldly told
him that he had neglected his duty, and
driven his son into the way of sin and
death; and that the seeds sown in domestic
bickering and unkindness had only brought
forth their natural fruit. The scales fell
from his eyes; all the past became clear to

him. His own righteousness was dreadful in his sight. He cried out with his whole soul, "God be merciful! God be merciful!"

The darkest despairs are the most silent. All the night long he was only able to utter that one heartbroken cry for pity and help. At the earliest daylight he was with his son. He was amazed to find him calm, almost cheerful. "The worst is over father," he said. "I have done a great wrong; I acknowledge the justice of the punishment, and am willing to suffer it."

"But after death! Oh, David, David—afterward!"

"I shall dare to hope—for Christ also has died, the just for the unjust."

Then the father, with a solemn earnestness, spoke to his son of that eternity whose shores his feet were touching. At this hour he would shirk no truth; he would encourage no false hope. And David listened; for this side of his father's character he had always had great respect, and in those first hours of remorse following the murder, not the least part of his suffering had been the fearful looking forward to the Divine vengeance which he could never fly from. But there had been *One* with him that night, *One* who is not very far from us at any time; and though David had but tremblingly understood His voice, and almost feared to accept its comfort, he was in those desperate circumstances when men cannot reason and philosophize, when nothing remains for them but to believe.

"Dinna get by the truth, my dear lad; you hae committed a great sin, there is nae doubt o' that."

"But God's mercy, I trust, is greater."

"And you hae nothing to bring him from a' the years o' your life! Oh, David, David!"

"I know," he answered sadly. "But neither had the dying thief. He only believed. Father, this is the sole hope and comfort left me now. Don't take it from me."

Lorimer turned away weeping; yes, and praying, too, as men must pray when they stand powerless in the stress of terrible sorrows. At noon the twelve men summoned dropped in one by one, and the informal court was opened. David Lorimer admitted the murder, and explained the long irritation and the final taunt which had produced it. The testimony of the returned drovers supplemented the tragedy. If there was any excuse to be made, it lay in the disgraceful epithet applied to David and the scornful mention of his mother's race.

There was, however, an unfavorable feeling from the first. The elder Lorimer, with his stern principles and severe manners, was not a popular man. David's proud, passionate temper had made him some active enemies; and there was not a man on the jury who did not feel as the sheriff had honestly expressed himself regarding David's conduct at the moment of the stampede. It touched all their prejudices and their interests very nearly; not one of them was inclined to blame Whaley for calling a man a coward who would not answer the demand for help at such an imperative moment.

As to the Spanish element, it had always been an offence to Texans. There were men on the jury whose fathers had died fighting it; beside, there was that unacknowledged but positive contempt which ever attaches itself to a race that has been subjugated. Long before the form of a trial was over, David had felt the hopelessness of hope, and had accepted his fate. Not so his father. He pleaded with all his soul for his son's life. But he touched no heart there. The jury had decided on the death-sentence before they left their seats.

And in that locality, and at that time, there was no delay in carrying it out. It would be inconvenient to bring together again a sufficient number of witnesses, and equally inconvenient to guard a prisoner for any length of time. David was to die at sunset.

Three hours yet remained to the miserable father. He threw aside all pride and all restraint. Remorse and tenderness wrung his heart. But these last hours had a comfort no others in their life ever had. What confessions of mutual faults were made! What kisses and forgivenesses were exchanged! At last the two poor souls who had dwelt in the chill of mistakes and ignorance knew that they loved each other. Sometimes the Lord grants such sudden unfoldings to souls long closed. They are of those royal compassions which astonish even the angels.

When his time was nearly over, David pushed a piece of paper toward his father. "It is my last request," he said, looking into his face with eyes whose entreaty was pathetic. "You must grant it, father, hard as it is."

Lorimer's hand trembled as he took the paper, but his face turned pale as ashes when he read the contents.

"I canna, I canna do it," he whispered.

"Yes, you will, father. It is the last favor I shall ask of you."

The request was indeed a bitter one; so bitter that David had not dared to voice it. It was this—

"Father, be my executioner. Do not let me be hung. The rope is all I dread in death; ere it touch me, let your rifle end my life."

For a few moments Lorimer sat like a man turned to stone. Then he rose and went to the jury. They were sitting together under some mulberry trees, smoking. Naturally silent, they had scarcely spoken since their verdict. Grave, fierce men, they were far from being cruel; they had no pleasure in the act which they believed to be their duty.

Lorimer went from one to the other and made known his son's request. He pleaded, "That as David had shot Whaley, justice would be fully satisfied in meting out the same death to the murderer as the victim."

But one man, a ranchero of great influence and wealth, answered that he must oppose such a request. It was the rope, he thought, made the punishment. He hoped no Texan feared a bullet. A clean, honorable death like that was for a man who had never wronged his manhood. Every rascally horse thief or Mexican assassin would demand a shot if they were given a precedent. And arguments that would have been essentially false in some localities had a compelling weight in that one. The men gravely nodded their heads in assent, and Lorimer knew that any further pleading was in vain. Yet when he returned to his son, he clasped his hand and looked into his eyes, and David understood that his request would be granted.

Just as the sun dropped the sheriff entered the room. He took the prisoner's arm and walked quietly out with him. There was a coil of rope on his other arm, and David cast his eyes on it with horror and abhorrence, and then looked at his father; and the look was returned with one of singular steadiness. When they reached the little grove of mulberries, the men, one by one, laid down their pipes and slowly rose. There was a large live oak at the end of the enclosure, and to it the party walked.

Here David was asked "if he was guilty?" and he acknowledged the sin: and when further asked "if he thought he had been fairly dealt with, and deserved death?" he answered, "that he was quite satisfied, and was willing to pay the penalty of his crime."

Oh, how handsome he looked at this moment to his heart-broken father! His bare head was just touched by the rays of the setting sun behind him; his fine face, calm and composed, wore even a faint air of exultation. At this hour the travel-stained garments clothed him with a touching and not ignoble pathos. Involuntarily they told of the weary days and nights of despairing flight, which after all had been useless.

Lorimer asked if he might pray, and there was a simultaneous though silent motion of assent. Every man bared his head, while the wretched father repeated the few verses of entreaty and hope which at that awful hour were his own strength and comfort. This service occupied but a few minutes; just as it ended out of the dead stillness rose suddenly a clear, joyful thrilling burst of song from a mocking bird in the branches above. David looked up with a wonderful light on his face; perhaps it meant more to him than anyone else understood.

The next moment the sheriff was turning back the flannel collar which covered the strong, pillar-like throat. In that moment David sought his father's eyes once more, smiled faintly, and called "Father! *Now!*" As the words reached the father's ears, the bullet reached the son's heart. He fell without a moan ere the rope had touched him. It was the father's groan which struck every heart like a blow; and there was a grandeur of suffering about him which no one thought of resisting.

He walked to his child's side, and kneeling down closed the eyes, and wept and prayed over him as a mother over her first-born. They were all fathers around him; not one of them but suffered with him. Silently they untied their horses and rode away; no one had the heart to say a word of dissent. If they had, Lorimer had reached a point far beyond care of man's approval or disapproval in the matter; for a great sorrow is indifferent to all outside itself.

When he lifted his head he was alone. The sheriff was waiting at the house door, Plato stood at a little distance, weeping. He motioned to him to approach, and in a few words understood that he had with him a companion and a rude bier. They laid the body upon it, and the sheriff having satisfied himself that the last penalty had been fully paid, Lorimer was permitted to claim his dead. He took him up to his own room and laid him on his own bed, and passed the night by his side. The dead opened the eyes of the living, and in that solemn companionship he saw all that he had been blind to for so many years. Then he understood what it must be to sit in the silent halls of eternal despair, and count over and over the wasted blessings of love and endure the agony of unavailing repentance.

In the morning he knew he must tell Lulu all; and this duty he dreaded. But in some way the girl already knew the full misery of the tragedy. Part she had divined, and part she had gathered from the servants' faces and words. She was quite aware *what* was in her uncle's lonely room. Just as he was thinking of the hard

necessity of going to her, she came to the
door. For the first time in his life he called
her "My daughter," and stooped and kissed
her. He had a letter for her—David's
dying message of love. He put it in her
hand, and left her alone with the dead.

At sunrise a funeral took place. In that
climate the necessity was an urgent one.
Plato had dug the grave under a tree in the
little clearing in the cypress swamp. It
had been a favorite place of resort; there
Lulu had often brought her work or book,
and passed long happy hours with the slain
youth. She followed his corpse to the
grave in a tearless apathy, more pitiful
than the most frantic grief. Lorimer took
her on his arm, the servants in long single
file, silent and terrified, walked behind
them. The sun was shining, but the chilly
wind blew the withered leaves across the
still prostrate figure, as it lay upon the
ground, where last it had stood in all the
beauty and unreasoning passion of youth.

When the last rites were over the servants went wailing home again, their dole-
ful, monotonous chant seeming to fill the
whole spaces of air with lamentation. But
neither Lorimer nor Lulu spoke a word.
The girl was white and cold as marble, and
absolutely irresponsive to her uncle's unusual tenderness. Evidently she had not
forgiven him. And as the winter went

wearily on she gradually drew more and more within her own consciousness. Lorimer seldom saw her. She was soon very ill, and kept her room entirely. He sent for eminent physicians, he surrounded her with marks of thoughtful love and care; but quietly, as a flower fades, she died.

One night she sent for him. "Uncle," she said, "I am going away very soon, now. If I have been hard and unjust to you, forgive me. And I want your promise about my sister's children; will you give me it?"

He winced visibly, and remained silent.

"There are six boys and two girls—they are poor, ignorant and unhappy. They are under very bad influences. For David's sake and my sake you must see that they are brought up right. There need be no mistakes this time; for two wrecked lives you may save eight. You will do it, uncle?"

"I will do my best, dear."

"I know you will. Send Plato to San Antonio for them at once. You will need company soon."

"Do you think you are dying, dear?"

"I know I am dying."

"And how is a' wi' you anent what is beyond death?"

She pointed with a bright smile to the New Testament by her side, and then closed her eyes wearily. She appeared so exhausted that he could press the question no further. And the next morning she had "gone away"—gone so silently and peacefully that Aunt Cassie, who was sitting by her side, knew not when she departed. He went and looked at her. The fair young face had a look austere and sorrowful, as if life had been too sore a burden for her. His anguish was great, but it was God's doing. What was there for him to say?

The charge that she had left him he faithfully kept—not very cheerfully at first, perhaps, and often feeling it to be a very heavy care; but he persevered, and the reward came. The children grew and prospered; they loved him, and he learned to love them, so much, finally, that he gave them his own name, and suffered them to call him father.

As the country settled, and little towns grew up around him, the tragedy of his earlier life was forgotten by the world, but it was ever present to his own heart; for though love and sorrow mellowed and chastened the stern creed in which he believed with all his soul, he had many an hour of spiritual agony concerning the beloved ones who had died and made no sign. Not till he got almost within the heavenly horizon did he understand that the Divine love and mercy is without limitations; and that He who could say, "Let there be

light," could also say, "Thy sins be forgiven thee;" and the pardoned child, or
ever he was aware, be come to the holy
land: for—

"Down in the valley of death
  A cross is standing plain;
Where strange and awful the shadows sleep,
  And the ground has a deep red stain.
This cross uplifted there
  Forbids, with voice Divine,
Our anguished hearts to break for the dead
  Who have died and made no sign.
As they turned at length from us,
  Dear eyes that were heavy and dim,
May have met his look, who was lifted there,
  May be sleeping safe in Him."

THE SEVEN WISE MEN OF PRESTON.

Let me introduce to our readers seven of the wisest men of the present century—the seven drafters and signers of the first teetotal pledge.

The movement originated in the mind of Joseph Livesey, and a short consideration of the circumstances and surroundings of his useful career will give us the best insight into the necessities and influences which gave it birth. He was born near Preston, in Lancashire, in the year 1795; the beginning of an era in English history which scarcely has a parallel for national suffering. The excitement of the French Revolution still agitated all classes, and commercial distress and political animosities made still more terrible the universal scarcity of food and the prostration of the manufacturing business.

His father and mother died early, and he was left to the charge of his grandfather, who, unfortunately, abandoned his farm and became a cotton spinner. Lancashire men had not then been whetted by daily attrition with steam to their present keen and shrewd character, and the elder Livesey lost all he possessed. The records of cotton printing and spinning mention with honor the Messrs. Livesey, of Preston, as the first who put into practice Bell's invention of cylindrical printing of calicoes in 1785; but whether the firms are identical or not I have no certain knowledge. It shows, however, that they were a race inclined to improvements and ready to test an advance movement.

That Joseph Livesey's youth was a hard and bitter one there is no doubt. The price of flour continued for years fabulously high; so much so that wealthy people generally pledged themselves to reduce their use of it one-third, and puddings or cakes were considered on any table, a sinful extravagance. When the government was offering large premiums to farmers for raising extra quantities and detailing soldiers to assist in threshing it, poor bankrupt spinners must have had a hard struggle for a bare existence.

Indeed, education was hardly thought possible, and, though Joseph managed, "by hook or crook," to learn how to read, write and count a little, it was through difficulties and discouragements that would have been fatal to any ordinary intelligence or will.

Until he was twenty-one years of age he worked patiently at his loom, which stood in one corner of a cellar, so cold and damp

that its walls were constantly wet.   But **he**
was hopeful, and even in those dark days
dared to fall in love.   On attaining his
majority, he received a legacy of £30.   Then
he married the poor girl who had made
brighter his hard apprenticeship, and lived
happily with her for fifty years.

But the troubles that had begun before
his birth—and which did not lighten until
after the passing of the Reform Bill, in
June, 1832—had then attained a proportion
which taxed the utmost energies of both
private charities and the national government.

The year of Joseph Livesey's marriage
saw the passage of the Corn Laws, and
the first of those famous mass meetings
in Peter's Field, near Manchester, which
undoubtedly molded the future temper and
status of the English weavers and spinners.
From one of these meetings, the following
year, thousands of starving men started *en
masse* to London.   They were followed by
the military and brought back for punishment or died miserably on the road, though
500 of them reached Macclesfield and a
smaller number Derby.

But Livesey, though probably suffering
as keenly as others, joined no body of riot-
ers.   He borrowed a sovereign and bought
two cheeses; then cutting them up into
small lots, he retailed them on the streets,

Saturday afternoons, when the men were released from work. The profit from this small investment exceeding what it was possible for him to make at his loom, he continued the trade, and from this small beginning founded a business, and made a fortune which enabled him to devote a long life to public usefulness and benevolence.

But his little craft must have needed skillful piloting, for his family increased rapidly during the disastrous years between 1816 and 1832; so disastrous that in 1825-26 the Bank of England was obliged to authorize the Chamber of Commerce to make loans to individuals carrying on large works of from £500 to £10,000. Bankruptcies were enormous, trade was everywhere stagnant, £60,000 were subscribed for meal and peas to feed the starving, and the government issued 40,000 articles of clothing. The quarrels between masters and spinners were more and more bitter, mills were everywhere burnt, and at Ashton in one day 30,000 "hands" turned out.

During these dreadful years every thoughtful person had noticed how much misery and ill-will was caused by the constant thronging to public houses, and temperance societies had been at work among the angry men of the working classes. Joseph Livesey had been actively engaged in this work. But these first efforts of the temperance cause were directed entirely against spirits. The use of wine and ale was considered then a necessity of life. Brewing was in most families as regular and important a duty as baking; the youngest children had their mug of ale; and clergymen were spoken of without reproach as ''one,'' ''two'' or ''three-bottle men.''

But Joseph Livesey soon became satisfied that these half measures were doing no good at all, and in 1831 a little circumstance decided him to take a stronger position. He had to go to Blackburn to see a person on business; and, as a matter of course, whiskey was put on the table. Livesey for the first time tasted it, and was very ill in consequence. He had then a large family of boys, and both for their sakes and that of others, he resolved to halt no longer between two opinions.

He spoke at once in all the temperance meetings of the folly of partial reforms, pointed out the hundreds of relapses, and urged upon the association the duty of absolute abstinence. His zeal warmed with his efforts and he insisted that in the matter of drinking ''the golden mean'' was the very sin for which the Laodicean Church had been cursed.

The disputes were very angry and bitter;

far more so than we at this day can believe possible, unless we take into account the universal national habits and its poetic and domestic associations with every phase of English life. But he gradually gained adherents to his views though it was not until the following year he was able to take another step forward.

It was on Thursday, August 23, 1832, that the first solemn pledge of total abstinence was taken. That afternoon Joseph Livesey, pondering the matter in his mind, saw John King pass his shop. He asked him to come in and talk the subject over with him. Before they parted Livesey asked King if he would join him in a pledge to abstain forever from all liquors; and King said he would. Livesey then wrote out a form and, laying it before King, said: "Thee sign it first, lad." King signed it, Livesey followed him, and the two men clasped hands and stood pledged to one of the greatest works humanity has ever undertaken.

A special meeting was then called, and after a stormy debate, the main part of the audience left, a small number remaining to continue the argument. But the end of it was that seven men came forward and drew up and signed the following document, which is still preserved:

"We agree to abstain from all liquors of an intoxicating quality, whether they be ale, porter, **wine or** ardent spirits, except as medicine.

> "JOHN GRATREX,
> EDWARD DICKINSON,
> JOHN BROADBENT,
> JNO. SMITH,
> JOSEPH LIVESEY,
> DAVID ANDERTON,
> JNO. KING."

All these reformers were virtually *working* men, though most of them rose to positions of respect and affluence. Still the humility of the origin of the movement was long a source of contempt, and its members, within my own recollection, had the stigma of vulgarity almost in right of their convictions.

But God takes hands with good men's efforts, and the cause prospered just where it was most needed—among the operatives and "the common people." One of these latter, a hawker of fish, called Richard Turner, stood, in a very amusing and unexpected way, sponsor for the society. Richard was fluent of speech, and, if his language was the broadest patois, it was, nevertheless, of the most convincing character. He always spoke well, and, if authorized words failed him, readily coined what he needed. One night while making a very fervent speech, he said: "No half-way measures here. Nothing but the *te-te total* will do.''

Mr. Livesey at once seized the word, and, rising, proposed it as the name of the society. The proposition was received with enthusiastic cheering, and these ''root and branch'' temperance men were thenceforward known as teetotalers. Richard remained all his life a sturdy advocate of the cause, and when he died, in 1846, I made one of the hundreds and thousands that crowded the streets of the beautiful town of Preston and followed him to his grave. The stone above it chronicles shortly his name and death, and the fact that he was the author of a word known now wherever Christianity and civilization are known.

MARGARET SINCLAIR'S SILENT MONEY.

''It was ma luck, Sinclair, an' I couldna win by it.''

''Ha'vers! It was David Vedder's whiskey that turned ma boat tapsalteerie, Geordie Twatt.''

''Thou had better blame Hacon; he turned the boat *Widdershins* an' what fule doesna ken that it is evil luck to go contrarie to the sun?''

''It is waur luck to have a drunken, superstitious pilot. Twatt, that Norse blood i' thy veins is o'er full o' freets. Fear God, an' mind thy wark, an' thou needna speir o' the sun what gate to turn the boat.''

''My Norse blood willna stand ony Scot stirring it up, Sinclair. I come o' a mighty kind—''

''Tush, man! Mules mak' an unco' full about their ancestors having been horses. It has come to this, Geordie: thou must be laird o' theesel' before I'll trust thee again with ony craft o' mine.'' Then Peter Sinclair lifted his papers, and, looking the discharged sailor steadily in the face, bid him "go on his penitentials an' think things o'er a bit."

Geordie Twatt went sullenly out, but Peter was rather pleased with himself; he believed that he had done his duty in a satisfactory manner. And if a man was in a good temper with himself, it was just the kind of even to increase his satisfaction. The gray old town of Kirkwall lay in supernatural glory, the wondrous beauty of the mellow gloaming blending with soft green and rosy-red spears of light that shot from east to west, or charged upward to the zenith. The great herring fleet outside the harbor was as motionless as "a painted *fleet* upon a painted ocean"—the men were sleeping or smoking upon the piers—not a foot fell upon the flagged streets, and the only murmur of sound was round the public fountains, where a few women were perched on the bowl's edge, knitting and gossiping.

Peter Sinclair was, perhaps, not a man inclined to analyze such things, but they had their influence over him; for, as he drifted slowly home in his skiff, he began to pity Geordie's four motherless babies, and to wonder if he had been as patient with him as he might have been. "An' yet," he murmured, "there's the loss on the goods, an' the loss o' time, and the boat to steek afresh forbye the danger to life! Na, na, I'm no called upon to put life i' peril for a glass o' whiskey."

Then he lifted his head, and there, on the white sands, stood his daughter Margaret. He was conscious of a great thrill of pride as he looked at her, for Margaret Sinclair, even among the beautiful women of the Orcades, was most beautiful of all. In a few minutes he had fastened his skiff at a little jetty, and was walking with her over the springy heath toward a very pretty house of white stone. It was his own house, and he was proud of it also, but not half so proud of the house as of its tiny garden; for there, with great care and at great cost, he had managed to rear a few pansies, snowdrops, lilies of the valley, and other hardy English flowers. Margaret and he stooped lovingly over them, and it was wonderful to see how Peter's face softened, and how gently the great rough hands, that had been all day handling smoked geese and fish, touched these frail, trembling blossoms.

"Eh, lassie! I could most greet wi' joy to see the bonnie bit things; when I can get time I'se e'en go wi' thee to Edinburgh; I'd like weel to see such fields an' gardens an' trees as I hear thee tell on."

Then Margaret began again to describe the greenhouses, the meadows and wheat fields, the forests of oaks and beeches she had seen during her school days in Edinburgh. Peter listened to her as if she was telling a wonderful fairy story, but he liked it, and, as he cut slice after slice from his smoked goose, he enjoyed her talk of roses and apple-blossoms, and smacked his lips for the thousandth time when she described a peach, and said, "It tasted, father, as if it had been grown in the Garden of Eden."

After such conversations Peter was always stern and strict. He felt an actual anger at Adam and Eve; their transgression became a keenly personal affair, for he had a very vivid sense of the loss they had entailed upon him. The vague sense of wrong made him try to fix it, and, after a short reflection, he said in an injured tone:

"I wonder when Ronald's coming hame again?"

"Ronald is all right, father."

"A' wrong, thou means, lassie. There's three vessels waiting to be loaded, an' the books sae far ahint that I kenna whether I'm losing or saving. Where is he?"

"Not far away. He will be at the Stones of Stennis this week some time with an Englishman he fell in with at Perth."

"I wonder, now, was it for my sins or his ain that the lad has sic auld world notions? There isna a pagan altar-stane 'tween John O'Groat's an' Lambaness he doesna run after. I wish he were as anxious to serve in the Lord's temple—I would build him a kirk an' a manse for it.''

"We'll be proud of Ronald yet, father. The Sinclairs have been fighting and making money for centuries: it is a sign of grace to have a scholar and a poet at last among them.''

Peter grumbled. His ideas of poetry were limited by the Scotch psalms, and, as for scholarship, he asserted that the books were better kept when he used his own method of tallies and crosses. Then he remembered Geordie Twatt's misfortune, and had his little grumble out on this subject: "Boat and goods might hae been a total loss, no to speak o' the lives o' Geordie an' the four lads wi' him; an' a' for the sake o' liquor!''

Margaret looked at the brandy bottle standing at her father's elbow, and, though she did not speak, the look annoyed Peter.

"You arna to even my glass wi' his, lassie. I ken when to stop—Geordie never does.''

"It is a common fault in more things than drinking, father. When Magnus Hay has struck the first blow he is quite ready to draw his dirk and strike the last one; and Paul Snackole, though he has made gold and to spare, will just go on making gold until death takes the balances out of his hands. There are few folks that in all things offend not.''

She looked so noble standing before him, so fair and tall, her hair yellow as down, her eyes cool and calm and blue as night; her whole attitude so serene, assured and majestic, that Peter rose uneasily, left his glass unfinished, and went away with a very confused "good night."

In the morning the first thing he did when he reached his office, was to send for the offending sailor.

"Geordie, my Margaret says there are plenty folk as bad as thou art; so, thou'lt just see to the steeking o' the boat, an' be ready to sail her—or upset her—i' ten days again."

"I'll keep her right side up for Margaret Sinclair's sake—tell her I said that, Master."

"I'se do no promising for thee, Geordie. Between wording an' working is a lang road, but Kirkwall an' Stromness kens thee for an honest lad, an' thou wilt mind this— *things promised are things due.*"

Insensibly this act of forbearance lightened Peter's whole day; he was good-tempered with the world, and the world returned the compliment. When night came, and he watched for Margaret on the sands, he was delighted to see that Ronald was with her. The lad had come home and nothing was now remembered against him. That night it was Ronald told him fairy-stories of great cities and universities, of miles of books and pictures, of wonderful machinery and steam engines, of delicious things to eat and drink. Peter felt as if he must start southward by the next mail packet, but in the morning he thought more unselfishly.

"There are forty families depending on me sticking to the shop an' the boats, Ronald, an' I canna go pleasuring till there is ane to step into my shoes."

Ronald Sinclair had all the fair, stately beauty and noble presence of his sister, but yet there was some lack about him easier to feel than to define. Perhaps no one was unconscious of this lack except Margaret; but women have a grand invention where their idols are concerned, and create readily for them every excellency that they lack. Her own two years' study in an Edinburgh boarding-school had been very superficial, and she knew it; but this wonderful Ronald could read Homer and Horace, could play and sketch, and recite Shakespeare and write poetry. If he could have done none of these things, if he had been dull and ugly, and content to trade in fish and wool, she would still have loved him tenderly; how much more then, this handsome Antinous, whom she credited with all the accomplishments of Apollo.

Ronald needed all her enthusiastic

support. He had left heavy college bills, and
he had quite made up his mind that he
would not be a minister and that he would
be a lawyer. He could scarcely have decided on two things more offensive to his
father. Only for the hope of having a
minister in the family had Peter submitted
to his son's continued demands for money.
For this end he had bought books, and
paid for all kinds of teachers and tours,
and sighed over the cost of Ronald's
different hobbies. And now he was not
only to have a grievous disappointment,
but also a great offence, for Peter Sinclair
shared fully in the Arcadean dislike and
distrust of lawyers, and would have been
deeply offended at any one requiring their
aid in any business transaction with him.

His son's proposal to be a "writer" he
took almost as a personal insult. He had
formed his own opinion of the profession
and the opinion of any other person who
would say a word in favor of a lawyer he
considered of no value. Margaret had a
hard task before her, that she succeeded at
all was due to her womanly tact. Ronald
and his father simply clashed against each
other and exchanged pointed truths which
hurt worse than wounds. At length, when
the short Arcadean summer was almost over,
Margaret won a hard and reluctant consent.

"The lad is fit for naething better, I

suppose''—and the old man turned away to
shed the bitterest tears of his whole life.
They shocked Margaret; she was terrified
at her success, and, falling humbly at his
feet, she besought him to forget and forgive her importunities, and to take back a
gift baptized with such ominous tears.

But Peter Sinclair, having been compelled to take such a step, was not the man
to retrace it; he shook his head in a dour,
hopeless way: ''He couldna say 'yes' an'
'no' in a breath, an' Ronald must e'en
drink as he brewed.''

These struggles, so real and sorrowful to
his father and sister, Ronald had no sympathy with—not that he was heartless, but
that he had taught himself to believe they
were the result of ignorance of the world
and old-fashioned prejudices. He certainly
intended to become a great man—perhaps
a judge—and, when he was one of ''the
Lords,'' he had no doubt his father would
respect his disobedience. He knew his
father as little as he knew himself. Peter
Sinclair was only Peter Sinclair's opinions
incorporate; and he could no more have
changed them than he could have changed
the color of his eyes or the shape of his
nose; and the difference between a common
lawyer and a ''lord,'' in his eyes, would
only have been the difference between a
little oppressor and a great one.

For the first time in all her life Margaret suspected a flaw in this perfect crystal of a brother; his gay debonnaire manner hurt her. Even if her father's objections were ignorant prejudices, they were positive convictions to him, and she did not like to see them smiled at, entertained by the cast of the eye, and the put-by of the turning hand. But loving women are the greatest of philistines: knock their idol down daily, rob it of every beauty, cut off its hands and head, and they will still "set it up in its place," and fall down and worship it.

Undoubtedly Margaret was one of the blindest of these characters, but the world may pause before it scorns them too bitterly. It is faith of this sublime integrity which, brought down to personal experience, believes, endures, hopes, sacrifices and loves on to the end, winning finally what never would have been given to a more prudent and reasonable devotion. So, if Margaret had her doubts, she put them arbitrarily down, and sent her brother away with manifold tokens of her love—among them, with a check on the Kirkwall Bank for sixty pounds, the whole of her personal savings.

To this frugal Arcadean maid it seemed a large sum, but she hoped by the sacrifice to clear off Ronald's college debts, and thus enable him to start his new race unweighted.

It was but a mouthful to each creditor, but it put them off for a time, and Ronald was not a youth inclined to "take thought" for their "to-morrow."

He had been entered for four years' study with the firm of Wilkes & Brechen, writers and conveyancers, of the city of Glasgow. Her father had paid the whole fee down, and placed in the Western Bank to his credit four hundred pounds for his four years' support. Whatever Ronald thought of the provision, Peter considered it a magnificent income, and it had cost him a great struggle to give up at once, and for no evident return, so much of his hardearned gold. To Ronald he said nothing of this reluctance; he simply put vouchers for both transactions in his hand, and asked him to "try an' spend the siller as weel as it had been earned."

But to Margaret he fretted not a little. "Fourteen hun'red pounds a' thegither, dawtie," he said in a tearful voice. "I warked early an' late through mony a year for it; an' it is gane a' at once, though I hae naught but words an' promises for it. I ken, Margaret, that I am an auld farrant trader, but I'se aye say that it is a bad well into which ane must put water."

When Ronald went, the summer went too. It became necessary to remove at once to their rock-built house in one of the narrow streets of Kirkwall. Margaret was glad of the change; her father could come into the little parlor behind the shop any time in the day and smoke his pipe beside her. He needed this consolation sorely; his son's conduct had grieved him far more deeply than he would allow, and Margaret often saw him gazing southward over the stormy Pentland Frith with a very mournful face.

But a good heart soon breaks bad fortune and Peter had a good heart, sound and sweet and true to his fellow-creatures and full of faith in God. It is true that his creed was of the very strictest and sternest; but men are always better than their theology and Margaret knew from the Scriptures chosen for their household worship that in the depth and stillness of his soul his human fatherhood had anchored fast to the fatherhood of God.

Arcadean winters are long and dreary, but no one need much pity the Arcadeans; they have learned how to make them the very festival of social life. And, in spite of her anxiety about Ronald, Margaret thoroughly enjoyed this one—perhaps the more because Captain Olave Thorkald spent two months of it with them in Kirkwall. There had been a long attachment between the young soldier and Margaret; and having obtained his commission, he had come to ask also for the public recognition of their engagement. Margaret was rarely beautiful and rarely happy, and she carried with a charming and kindly grace the full cup of her felicity. The Arcadeans love to date from a good year, and all her life afterward Margaret reckoned events from this pleasant winter.

Peter Sinclair's house being one of the largest in Kirkwall, was a favorite gathering place, and Peter took his full share in all the home-like, innocent amusements which beguiled the long, dreary nights. No one in Orkney or Zetland could recite Ossian with more passion and tenderness, and he enjoyed his little triumph over the youngsters who emulated him. No one could sing a Scotch song with more humor, and few of the lads and lassies could match Peter in a blithe foursome reel or a rattling strathspey. Some, indeed, thought that good Dr. Ogilvie had a more graceful spring and a longer breath, but Peter always insisted that his inferiority to the minister was a voluntary concession to the Dominie's superior dignity. It was, however, a rivalry that always ended in a firmer grip at parting. These little festivals, in which young and old freely mingled, cultivated to perfection the best and kindest feelings of both classes. Age mellowed to perfect sweetness in the sunshine of youthful gayety, and youth learned from age how at once to be merry and wise.

At length June arrived; and though winter lingered in *spates*, the song of the skylark and the thrush heralded the spring. When the dream-like voice of the cuckoo should be heard once more, Peter and Margaret had determined to take a long summer trip. They were to go first to Perth, where Captain Thorkald was stationed, and then to Glasgow and see Ronald. But God had planned another journey for Peter, even one to a "land very far off." A disease, to which he had been subject at intervals for many years, suddenly assumed a fatal character and Peter needed no one to tell him that his days were numbered.

He set his house in order, and then, going with Margaret to his summer dwelling, waited quietly. He said little on the subject, and as long as he was able, gave himself up with the delight of a child to watching the few flowers in his garden; but still one solemn, waylaying thought made these few last weeks of life peculiarly hushed and sacred. Ronald had been sent for, and the old man, with the clear prescience that sometimes comes before death, divined much and foresaw much he did not care to speak about—only that in some subtle way he made Margaret perceive that

12

Ronald was to be cared for and watched over, and that to her this charge was committed.

Before the summer was quite over Peter Sinclair went away. In his tarrying by the eternal shore he became, as it were, purified of the body, and one lovely night, when gloaming and dawning mingled, and the lark was thrilling the midnight skies, he heard the Master call him, and promptly answered, "Here am I." Then "Death, with sweet enlargement, did dismiss him hence."

He had been considered a rich man in Orkney, and, therefore, Ronald—who had become accustomed to a Glasgow standard of wealth—was much disappointed. His whole estate was not worth over six thousand pounds; about two thousand pounds of this was in gold, the rest was invested in his houses in Kirkwall, and in a little cottage in Stromness, where Peter's wife had been born. He gave to Ronald £1800, and to Margaret £200 and the life rent of the real property. Ronald had already received £1400, and, therefore, had no cause of complaint, but somehow he felt as if he had been wronged. He was older than his sister, and the son of the house, and use and custom were not in favor of recognizing daughters as having equal rights. But he kept such thoughts to himself, and when he went back to Glasgow took with him solid proof of his sister's devotion.

It was necessary, now, for Margaret to make a great change in her life. She determined to remove to Stromness and occupy the little four-roomed cottage that had been her mother's. It stood close to that of Geordie Twatt, and she felt that in any emergency she was thus sure of one faithful friend. "A lone woman" in Margaret's position has in these days numberless objects of interest of which Margaret never dreamed. She would have thought it a kind of impiety to advise her minister, or meddle in church affairs. These simple parents attended themselves to the spiritual training of their children— there was no necessity for Sunday Schools, and they did not exist. She was not one of those women whom their friends call "beings," and who have deep and mysterious feelings that interpret themselves in poems and thrilling stories. She had no taste for philosophy or history or social science, and had been taught to regard novels as dangerously sinful books.

But no one need imagine that she was either wretched or idle. In the first place, she took life much more calmly and slowly than we do; a very little pleasure or employment went a long way. She read her Bible and helped her old servant Helga to

keep the house in order. She had her flowers
to care for,—and her brother and lover to
write to. She looked after Geordie Twatt's
little motherless lads, went to church and
to see her friends, and very often had her
friends to see her. It happened to be a
very stormy winter, and the mails were
often delayed for weeks together. This
was her only trouble. Ronald's letters
were more and more unsatisfactory; he was
evidently unhappy and dissatisfied and
heartily tired of his new study. Posts were
so irregular that often their letters seemed
to be playing at cross purposes. She determined as soon as spring opened to go and
have a straightforward talk with him.

So the following June Geordie Twatt
took her in his boat to Thurso, where Captain Thorkald was waiting for her. They
had not met since Peter Sinclair's death,
and that event had materially affected their
prospects. Before it their marriage had
been a possible joy in some far future; now
there was no greater claim on her care and
love than the captain's, and he urged their
early marriage.

Margaret had her two hundred pounds
with her, and she promised to buy her
"plenishing" during her visit to Glasgow.
In those days girls made their own trous-
seau, sewing into every garment solemn and
tender hopes and joys. Margaret thought

that proper attention to this dear stitching as well as proper respect for her father's memory, asked of her yet at least another year's delay; and for the present Captain Thorkald thought it best not to urge her further.

Ronald received his sister very joyfully. He had provided lodgings for her with their father's old correspondent, Robert Gorie, a tea merchant in the Cowcaddens. The Cowcaddens was then a very respectable street, and Margaret was quite pleased with her quarters. She was not pleased with Ronald, however. He avowed himself thoroughly disgusted with the law, and declared his intention of forfeiting his fee and joining his friend Walter Cashell in a manufacturing scheme.

Margaret could *feel* that he was all wrong, but she could not reason about a business of which she knew nothing, and Ronald took his own way. But changing and bettering are two different things, and, though he was always talking of his "good luck" and his "good bargains," Margaret was very uneasy. Perhaps Robert Gorie was partly to blame for this; his pawky face and shrewd little eyes made visible dissents to all such boasts; nor did he scruple to say, "Guid luck needs guid elbowing, Ronald, an' it is at the *guid bargains* I aye pause an' ponder."

The following winter was a restless, unhappy one; Ronald was either painfully elated or very dull; and, soon after the New Year, Walter Cashell fell into bad health, went to the West Indies, and left Ronald with the whole business to manage. He soon now began to come to his sister, not only for advice, but for money. Margaret believed at first that she was only supplying Walter's sudden loss, but when her cash was all gone, and Ronald urged her to mortgage her rents she resolutely shut her ears to all his plausible promises, and refused to ''throw more good money after bad.''

It was the first ill-blood between them, and it hurt Margaret sorely. She was glad when the fine weather came, and she could escape to her island home, for Ronald was cool to her, and said cruel things of Captain Thorkald, for whose sake he declared his sister had refused to help him.

One day, at the end of the following August, when most of the towns-people—men and women—had gone to the moss to cut the winter's peat, she saw Geordie Twatt coming toward the house. Something about his appearance troubled her, and she went to the open door and stood waiting for him.

''What is it, Geordie?''

''I am bidden to tell thee, Margaret

Sinclair, to be at the Stanes o' Stennis to-night at eleven o'clock.''

''Who trysts me there, Geordie, at such an hour?''

''Thy brother; but thou'lt come—yes, thou wilt.''

Margaret's very lips turned white as she answered: ''Il'l be there—see thou art, too.''

''Sure as death! If naebody spiers after me, thou needna say I was here at a', thou needna.''

Margaret understood the caution, and nodded her head. She could not speak, and all day long she wandered about like a soul in a restless dream.

Fortunately, every one was weary at night, and went early to rest, and she found little difficulty in getting outside the town without notice; and one of the ponies on the common took her speedily across the moor.

Late as it was, twilight lingered over the silent moor, with its old Pictish mounds and burial places, giving them an indescribable aspect of something weird and eerie. No one could have been insensible to the mournful, brooding light and the unearthly stillness, and Margaret was trembling with a supernatural terror as she stood amid the solemn circle of gray stones and looked over the lake of Stennis and the low, brown hills of Harray.

From behind one of these gigantic pillars Ronald came toward her—Ronald, and yet not Ronald. He was dressed as a common sailor, and otherwise shamefully disguised. There was no time to soften things—he told his miserable story in a few plain words:

His business had become so entangled that he knew not which way to turn, and, sick of the whole affair, he had taken a passage for Australia, and then forged a note on the Western Bank for £900. He had hoped to be far at sea with his ill-gotten money before the fraud was discovered, but suspicion had gathered around him so quickly, that he had not even dared to claim his passage. Then he fled north, and, fortunately, discovering Geordie's boat at Wick, had easily prevailed on him to put off at once with him.

What cowards sin makes of us! Margaret had seen this very lad face death often, among the sunken rocks and cruel surfs, that he might save the life of a shipwrecked sailor, and now, rather than meet the creditors whom he had wronged, he had committed a robbery and was flying from the gallows.

She was shocked and stunned, and stood speechless, wringing her hands and moaning pitifully. Her brother grew impatient. Often the first result of a bitter sense of sin is to make the sinner peevish and irritable.

"Margaret," he said, almost angrily, "I came to bid you farewell, and to promise you, *by my father's name!* to retrieve all this wrong. If you can speak a kind word speak it, for God's sake—if not, I must go without it!"

Then she fell upon his neck, and, amid sobs and kisses, said all that love so sorely and suddenly tried could say. He could not even soothe her anguish by any promise to write, but he did promise to come back to her sooner or later with restitution in his hand. All she could do now for this dear brother was to call Geordie to her side and put him in his care; taking what consolation she could from his assurance that "he would keep him out at sea until the search was cold, and if followed carry him into some of the dangerous 'races' between the islands." If any sailor could keep his boat above water in them, she knew Geordie could; *and if not*—she durst follow that thought no further, but, putting her hands before her face, stood praying, while the two men pulled silently away in the little skiff that had brought them up the outlet connecting the lake of Stennis with the sea. Margaret would have turned away from Ronald's open grave less heart-broken.

It was midnight now, but her real terror absorbed all imaginary ones; she did not even call a pony, but with swift, even steps

walked back to Stromness. Ere she had
reached it, she had decided what was to be
done, and next day she left Kirkwall in the
mail packet for the mainland. Thence by
night and day she traveled to Glasgow, and
a week after her interview with Ronald she
was standing before the directors of the de-
frauded bank and offering them the entire
proceeds of her Kirkwall property until the
debt was paid.

The bank had thoroughly respected Peter
Sinclair, and his daughter's earnest, decided
offer won their ready sympathy. It was
accepted without any question of interest,
though she could not hope to clear off the
obligation in less than nine years. She did
not go near any of her old acquaintances;
she had no heart to bear their questions and
condolences, and she had no money to stay
in Glasgow at charges. Winter was coming on rapidly, but before it broke over the
lonely islands she had reached her cottage
in Stromness again.

There had been, of course, much talk
concerning her hasty journey, but no one
had suspected its cause. Indeed, the pursuit after Ronald had been entirely the
bank's affair, had been committed to private
detectives and had not been nearly so hot
as the frightened criminal believed. His
failure and flight had indeed been noticed
in the Glasgow newspapers, but this

information did not reach Kirkwall until the following spring, and then in a very indefinite form.

About a week after her return, Geordie Twatt came into port. Margaret frequently went to his cottage with food or clothing for the children, and she contrived to meet him there.

"Yon lad is a' right, indeed is he," he said, with an assumption of indifference.

"Oh, Geordie! where?"

"A ship going westward took him off the boat."

"Thank God! You will say naught at all, Geordie?"

"I ken naught at a' save that his father's son was i' trouble, an' trying to gie thae weary, unchancy lawyers the go-by. I was fain eneuch mesel' to balk them."

But Margaret's real trials were all yet to come. The mere fact of doing a noble deed does not absolve one often from very mean and petty consequences. Before the winter was half over she had found out how rapid is the descent from good report. The neighbors were deeply offended at her for giving up the social tea parties and evening gatherings that had made the house of Sinclair popular for more than one generation. She gave still greater offence by becoming a workingwoman, and spending her days in braiding straw into the (once) famous Orkney Tuscans, and her long evenings in the manufacture of those delicate knitted goods peculiar to the country.

It was not alone that they grudged her the money for these labors, as so much out of their own pockets—they grudged her also the time; for they had been long accustomed to rely on Margaret Sinclair for their children's garments, for nursing the sick and for help in weddings, funerals and all the other extraordinary occasions of sympathy among a primitively social people.

Little by little, all winter, the sentiment of disapproval and dislike gathered. Some one soon found out that Margaret's tenants "just sent every bawbee o' the rent-siller to the Glasgow Bank;" and this was a double offence, as it implied a distrust of her own townsfolk and institutions. If from her humble earnings she made a little gift to any common object its small amount was a fresh source of anger and contempt; for none knew how much she had to deny herself even for such curtailed gratuities.

In fact, Margaret Sinclair's sudden stinginess and indifference to her townsfolk was the common wonder and talk of every little gathering. Old friends began to either pointedly reprove her, or pointedly ignore her; and at last even old Helga took the popular tone and said, "Margaret

Sinclair had got too scrimping for an auld wife like her to bide wi' langer."

Through all this Margaret suffered keenly. At first she tried earnestly to make her old friends understand that she had good reasons for her conduct; but as she would not explain these good reasons, she failed in her endeavor. She had imagined that her good conscience would support her, and that she could live very well without love and sympathy; she soon found out that it is a kind of negative punishment worse than many stripes.

At the end of the winter Captain Thorkald again earnestly pressed their marriage, saying that, "his regiment was ordered to Chelsea, and any longer delay might be a final one." He proposed also, that his father, the Udaller Thorkald of Serwick, should have charge of her Orkney property, as he understood its value and changes. Margaret wrote and frankly told him that her property was not hers for at least seven years, but that it was under good care, and he must accept her word without explanation. Out of this only grew a very unsatisfactory correspondence. Captain Thorkald went south without Margaret, and a very decided coolness separated them farther than any number of miles.

Udaller Thorkald was exceedingly angry, and his remarks about Margaret Sinclair's refusal "to trust her bit property in as guid hands as her own" increased very much the bitter feeling against the poor girl. At the end of three years the trial became too great for her; she began to think of running away from it.

Throughout these dark days she had purposely and pointedly kept apart from her old friend Dr. Ogilvie, for she feared his influence over her might tempt her to confidence. Latterly the doctor had humored her evident desire, but he had never ceased to watch over and, in a great measure, to believe in her; and, when he heard of this determination to quit Orkney forever, he came to Stromness with a resolution to spare no efforts to win her confidence.

He spoke very solemnly and tenderly to her, reminded her of her father's generosity and good gifts to the church and the poor, and said: "O, Margaret, dear lass! what good at a' will thy silent money do thee in *that Day?* It ought to speak for thee out o' the mouths o' the sorrowfu' an' the needy, the widows an' the fatherless—indeed it ought. And thou hast gien naught for thy Master's sake these three years! I'm fair 'shamed to think thou bears sae kind a name as thy father's."

What could Margaret do? She broke into passionate sobbing, and, when the good old man left the cottage an hour afterward

there was a strange light on his face,
and he walked and looked as if he had
come from some interview that had set him
for a little space still nearer to the angels.
Margaret had now one true friend, and
in a few days after this she rented her
cottage and went to live with the dominie.
Nothing could have so effectually re-
instated her in public opinion; wherever
the dominie went on a message of help or
kindness Margaret went with him. She
fell gradually into a quieter but still more
affectionate regard—the aged, the sick and
the little children clung to her hands, and
she was comforted.

Her life seemed, indeed, to have wonderfully narrowed, but when the tide is fairly
out, it begins to turn again. In the fifth year
of her poverty there was from various causes,
such an increase in the value of real estate,
that her rents were nearly doubled, and by
the end of the seventh year she had paid
the last shilling of her assumed debt, and
was again an independent woman.

It might be two years after this that she
one day received a letter that filled her
with joy and amazement. It contained a
check for her whole nine hundred pounds
back again. "The bank had just received
from Ronald Sinclair, of San Francisco, the
whole amount due it, with the most satisfactory acknowledgment and interest."

It was a few minutes before Margaret could take in all the joy this news promised her; but when she did, the calm, well-regulated girl had never been so near committing extravagances.

She ran wildly upstairs to the dominie, and, throwing herself at his knees, cried out, amid tears and smiles: "Father! father! Here is your money! Here is the poor's money and the church's money! God has sent it back to me! Sent it back with such glad tidings!"—and surely if angels rejoice with repenting sinners, they must have felt that day a far deeper joy with the happy, justified girl.

She knew now that she also would soon hear from Ronald, and she was not disappointed. The very next day the dominie brought home the letter. Margaret took it upstairs to read it upon her knees, while the good old man walked softly up and down his study praying for her. Presently she came to him with a radiant face.

"Is it weel wi' the lad, ma dawtie?"

"Yes, father; it is very well." Then she read him the letter.

Ronald had been in New Orleans and had the fever; he had been in Texas, and spent four years in fighting Indians and Mexicans and in herding cattle. He had suffered many things, but had worked night and day, and always managed to grow a little richer every year. Then, suddenly, the word ''California!'' rung through the world, and he caught the echo even on the lonely southwestern prairies. Through incredible hardships he had made his way thither, and a sudden and wonderful fortune had crowned his labors, first in mining and afterward in speculation and merchandising. He said that he was indeed afraid to tell her how rich he was lest to her Arcadean views the sum might appear incredible.

Margaret let the letter fall on her lap and clasped her hands above it. Her face was beautiful. If the prodigal son had a sister she must have looked just as Margaret looked when they brought in her lost brother, in the best robe and the gold ring.

The dominie was not so satisfied. A good many things in the letter displeased him, but he kissed Margaret tenderly and went away from her. ''It is a' *I* did this, an' *I* did that, an' *I* suffered you; there is nae word o' God's help, or o' what ither folk had to thole. I'll no be doing ma duty if I dinna set his sin afore his e'en.''

The old man was little used to writing, and the effort was a great one, but he bravely made it, and without delay. In a few curt, idiomatic sentences he told Ronald Margaret's story of suffering and wrong and poverty; her hard work for daily bread;

her loss of friends, of her good name and
her lover, adding: "It is a puir success,
ma lad, that ye dinna acknowledge God in;
an' let me tell thee, thy restitution is o'er
late for thy credit. I wad hae thought
better o' it had thou made it when it took
the last plack i' thy pouch. Out o' thy
great wealth, a few hun'red pounds is nae
matter to speak aboot."

But people did speak of it. In spite of
our chronic abuse of human nature it is,
after all, a kindly nature, and rejoices in
good more than in evil. The story of
Ronald's restitution is considered honorable
to it, and it was much made of in the daily
papers. Margaret's friends flocked round
her again, saying, "I'm sorry, Margaret!"
as simply and honestly as little children,
and the dominie did not fail to give them
the lecture on charity that Margaret neglected.

Whether the Udaller Thorkald wrote to
his son anent these transactions, or whether
the captain read in the papers enough to
satisfy him, he never explained; but one
day he suddenly appeared at Dr. Ogilvie's
and asked for Margaret. He had probably
good excuses for his conduct to offer; if
not, Margaret was quite ready to invent
for him—as she had done for Ronald—all
the noble qualities he lacked. The captain
was tired of military life, and anxious to

return to Orkney; and, as his own and Margaret's property was yearly increasing in value, he foresaw profitable employment for his talents. He had plans for introducing many southern improvements—for building a fine modern house, growing some of the hardier fruits and for the construction of a grand conservatory for Margaret's flowers.

It must be allowed that Captain Thorkald was a very ordinary lord for a woman like Margaret Sinclair to "love, honor and obey;" but few men would have been worthy of her, and the usual rule which shows us the noblest women marrying men manifestly their inferiors is doubtless a wise one.

A lofty soul can have no higher mission than to help upward one upon a lower plane, and surely Captain Thorkald, being, as the dominie said, *"no that bad,"* had the fairest opportunities to grow to Margaret's stature in Margaret's atmosphere.

While these things were occurring, Ronald got Margaret's letter. It was full of love and praise, and had no word of blame or complaint in it. He noticed, indeed, that she still signed her name "Sinclair," and that she never alluded to Captain Thorkald, and the supposition that the stain on his character had caused a rupture did, for a moment, force itself upon his notice; but he put it instantly away with the reflection that "Thorkald was but a poor fellow, after all, and quite unworthy of his sister."

The very next mail-day he received the dominie's letter. He read it once, and could hardly take it in; read it again and again, until his lips blanched, and his whole countenance changed. In that moment he saw Ronald Sinclair for the first time in his life. Without a word, he left his business, went to his house and locked himself in his own room.

Then Margaret's silent money began to speak. In low upbraidings it showed him the lonely girl in that desolate land trying to make her own bread, deserted of lover and friends, robbed of her property and good name, silently suffering every extremity, never reproaching him once, not even thinking it necessary to tell him of her sufferings, or to count their cost unto him.

What is this bitterness we call remorse? This agony of the soul in all its senses? This sudden flood of intolerable light in the dark places of our hearts? This truth-telling voice which leaves us without a particle of our self-complacency? For many days Ronald could find no words to speak but these, "O, wretched man that I am!"

But at length the Comforter came as

swiftly and surely and mysteriously as the accuser had come, and once more that miracle of grace was renewed—"that day Jesus was guest in the house of one who was a sinner."

Margaret's "silent money" now found a thousand tongues. It spoke in many a little feeble church that Ronald Sinclair held in his arms until it was strong enough to stand alone. It spoke in schools and colleges and hospitals, in many a sorrowful home and to many a lonely, struggling heart—and at this very day it has echoes that reach from the far West to the lonely islands beyond the stormy Pentland Firth, and the sea-shattering precipices of Duncansbay Head.

It is not improbable that some of my readers may take a summer's trip to the Orkney Islands; let me ask them to wait at Thurso—the old town of Thor—for a handsome little steamer that leaves there three times a week for Kirkwall. It is the sole property of Captain Geordie Twatt, was a gift from an old friend in California, and is called "The Margaret Sinclair."

JUST WHAT HE DESERVED.

There is not in its own way a more dis-
tinctive and interesting bit of Scotland than
the bleak Lothian country, with its wide
views, its brown ploughed fields, and its
dense swaying plantations of fir. The
Lammermoor Hills and the Pentlands and
the veils of smoke that lie about Edinburgh
are on its horizon, and within that circle
all the large quietude of open grain fields,
wide turnip lands, where sheep feed, and
far-stretching pastures where the red and
white cows ruminate. The patient pro-
cesses of nature breed patient minds; the
gray cold climate can be read in the faces
of the people, and in their hearts the
seasons take root and grow; so that they
have a grave character, passive, yet endur-
ing; strong to feel and strong to act when
the time is full ready for action.

Of these natural peculiarities Jean Anderson had her share. She was a Lothian
lassie of many generations, usually un-
demonstrative, but with large possibilities
of storm beneath her placid face and gentle
manner. Her father was the minister of
Lambrig and the manse stood in a very
sequestered corner of the big parish, facing

the bleak east winds, and the salt showers
of the German ocean. It was sheltered by
dark fir woods on three sides, and in front
a little walled-in garden separated it from
the long, dreary, straight line of turnpike
road. But Jean had no knowledge of any
fairer land; she had read of flowery pastures
and rose gardens and vineyards, but these
places were to her only in books, while the
fields and fells that filled her eyes were her
home, and she loved them.

She loved them all the more because the
man she loved was going to leave them, and
if Gavin Burns did well, and was faithful
to her, then it was like to be that she also
would go far away from the blue Lammer-
muirs, and the wide still spaces of the
Lothians. She stood at the open door of
the manse with her lover thinking of these
things, but with no real sense of what pain
or deprivation the thought included. She
was tall and finely formed, a blooming girl,
with warmly-colored cheeks, a mouth rather
large and a great deal of wavy brown hair.
But the best of all her beauty was the soul
in her face; its vitality, its vivacity and
immediate response.

However, the time of love had come to
her, and though her love had grown as
naturally as a sapling in a wood, who could
tell what changes it would make? For
Gavin Burns had been educated in the

minister's house and Jean and he had
studied and fished and rambled together
all through the years in which Jean had
grown from childhood into womanhood.
Now Gavin was going to New York to
make his fortune. They stepped through
the garden and into the long dim road,
walking slowly in the calm night, with
thoughtful faces and clasped hands.
There was at this last hour little left
to say. Every promise known to Love
had been given; they had exchanged Bibles
and broken a piece of silver and vowed an
eternal fidelity. So, in the cold sunset they
walked silently by the river that was running in flood like their own hearts. At the
little stone bridge they stopped, and leaning over the parapet watched the drumly
water rushing below; and there Jean reiterated her promise to be Gavin's wife as
soon as he was able to make a home for her.

''And I am not proud, Gavin,'' she said;
''a little house, if it is filled with love, will
make me happy beyond all.''

They were both too hopeful and trustful
and too habitually calm to weep or make
much visible lament over their parting; and
yet when Gavin vanished into the dark of
the lonely road, Jean shut the heavy house
door very slowly. She felt as if she was
shutting part of herself out of the old home
forever, and she was shocked by this first

breaking of the continuity of life; this sharp cutting of regular events asunder. Gavin's letters were at first frequent and encouraging, but as the months went by he wrote more and more seldom. He said "he was kept so busy; he was making himself indispensable, and could not afford to be less busy. He was weary to death on the Saturday nights, and he could not bring his conscience to write anent his own personal and earthly happiness on the Sabbath day; but he was sure Jean trusted in him, whether he wrote or not; and they were past being bairns, always telling each other the love they were both so sure of."

Late in the autumn the minister died of typhoid fever, and Jean, heartbroken and physically worn out, was compelled to face for her mother and herself, a complete change of life. It had never seemed to these two women that anything could happen to the father and head of the family; in their loving hearts he had been immortal, and though the disease had run its tedious course before their eyes, his death at the last was a shock that shook their lives and their home to the very centre. A new minister was the first inevitable change, and then a removal from the comfortable manse to a little cottage in the village of Lambrig.

While this sad removal was in progress

they had felt the sorrow of it, all that they could bear; and neither had dared to look into the future or to speculate as to its necessities. Jean in her heart expected Gavin would at once send for them to come to America. He had a fair salary, and the sale of their furniture would defray their traveling expenses.

She was indeed so sure of this journey, that she did not regard the cottage as more than a temporary shelter during the approaching winter. In the spring, no doubt, Gavin would have a little home ready, and they would cross the ocean to it. The mother had the same thought. As they sat on their new hearthstone, lonely and poor, they talked of this event, and if any doubts lurked unconsciously below their love and trust they talked them away, while they waited for Gavin's answer to the sorrowful letter Jean had sent him on the night of her father's burial.

It was longer in coming than they expected. For a week they saw the postman pass their door with an indifference that seemed cruel; for a week Jean made new excuses and tried to hold up her mother's heart, while her own was sinking lower and lower. Then one morning the looked-for answer came. Jean fled to a room apart to read it alone; Mrs. Anderson sat down and waited, with dropped eyes and hands tightly clasped. She knew, before Jean said a word, that the letter had disappointed her. She had remained alone too long. If all had been as they hoped the mother was certain Jean would not have deferred the good tidings a moment. But a quarter of an hour had passed before Jean came to her side, and then when she lifted her eyes she saw that her daughter had been weeping.

"It is a disappointment, Jean, I see," she said sadly. "Never mind, dearie."

"Yes, mother; Gavin has failed us."

"We have been two foolish women, Jean. Oh, my dear lassie, we should have lippened to God, and He would not have disappointed us! What does Gavin Burns say?"

"It is what he does *not* say, that hurts me, mother. I may as well tell you the whole truth. When he heard how ill father was, he wrote to me, as if he had foreseen what was to happen. He said, 'there will be a new minister and a break-up of the old home, and you must come at once to your new home here. I am the one to care for you when your father is gone away; and what does it matter under what sun or sky if we are but together?' So, then, mother, when the worst had come to us I wrote with a free heart to Gavin. I said, 'I will come to you gladly, Gavin, but you know well that my mother is very dear to me, and where I am there she also must be.'

And he says, in this letter, that it is me he is wanting, and that you have a brother in Glasgow that is unmarried and who will be willing, no doubt, to have you keep his house for him. There is a wale of fine words about it, mother, but they come to just this, and no more—Gavin is willing to care for me but not for you, and I will not trust myself with a man that cannot love you for my sake. We will stay together, mammy darling! Whatever comes or goes we will stay together. The man isna born that can part us two!"

"He is your lover, Jean. A girl must stick to her lover."

"You are my mother. I am bone of your bone, and flesh of your flesh and love of your love. May God forsake me when I forsake you!"

She had thrown herself at her mother's knees and was clasping and kissing the sad face so dear to her, as she fervently uttered the last words. And the mother was profoundly touched by her child's devotion. She drew her close to her heart, and said firmly:

"No! No, my dearie! What could we two do for ourselves? And I'm loth to part you and Gavin. I simply cannot take the sacrifice you so lovingly offer me. I will write to my brother David. Gavin isna far wrong there; David is a very close man, but he willna see his sister suffer, there is no fear of that.''

"It is Jean that will not see you suffer.''

"But the bite and the sup, Jean? How are we to get them?''

"I can make my own dresses and cloaks, so then I can make dresses and cloaks for other people. I shall send out a card to the ladies near-by and put an advertisement in the Haddington newspaper, and God can make my needle sharp enough for the battle. Don't cry, mother! Oh, darling, don't cry! We have God and each other, and none can call us desolate.''

"But you will break your heart, Jean. You canna help it. And I canna take your love and happiness to brighten my old age. It isna right. I'll not do it. You must go to Gavin. I will go to my brother David.''

"I will not break my heart, mother. I will not shed a tear for the false, mean lad, that you were so kind to for fourteen years, when there was no one else to love him. Aye, I know he paid for his board and schooling, but he never could pay for the mother-love you gave him, just because he was motherless. And who has more right to have their life brightened by my love than you have? Beside, it is my happiness to brighten it, and so, what will you say against it? And I will not go to Gavin.

Not one step. If he wants me now, he will come for me, and for you, too. This is sure as death! Oh, mammy! Mammy, darling, a false lad shall not part us! Never! Never! Never!"

"Jean! Jean! What will I say at all?"

"What would my father say, if he was here this minute? He would say, 'you are right, Jean! And God bless you, Jean! And you may be sure that it is all for the best, Jean! So take the right road with a glad heart, Jean!' That is what father would say. And I will never do anything to prevent me looking him straight in the face when we meet again. Even in heaven I shall want him to smile into my eyes and say, 'Well done, Jean!'"

CHAPTER II.

Jean's plans for the future were humble and reasonable enough to insure them some measure of success, and the dreaded winter passed not uncomfortably away. Then in the summer Uncle David Nicoll came to Lambrig and boarded with his sister, paying a pound a week, and giving her, on his departure, a five-pound note to help the next winter's expenses. This order of things went on without change or intermission for five years, and the little cottage gradually gathered in its clean, sweet rooms, many articles of simple use and beauty. Mrs. Anderson took entire charge of the housekeeping. Jean's needle flew swiftly from morning to night, and though the girl had her share of the humiliations and annoyances incident to her position, these did not interfere with the cheerful affection and mutual help which brightened their lonely life.

She heard nothing from Gavin. After some painful correspondence, in which neither would retract a step from the stand they had taken, Gavin ceased writing, and Jean ceased expecting, though before this calm was reached she had many a bitter hour the mother never suspected. But such hours were to Jean's soul what the farmers call "growing weather;" in them much rich thought and feeling sprang up insensibly; her nature ripened and mellowed and she became a far lovelier woman than her twentieth year had promised.

One gray February afternoon, when the rain was falling steadily, Jean felt unusually depressed and weary. An apprehension of some unhappiness made her sad, and she could not sew for the tears that would dim her eyes. Suddenly the door opened and Gavin's sister Mary entered. Jean did not know her very well, and she did not like her at all, and she wondered what she had come to tell her.

"I am going to New York on Saturday, Jean," she said, "and I thought Gavin would like to know how you looked and felt these days."

Jean flushed indignantly. "You can see how I look easy enough, Mary Burns," she answered; "but as to how I feel, that is a thing I keep to myself these days."

"Gavin has furnished a pretty house at the long last, and I am to be the mistress of it. You will have heard, doubtless, that the school where I taught so long has been broken up, and so I was on the world, as one may say, and Gavin could not bear that. He is a good man, is Gavin, and I'm thinking I shall have a happy time with him in America."

"I hope you will, Mary. Give him a kind wish from me; and I will bid you 'good bye' now, if you please, seeing that I have more sewing to do to-night than I can well manage."

This event wounded Jean sorely. She felt sure Mary had only called for an unkind purpose, and that she would cruelly misrepresent her appearance and condition to Gavin. And no woman likes even a lost lover to think scornfully of her. But she brought her sewing beside her mother and talked the affair over with her, and so, at the end of the evening, went to bed resigned, and even cheerful. Never had they spent a more confidential, loving night together, and this fact was destined to be a comfort to Jean during all the rest of her life. For in the morning she noticed a singular look on her mother's face and at noon she found her in her chair fast in that sleep which knows no wakening in this world.

It was a blow which put all other considerations far out of Jean's mind. She mourned with a passionate sorrow her loss, and though Uncle David came at once to assist her in the necessary arrangements, she suffered no hand but her own to do the last kind offices for her dear dead. And oh! how empty and lonely was now the little cottage, while the swift return to all the ordinary duties of life seemed such a cruel effacement. Uncle David watched her silently, but on the evening of the third day after the funeral he said, kindly:

"Dry your eyes, Jean. There is naething to weep for. Your mother is far beyond tears."

"I cannot bear to forget her a minute, uncle, yet folks go and come and never name her; and it is not a week since she had a word and a smile for everybody."

> "Death is forgetfulness, Jean;
> .   .   .   'one lonely way
> We go: and is she gone?
> Is all our best friends say.'"

14

You must come home with me now, Jean.
I canna be what your mother has been to
you, but I'll do the best I can for you,
lassie. Sell these bit sticks o' furniture
and shut the door on the empty house and
begin a new life. You've had sorrow about
a lad; let him go. All o' the past worth
your keeping you can save in your memory.''

''I will be glad to go with you, uncle.
I shall be no charge on you. I can find my
own bread if you will just love me a little.''

''I'm no that poor, Jean. You are welcome to share my loaf. Put that weary
thimble and needle awa'; I'll no see you
take another stitch.''

So Jean followed her uncle's advice and
went back with him to Glasgow. He had
never said a word about his home, and
Jean knew not what she expected—certainly nothing more than a small floor in
some of the least expensive streets of the
great city. It was dark when they reached
Glasgow, but Jean was sensible of a great
change in her uncle's manner as soon as
they left the railway. He made an imperative motion and a carriage instantly
answered it; and they were swiftly driven
to a large dwelling in one of the finest
crescents of the West end. He led her into
a handsome parlor and called a servant,
and bid her ''show Miss Anderson her

rooms;'' and thus, without a word of preparation, Jean found herself surrounded by undreamed of luxury.

Nothing was ever definitely explained to her, but she gradually learned to understand the strange old man who assumed the guardianship of her life. His great wealth was evident, and it was not long ere she discovered that it was largely spent in two directions—scientific discovery and the Temperance Crusade. Men whose lives were devoted to chemistry or to electrical investigations, or passionate apostles of total abstinence from intoxicants were daily at his table; and Jean could not help becoming an enthusiastic partisan on such matters. One of the savants, a certain Professor Sharp, fell deeply in love with her; and she felt it difficult to escape the influence of his wooing, which had all the persistent patience of a man accustomed ''to seek till he found, and so not lose his labor.''

Her life was now very happy. Cautious in giving his love, David Nicoll gave it freely as soon as he had resolved to adopt his niece. Nor did he ever regret the gift. "Jean entered my house and she made it a home," he said to his friends. No words could have better explained the position. In the winter they entertained with a noble hospitality; in the summer they sailed far

north to the mystical isles of the Western
seas; to Orkney and Zetland and once even
as far as the North Cape by the light of the
midnight sun. So the time passed wonderfully away, until Jean was thirty-two years
old. The simple, unlettered girl had then
become a woman of great culture and of
perfect physical charm. Wise in many
ways, she yet kept her loving heart, and her
uncle delighted in her. ''You have made
my auld age parfectly happy, Jean,'' he
said to her on the last solemn night of his
life; ''and I thank God for the gift o' your
honest love! Now that I am going the way
of all flesh, I have gi'en you every bawbee
I have. I have put no restrictions on you,
and I have left nae dead wishes behind me.
You will do as you like wi' the land and
the siller, and you will do right in a'
things, I ken that, Jean. If it should come
into your heart to tak' the love Professor
Sharp offers you, I'll be pleased, for he'll
never spend a shilling that willna be weel
spent; and he is a clever man, and a good
man and he loves you. But it is a' in your
ain will; do as you like, anent either this
or that.''

This was the fourth great change in
Jean's life. Gavin's going away had opened
the doors of her destiny; her father's death
had sent her to the school of self-reliant
poverty; her mother's death given her a

home of love and luxury, and now her uncle put her in a position of vast, untrammeled responsibility. But if love is the joy of life, this was not the end; the crowning change was yet to come; and now, with both her hands full, her heart involuntarily turned to her first lover.

About this time, also, Gavin was led to remember Jean. His sister Mary was going to marry, and the circumstance annoyed him. "I'll have to store my furniture and pay for the care of it; or I'll have to sell it at a loss; or I'll have to hire a servant lass, and be robbed on the right hand and the left," he said fretfully. "It was not in the bargain that you should marry, and it is very bad behavior in you, Mary."

"Well, Gavin, get married yourself, and the furnishing will not be wasted," answered Mary. "There is Annie Riley, just dying for the love of you, and no brighter, smarter girl in New York city."

"She isn't in love with me; she is tired of the Remington all day; and if I wanted a wife, there is some one better than Annie Riley."

"Jean Anderson?"

"Ay."

"Send for her picture, and you will see what a plain, dowdy old maid she is. She is not for the like of you, Gavin—a bit country dressmaker, poor, and past liking."

Gavin said no more, but that night he wrote Jean Anderson the following letter: "Dear Jean. I wish you would send me a picture of yourself. If you will not write me a word, you might let me have your face to look at. Mary is getting herself married, and I will be alone in a few days." That is enough, he thought; "she will understand that there is a chance for her yet, if she is as bonnie as in the old days. Mary is not to be trusted. She never liked Jean. I'll see for myself."

Jean got this letter one warm day in spring, and she "understood" it as clearly as Gavin intended her to. For a long time she sat thinking it over, then she went to a drawer for a photo, taken just before her mother's death. It showed her face without any favor, without even justice, and the plain merino gown, which was then her best. And with this picture she wrote— "Dear Gavin. The enclosed was taken five years since, and there have been changes since."

She did not say what the changes were, but Gavin was sure they were unfavorable. He gazed at the sad, thoughtful face, the poor plain dress, and he was disappointed. A girl like that would do his house no honor; he would not care to introduce her to his fellow clerks; they would not envy him a bit. Annie Riley was far better looking, and far more stylish. He decided in favor of Annie Riley.

Jean was not astonished when no answer came. She had anticipated her failure to please her old lover; but she smiled a little sadly at *his* failure. Then there came into her mind a suspicion of Mary, an uncertainty, a lingering hope that some circumstance, not to be guessed at from a distance, was to blame for Gavin's silence and utter want of response. It was midsummer, she wanted a breath of the ocean; why should she not go to New York and quietly see how things were for herself? The idea took possession of her, and she carried it out.

She knew the name of the large dry goods firm that Gavin served, and the morning after her arrival in New York she strolled into it for a pair of gloves. As they were being fitted on she heard Gavin speak, and moving her position slightly, she saw him leaning against a pile of summer blankets. He was talking to one of his fellows, and evidently telling a funny story, at which both giggled and snickered, ere they walked their separate ways. Being midsummer the store was nearly empty, and Jean, by varying her purchases, easily kept Gavin in sight. She never for one moment found the sight a pleasant one. Gavin had deteriorated in every way. He was no longer

handsome; the veil of youth had fallen from
him, and his face, his hands, his figure,
his slouching walk, his querulous authoritative voice, all revealed a man whom Jean
repelled at every point. Years had not re-
fined, they had vulgarized him. His clothing careless and not quite fresh, offended
her taste; in fact, his whole appearance
was of that shabby genteel character, which
is far more mean and plebeian than can be
given by undisguised working apparel. As
Jean was taking note of these things a girl,
with a flushed, angry face, spoke to him.
She was evidently making a complaint, and
Gavin answered her in a manner which
made Jean burn from head to feet. The
disillusion was complete; she never looked
at him again, and he never knew she had
looked at him at all.

But after Mary's marriage he heard news
which startled him. Mary, under her new
name, wrote to an acquaintance in Lambrig, and this acquaintance in reply said,
"You will have heard that Jean Anderson
was left a great fortune by her uncle, David
Nicoll. She is building a home near Lambrig that is finer than Maxwell Castle; and
Lord Maxwell has rented the castle to her
until her new home is finished. You
wouldn't ken the looks of her now, she is
that handsome, but weel-a-way, fine feathers
aye make fine birds!"

Gavin fairly trembled when he heard this news, and as he had been with the firm eleven years and never asked a favor, he resolved to tell them he had important business in Scotland, and ask for a month's holiday to attend to it. If he was on the ground he never doubted his personal influence. "Jean was aye wax in my fingers," he said to Mary.

"There is Annie Riley," answered Mary.

"She will have to give me up. I'll not marry her. I am going to marry Jean, and settle myself in Scotland."

"Annie is not the girl to be thrown off that kind of way, Gavin. You have promised to marry her."

"I shall marry Jean Anderson, and then what will Annie do about it, I would like to know?"

"I think you will find out."

In the fall he obtained permission to go to Scotland for a month, and he hastened to Lambrig as fast as steam could carry him. He intended no secret visit; he had made every preparation to fill his old townsmen with admiration and envy. But things had changed, even in Lambrig. There was a new innkeeper, who could answer none of his questions, and who did not remember Minister Anderson and his daughter, Jean. He began to fear he had come on a fool's errand, and after a leisurely, late breakfast, he strolled out to make his own investigations.

There was certainly a building on a magnificent scale going up on a neighboring hill, and he walked toward it. When half way there a finely-appointed carriage passed him swiftly, but not too swiftly for him to see that Jean and a very handsome man were its occupants. "It will be her lawyer or architect," he thought; and he walked rapidly onward, pleased with himself for having put on his very best walking suit. There were many workmen on the building, and he fell into conversation with a man who was mixing mortar; but all the time he was watching Jean and her escort stepping about the great uncovered spaces of the new dwelling-house with such an air of mutual trust and happiness that it angered him.

"Who is the lady?" he asked at length; "she seems to have business here."

"What for no? The house is her ain. She is Mistress Sharp, and that is the professor with her. He is a great gun in the Glasgow University."

"They are married, then?"

"Ay, they are married. What are you saying at all? They were married a month syne, and they are as happy as robins in spring, I'm thinking. I'll drink their health, sir, if you'll gie me the bit o' siller."

Gavin gave the silver and turned away dazed and sick at heart. His business in Scotland was over. The quiet Lothian country sickened him; he turned his face to London, and very soon went back to New York. He had lost Jean, and he had lost Jean's fortune; and there were no words to express his chagrin and disappointment. His sister felt the first weight of it. He blamed her entirely. She had lied to him about Jean's beauty. He believed he would have liked the photo but for Mary. And all for Annie Riley! He hated Annie Riley! He was resolved never to marry her, and he let the girl feel his dislike in no equivocal manner.

For a time Annie was tearful and conciliating. Then she wrote him a touching letter, and asked him to tell her frankly if he had ceased to love her, and was resolved to break their marriage off. And Gavin did tell her, with almost brutal frankness, that he no longer loved her, and that he had firmly made up his mind not to marry her. He said something about his heart being in Scotland, but that was only a bit of sentiment that he thought gave a better air to his unfaithfulness.

Annie did not answer his letter, but Messrs. Howe & Hummel did, and Gavin

soon found himself the centre of a breach
of promise trial, with damages laid at fifty
thousand dollars.   All his fine poetical love
letters were in the newspapers; he was
ashamed to look men and women in the
face; he suffered a constant pillory for
weeks; through his vanity, his self-con-
sciousness, his egotism he was perpetually
wounded.   But pretty Annie Riley was the
object of public pity and interest, and she
really seemed to enjoy her notoriety.   The
verdict was righteously enough in her favor.
The jury gave her ten thousand dollars,
and all expenses, and Gavin Burns was a
ruined man.   His eleven years savings
only amounted to nine thousand dollars,
and for the balance he was compelled to sell
his furniture and give notes payable out of
his next year's salary.   He wept like a
child as he signed these miserable vouchers
for his folly, and for some days was completely prostrated by the evil he had called
unto himself.   Then the necessities of his
position compelled him to go to work again,
though it was with a completely broken
spirit.

"I'm getting on to forty," he said to his
sister, "and I am beginning the world over
again!   One woman has given me a disappointment that I will carry to the grave;
and another woman is laughing at me, for
she has got all my saved siller, and more

too; forbye, she is like to marry Bob Severs
and share it with him. Then I have them
weary notes to meet beyond all. There
never was a man so badly used as I have
been!''

No one pitied him much. Whatever his
acquaintances said to his face he knew
right well their private opinion was that he
had received *just what he deserved*.

AN ONLY OFFER.

"Aunt Phoebe, were you ever pretty?"

"When I was sixteen I was considered so. I was very like you then, Julia. I am forty-three now, remember."

"Did you ever have an offer—an offer of marriage, I mean, aunt?"

"No. Well, that is not true; I did have one offer."

"And you refused it?"

"No."

"Then he died, or went away?"

"No."

"Or deserted you?"

"No."

"Then you deceived him, I suppose?"

"I did not."

"What ever happened, then? Was he poor, or crippled or something dreadful?"

"He was rich and handsome."

"Suppose you tell me about him."

"I never talk about him to any one."

"Did it happen at the old place?"

"Yes, Julia. I never left Ryelands until I was thirty. This happened when I was sixteen."

"Was he a farmer's son in the neighborhood?"

"He was a fine city gentleman."

"Oh, aunt, how interesting! Put down your embroidery and tell me about it; you cannot see to work longer."

Perhaps after so many years of silence a sudden longing for sympathy and confidence seized the elder lady, for she let her work fall from her hands, and smiling sadly, said:

"Twenty-seven years ago I was standing one afternoon by the gate at Ryelands. All the work had been finished early, and my mother and two elder sisters had gone to the village to see a friend. I had watched them a little way down the hillside, and was turning to go into the house, when I saw a stranger on horseback coming up the road. He stopped and spoke to mother, and this aroused my curiosity; so I lingered at the gate. He stopped when he reached it, fastened his horse, and asked, 'Is Mr. Wakefield in?'

"I said, 'father was in the barn, and I could fetch him,' which I immediately did.

"He was a dark, unpleasant-looking man, and had a masterful way with him, even to father, that I disliked; but after a short, business-like talk, apparently satisfactory to both, he went away without entering the house. Father put his hands in his pockets and watched him out of sight;

then, looking at me, he said, 'Put the spare rooms in order, Phoebe.'

" 'They are in order, father; but is that man to occupy them?'

" 'Yes, he and his patient, a young gentleman of fine family, who is in bad health.'

" 'Do you know the young gentleman, father?'

" 'I know it is young Alfred Compton— that is enough for me.'

" 'And the dark man who has just left? I don't like his looks, father.'

" 'Nobody wants thee to like his looks. He is Mr. Alfred's physician—a Dr. Orman, of Boston. Neither of them are any of thy business, so ask no more questions;' and with that he went back to the barn.

"Mother was not at all astonished. She said there had been letters on the subject already, and that she had been rather expecting the company. 'But,' she added, 'they will pay well, and as Melissa is to be married at Christmas, ready money will be very needful.'

"About dark a carriage arrived. It contained two gentlemen and several large trunks. I had been watching for it behind the lilac trees and I saw that our afternoon visitor was now accompanied by a slight, very fair-man, dressed with extreme care in the very highest fashion. I saw also that he was handsome, and I was quite sure he must be rich, or no doctor would wait upon him so subserviently.

"This doctor I had disliked at first sight, and I soon began to imagine that I had good cause to hate him. His conduct to his patient I believed to be tyrannical and unkind. Some days he insisted that Mr. Compton was too ill to go out, though the poor gentleman begged for a walk; and again, mother said, he would take from him all his books, though he pleaded urgently for them.

"One afternoon the postman brought Dr. Orman a letter, which seemed to be important, for he asked father to drive him to the next town, and requested mother to see that Mr. Compton did not leave the house. I suppose it was not a right thing to do, but this handsome sick stranger, so hardly used, and so surrounded with mystery, had roused in me a sincere sympathy for his loneliness and suffering, and I walked through that part of the garden into which his windows looked. We had been politely requested to avoid it, 'because the sight of strangers increased Mr. Compton's nervous condition.' I did not believe this, and I determined to try the experiment.

"He was leaning out of the window, and a sadder face I never saw. I smiled and

15

courtesied, and he immediately leaped the low sill, and came toward me. I stooped and began to tie up some fallen carnations; he stooped and helped me, saying all the while I know not what, only that it seemed to me the most beautiful language I ever heard. Then we walked up and down the long peach walk until I heard the rattle of father's wagon.

After this we became quietly, almost secretly, as far as Dr. Orman was concerned, very great friends. Mother so thoroughly pitied Alfred, that she not only pretended oblivion of our friendship, but even promoted it in many ways; and in the course of time Dr. Orman began to recognize its value. I was requested to walk past Mr. Compton's windows and say 'Good morning' or offer him a flower or some ripe peaches, and finally to accompany the gentlemen in their short rambles in the neighborhood.

"I need not tell you how all this restricted intercourse ended. We were soon deeply in love with each other, and love ever finds out the way to make himself understood. We had many a five minutes' meeting no one knew of, and when these were impossible, a rose bush near his window hid for me the tenderest little love-letters. In fact, Julia, I found him irresistible; he was so handsome and gentle, and though he must have been thirty-five years old, yet, to my thinking, he looked handsomer than any younger man could have done.

"As the weeks passed on, the doctor seemed to have more confidence in us, or else his patient was more completely under control. They had much fewer quarrels, and Alfred and I walked in the garden, and even a little way up the hill without opposition or remark. I do not know how I received the idea, but I certainly did believe that Dr. Orman was keeping Alfred sick for some purpose of his own, and I determined to take the first opportunity of arousing Alfred's suspicions. So one evening, when we were walking alone, I asked him if he did not wish to see his relatives.

"He trembled violently, and seemed in the greatest distress, and only by the tenderest words could I soothe him, as, half sobbing, he declared that they were his bitterest enemies, and that Dr. Orman was the only friend he had in the world. Any further efforts I made to get at the secret of his life were equally fruitless, and only threw him into paroxysms of distress. During the month of August he was very ill, or at least Dr. Orman said so. I scarcely saw him, there were no letters in the rose bush, and frequently the disputes between the two men rose to a pitch which father seriously disliked.

"One hot day in September everyone was in the fields or orchard; only the doctor and Alfred and I were in the house. Early in the afternoon a boy came from the village with a letter to Dr. Orman, and he seemed very much perplexed, and at a loss how to act. At length he said, 'Miss Phoebe, I must go to the village for a couple of hours; I think Mr. Alfred will sleep until my return, but if not, will you try and amuse him?'

"I promised gladly, and Dr. Orman went back to the village with the messenger. No sooner was he out of sight than Alfred appeared, and we rambled about the garden, as happy as two lovers could be. But the day was extremely hot, and as the afternoon advanced, the heat increased. I proposed then that we should walk up the hill, where there was generally a breeze, and Alfred was delighted at the larger freedom it promised us.

"But in another hour the sky grew dark and lurid, and I noticed that Alfred grew strangely restless. His cheeks flushed, his eyes had a wild look of terror in them, he trembled and started, and in spite of all my efforts to soothe him, grew irritable and gloomy. Yet he had just asked me to marry him, and I had promised I would. He had called me 'his wife,' and I had told him again my suspicions about Dr. Orman,

and vowed to nurse him myself back to perfect health.   We had talked, too, of going to
Europe, and in the eagerness and delight
of our new plans, had wandered quite up
to the little pine forest at the top of the hill.

"Then I noticed Alfred's excited condition, and saw also that we were going to
have a thunder storm.   There was an
empty log hut not far away, and I urged
Alfred to try and reach it before the storm
broke.   But he became suddenly like a
child in his terror, and it was only with
the greatest difficulty I got him within its
shelter.

"As peal after peal of thunder crashed
above us, Alfred seemed to lose all control
of himself, and, seriously offended, I left
him, nearly sobbing, in a corner, and went
and stood by myself in the open door.   In
the very height of the storm I saw my
father, Dr. Orman and three of our workmen coming through the wood.   They evidently suspected our sheltering-place, for
they came directly toward it.

"'Alfred!' shouted Dr. Orman, in the
tone of an angry master, 'where are you,
sir?   Come here instantly.'

"My pettedness instantly vanished, and
I said: 'Doctor, you have no right to speak
to Alfred in that way.   He is going to be
my husband, and I shall not permit it any
more.'

"'Miss Wakefield,' he answered, 'this is sheer folly.   Look here!'

"I turned, and saw Alfred crouching in a corner, completely paralyzed with terror; and yet, when Dr. Orman spoke to him, he rose mechanically as a dog might follow his master's call.

"'I am sorry, Miss Wakefield, to destroy your fine romance.   Mr. Alfred Compton is, as you perceive, not fit to marry any lady.   In fact, I am his—*keeper.*'"

"Oh, Aunt Phoebe!   Surely he was not a lunatic!"

"So they said, Julia.   His frantic terror was the only sign I saw of it; but Dr. Orman told my father that he was at times really dangerous, and that he was annually paid a large sum to take charge of him, as he became uncontrollable in an aslyum."

"Did you see him again?"

"No.   I found a little note in the rose bush, saying that he was not mad; that he remembered my promise to be his wife, and would surely come some day and claim me. But they left in three days, and Melissa, whose wedding outfit was curtailed in consequence, twitted me very unkindly about my fine crazy lover.   It was a little hard on me, for he was the only lover I ever had. Melissa and Jane both married, and went west with their husbands; I lived on at Ryelands, a faded little old maid, until my uncle Joshua sent for me to come to New York and keep his fine house for him.   You know that he left me all he had when he died, nearly two years ago.   Then I sent for you.   I remembered my own lonely youth, and thought I would give you a fair chance, dear.''

''Did you ever hear of him again, aunt?''

''Of him, never.   His elder brother died more than a year ago.   I suppose Alfred died many years since; he was very frail and delicate.   I thought it was refinement and beauty then; I know now it was ill health.''

''Poor aunt!''

''Nay, child; I was very happy while my dream lasted; and I never will believe but that Alfred in his love for me was quite sane, and perhaps more sincere than many wiser men.''

After this confidence Miss Phoebe seemed to take a great pleasure in speaking of the little romance of her youth.   Often the old and the young maidens sat in the twilight discussing the probabilities of poor Alfred Compton's life and death, and every discussion left them more and more positive that he had been the victim of some cruel plot.   The subject never tired Miss Phoebe, and Julia, in the absence of a lover of her own, found in it a charm quite in keeping with her own youthful dreams.

One cold night in the middle of January they had talked over the old subject until both felt it to be exhausted—at least for that night. Julia drew aside the heavy satin curtains, and looking out said, "It is snowing heavily, aunt; to-morrow we can have a sleigh ride. Why, there is a sleigh at our door! Who can it be? A gentleman, aunt, and he is coming here."

"Close the curtains, child. It is my lawyer, Mr. Howard. He promised to call to-night."

"Oh, dear! I was hoping it was some nice strange person."

Miss Phoebe did not answer; her thoughts were far away. In fact, she had talked about her old lover until there had sprung up anew in her heart a very strong sentimental affection for his memory; and when the servant announced a visitor on business, she rose with a sigh from her reflections, and went into the reception-room.

In a few minutes Julia heard her voice, in rapid, excited tones, and ere she could decide whether to go to her or not, Aunt Phoebe entered the room, holding by the hand a gentleman whom she announced as Mr. Alfred Compton. Julia was disappointed, to say the least, but she met him with enthusiasm. Perhaps Aunt Phoebe had quite unconsciously magnified the beauty of the youthful Alfred: certainly this one was not handsome. He was sixty, at least, his fair curling locks had vanished, and his fine figure was slightly bent. But the clear, sensitive face remained, and he was still dressed with scrupulous care.

The two women made much of him. In half an hour Delmonico had furnished a delicious little banquet, and Alfred had proposed, with old-fashioned grace, the health of "his promised wife, Miss Phœbe Wakefield, best and loveliest of women."

Miss Phoebe laughed, but she dearly liked it; and hand in hand the two old lovers sat, while Alfred told his sad little story of life-long wrong and suffering; of an intensely nervous, self-conscious nature, driven to extremity by cruel usage and many wrongs. At the mention of Dr. Orman Miss Phoebe expressed herself a little bitterly.

"Nay, Phoebe," said Alfred; "whatever he was when my brother put me in his care, he became my true friend. To his skill and patience I owe my restoration to perfect health; and to his firm advocacy of my right and ability to manage my own estate I owe the position I now hold, and my ability to come and ask Phoebe to redeem her never-forgotten promise."

Perhaps Julia got a little tired of these old-fashioned lovers, but they never tired of each other. Miss Phoebe was not the least abashed by any contrast between her ideal and her real Alfred, and Alfred was never weary of assuring her that he found her infinitely more delightful and womanly than in the days of their first courtship.

She cannot even call them a "silly" or "foolish" couple, or use any other relieving phrase of that order, for Miss Phoebe—or rather Mrs. Compton—resents any word as applied to Mr. Alfred Compton that would imply less than supernatural wisdom and intelligence. "No one but those who have known him as long as I have," she continually avers, "can possibly estimate the superior information and infallible judgment of my husband."

TWO FAIR DECEIVERS.

What do young men talk about when they sit at the open windows chatting on summer evenings? Do you suppose it is of love? Indeed, I suspect it is of money; or, if not of money, then, at least, of something that either makes money or spends it.

Cleve Sullivan has been spending his for four years in Europe, and he has just been telling his friend John Selden how he spent it. John has spent his in New York—he is inclined to think just as profitably. Both stories conclude in the same way.

"I have not a thousand dollars left, John."

"Nor I, Cleve."

"I thought your cousin died two years ago; surely you have not spent all the old gentleman's money already?"

"I only got $20,000; I owed half of it."

"Only $20,000! What did he do with it?"

"Gave it to his wife. He married a beauty about a year after you went away, died in a few months afterward, and left her his whole fortune. I had no claim on him. He educated me, gave me a profession, and $20,000. That was very well: he was only my mother's cousin."

"And the widow—where is she?"

"Living at his country-seat. I have never seen her. She was one of the St. Maurs, of Maryland."

"Good family, and all beauties. Why don't you marry the widow?"

"Why, I never thought of such a thing."

"You can't think of anything better. Write her a little note at once; say that you and I will soon be in her neighborhood, and that gratitude to your cousin, and all that kind of thing—then beg leave to call and pay respects," etc., etc.

John demurred a good deal to the plan, but Cleve was masterful, and the note was written, Cleve himself putting it in the post-office.

That was on Monday night. On Wednesday morning the widow Clare found it with a dozen others upon her breakfast table. She was a dainty, high-bred little lady, with

"Eyes that drowse with dreamy splendor,
Cheeks with rose-leaf tintings tender,
Lips like fragrant posy,"

and withal a kind, hospitable temper, well inclined to be happy in the happiness of others.

But this letter could not be answered with the usual polite formula. She was quite aware that John Selden had regarded himself for many years as his cousin's heir, and that her marriage with the late Thomas Clare had seriously altered his prospects. Women easily see through the best laid plans of men, and this plan was transparent enough to the shrewd little widow. John would scarcely have liked the half-contemptuous shrug and smile which terminated her private thoughts on the matter.

"Clementine, if you could spare a moment from your fashion paper, I want to consult you, dear, about a visitor."

Clementine raised her blue eyes, dropped her paper, and said, "Who is it, Fan?"

"It is John Selden. If Mr. Clare had not married me, he would have inherited the Clare estate. I think he is coming now in order to see if it is worth while asking for, encumbered by his cousin's widow."

"What selfishness! Write and tell him that you are just leaving for the Suez Canal, or the Sandwich Islands, or any other inconvenient place."

"No; I have a better plan than that—Clementine, do stop reading a few minutes. I will take that pretty cottage at Ryebank for the summer, and Mr. Selden and his friend shall visit us there. No one knows us in the place, and I will take none of the servants with me."

"Well?"

"Then, Clementine, you are to be the widow Clare, and I your poor friend and companion."

"Good! very good! 'The Fair Deceivers' —an excellent comedy. How I shall snub you, Fan! And for once I shall have the pleasure of outdressing you. But has not Mr. Selden seen you?"

"No; I was married in Maryland, and went immediately to Europe. I came back a widow two years ago, but Mr. Selden has never remembered me until now. I wonder who this friend is that he proposes to bring with him?"

"Oh, men always think in pairs, Fan. They never decide on anything until their particular friend approves. I dare say they wrote the letter together. What is the gentleman's name?"

The widow examined the note. " 'My friend Mr. Cleve Sullivan.' Do you know him, Clementine?"

"No; I am quite sure that I never saw Mr. Cleve Sullivan. I don't fall in love with the name—do you? But pray accept the offer for both gentlemen, Fan, and write this morning, dear." Then Clementine returned to the consideration of the lace in *coquilles* for her new evening dress.

The plan so hastily sketched was subsequently thoroughly discussed and carried out. The cottage at Ryebank was taken, and one evening at the end of June the two ladies took possession of it. The new widow Clare had engaged a maid in New York, and fell into her part with charming ease and a very pretty assumption of authority; and the real widow, in her plain dress and pensive, quiet manners, realized effectively the idea of a cultivated but dependent companion. They had two days in which to rehearse their parts and get all the household machinery in order, and then the gentlemen arrived at Ryebank.

Fan and Clementine were quite ready for their first call; the latter in a rich and exquisite morning costume, the former in a simple dress of spotted lawn. Clementine went through the introductions with consummate ease of manner, and in half an hour they were a very pleasant party. John's "cousinship" afforded an excellent basis for informal companionship, and Clementine gave it full prominence. Indeed, in a few days John began to find the relationship tiresome; it had been "Cousin John, do this," and "Cousin John, come here," continually; and one night when Cleve and he sat down to smoke their final cigar, he was irritable enough to give his objections the form of speech.

"Cleve, to tell you the honest truth, I do not like Mrs. Clare."

"I think she is a very lovely woman, John."

"I say nothing against her beauty, Cleve; I don't like her, and I have no mind to occupy the place that beautiful ill-used Miss Marat fills. The way Cousin Clare ignores or snubs a woman to whom she is every way inferior makes me angry enough, I assure you."

"Don't fall in love with the wrong woman, John."

"Your advice is too late, Cleve; I am in love. There is no use in us deceiving ourselves or each other. You seem to like the widow—why not marry her? I am quite willing you should."

"Thank you, John; I have already made some advances that way. They have been favorably received, I think."

"You are so handsome, a fellow has no chance against you. But we shall hardly quarrel, if you do not interfere between lovely little Clement and myself."

"I could not afford to smile on her, John; she is too poor. And what on earth are you going to do with a poor wife? Nothing added to nothing will not make a decent living."

"I am going to ask her to be my wife, and if she does me the honor to say 'Yes,' I will make a decent living out of my profession."

From this time forth John devoted himself with some ostentation to his supposed cousin's companion. He was determined to let the widow perceive that he had made his choice, and that he could not be bought with her money. Mr. Selden and Miss Marat were always together, and the widow did not interfere between her companion and her cousin. Perhaps she was rather glad of their close friendship, for the handsome Cleve made a much more delightful attendant. Thus the party fell quite naturally into couples, and the two weeks that the gentlemen had first fixed as the limit of their stay lengthened into two months.

It was noticeable that as the ladies became more confidential with their lovers, they had less to say to each other; and it began at last to be quite evident to the real widow that the play must end for the present, or the *dénouement* would come prematurely. Circumstances favored her determination. One night Clementine, with a radiant face, came into her friend's room, and said, "Fan, I have something to tell you. Cleve has asked me to marry him."

"Now, Clement, you have told him all; I know you have."

"Not a word, Fan. He still believes me the widow Clare."

"Did you accept him?"

"Conditionally. I am to give him a final answer when we go to the city in October.

16

You are going to New York this winter, are you not?"

"Yes. Our little play progresses finely. John Selden asked me to be his wife to-night."

"I told you men think and act in pairs."

"John is a noble fellow. I pretended to think that his cousin had ill-used him, and he defended him until I was ashamed of myself; absolutely said, Clement, that *you* were a sufficient excuse for Mr. Clare's will. Then he blamed his own past idleness so much, and promised if I would only try and endure 'the slings and arrows' of your out-rageous temper, Clement, for two years longer, he would have made a home for me in which I could be happy. Yes, Clement, I should marry John Selden if we had not a five-dollar bill between us."

"I wish Cleve had been a little more ex-plicit about his money affairs. However, there is time enough yet. When they leave to-morrow, what shall we do?"

"We will remain here another month; Levine will have the house ready for me by that time. I have written to him about refurnishing the parlors."

So next day the lovers parted, with many promises of constant letters and future happy days together. The interval was long and dull enough; but it passed, and one morning both gentlemen received notes of invitation to a small dinner party at the widow Clare's mansion in —— street. There was a good deal of dressing for this party. Cleve wished to make his entrance into his future home as became the prospective master of a million and a half of money, and John was desirous of not suffering in Clement's eyes by any comparison with the other gentlemen who would probably be there.

Scarcely had they entered the drawing-room when the ladies appeared, the true widow Clare no longer in the unassuming toilet she had hitherto worn, but magnificent in white crêpe lisse and satin, her arms and throat and pretty head flashing with sapphires and diamonds. Her companion had assumed now the rôle of simplicity, and Cleve was disappointed with the first glance at her plain white Chambéry gauze dress.

John had seen nothing but the bright face of the girl he loved and the love-light in her eyes. Before she could speak he had taken both her hands and whispered, "Dearest and best and loveliest Clement."

Her smile answered him first. Then she said: "Pardon me, Mr. Selden, but we have been in masquerade all summer, and now we must unmask before real life begins. My name is not Clementine Marat, but Fanny Clare. *Cousin John*, I hope you are not disappointed." Then she put her hand into John's, and they wandered off into the conservatory to finish their explanation.

Mr. Cleve Sullivan found himself at that moment in the most trying circumstance of his life. The real Clementine Marat stood looking down at a flower on the carpet, and evidently expecting him to resume the tender attitude he had been accustomed to bear toward her. He was a man of quick decisions where his own interests were concerned, and it did not take him half a minute to review his position and determine what to do. This plain blonde girl without fortune was not the girl he could marry; she had deceived him, too—he had a sudden and severe spasm of morality; his confidence was broken; he thought it was very poor sport to play with a man's most sacred feelings; he had been deeply disappointed and grieved, etc., etc.

Clementine stood perfectly still, with her eyes fixed on the carpet and her cheeks gradually flushing, as Cleve made his awkward accusations. She gave him no help and she made no defence, and it soon becomes embarrassing for a man to stand in the middle of a large drawing-room and talk to himself about any girl. Cleve felt it so.

"Have you done, sir?" at length she asked, lifting to his face a pair of blue eyes, scintillating with scorn and anger. "I

promised you my final answer to your suit
when we met in New York. You have
spared me that trouble. Good evening,
sir.''

Clementine showed to no one her disappointment, and she probably soon recovered
from it. Her life was full of many other
pleasant plans and hopes, and she could
well afford to let a selfish lover pass out of it.
She remained with her friend until after
the marriage between her and John Selden
had been consummated; and then Cleve
saw her name among the list of passengers
sailing on one particular day for Europe.
As John and his bride left on the same
steamer Cleve supposed, of course, she had
gone in their company.

''Nice thing it would have been for Cleve
Sullivan to marry John Selden's wife's
maid, or something or other? John always
was a lucky fellow. Some fellows are always unlucky in love affairs—I always am.''

Half a year afterward he reiterated this
statement with a great deal of unnecessary
emphasis. He was just buttoning his
gloves preparatory to starting for his afternoon drive, when an old acquaintance
hailed him.

''Oh, it's that fool Belmar,'' he muttered;
''I shall have to offer him a ride. I thought
he was in Paris. Hello, Belmar, when did
you get back? Have a ride?''

"No, thank you. I have promised my wife to ride with her this afternoon."

"Your wife! When were you married?"

"Last month, in Paris."

"And the happy lady was—"

"Why, I thought you knew; everyone is talking about my good fortune. Mrs. Belmar is old Paul Marat's only child."

"What?"

"Miss Clementine Marat. She brings me nearly $3,000,000 in money and real estate, and a heart beyond all price."

"How on earth did you meet her?"

"She was traveling with Mr. and Mrs. Selden—you know John Selden. She has lived with Mrs. Selden ever since she left school; they were friends when they were girls together."

Cleve gathered up his reins, and nodding to Mr. Frank Belmar, drove at a finable rate up the avenue and through the park. He could not trust himself to speak to any one, and when he did, the remark which he made to himself in strict confidence was not flattering. For once Mr. Cleve Sullivan told Mr. Cleve Sullivan that he had been badly punished, and that he well deserved it.

THE TWO MR. SMITHS.

"It is not either her money or her position that dashes me, Carrol; it is my own name. Think of asking Eleanor Bethune to become Mrs. William Smith! If it had been Alexander Smith—"

"Or Hyacinth Smith."

"Yes, Hyacinth Smith would have done; but plain William Smith!"

"Well, as far as I can see, you are not to blame. Apologize to the lady for the blunder of your godfathers and godmothers. Stupid old parties! They ought to have thought of Hyacinth;" and Carrol forthwith began to buckle on his spurs.

"Come with me, Carrol."

"No, thank you. It is against my principles to like anyone better than myself, and Alice Fontaine is a temptation to do so."

"*I* don't like Alice's style at all."

"Of course not. Alice's beauty, as compared with Mrs. Bethune's settled income, is skin-deep."

If sarcasm was intended, Smith did not perceive it. He took the criticism at its face value, and answered, "Yes, Eleanor's income is satisfactory; and besides that, she has all kinds of good qualities, and several accomplishments. If I only could offer her, with myself, a suitable name for them!''

''Could you not, in taking Mrs. Bethune and her money, take her name also?''

''N-n-no. A man does not like to lose all his individuality in his wife's, Carrol.''

''Well, then, I have no other suggestion, and I am going to ride.''

So Carrol went to the park, and Smith went to his mirror. The occupation gave him the courage he wanted. He was undoubtedly a very handsome man, and he had, also, very fine manners; indeed, he would have been a very great man if the world had only been a drawing-room, for, polished and fastidious, he dreaded nothing so much as an indecorum, and had the air of being uncomfortable unless his hands were in kid gloves.

Smith had a standing invitation to Mrs. Bethune's five-o'clock teas, and he was always considered an acquisition. He was also very fond of going to them; for under no circumstances was Mrs. Bethune so charming. To see her in this hour of perfect relaxation was to understand how great and beautiful is the art of idleness. Her ease and grace, her charming aimlessness, her indescribable air of inaction, were all so many proofs of her having been born in the purple of wealth and fashion; no parvenu could ever hope to imitate them.

Alice Fontaine never tried. She had been taken from a life of polite shifts and struggles by her cousin, Mrs. Bethune, two years before; and the circumstances that were to the one the mere accidents of her position were to the other a real holiday-making.

Alice met Mr. Smith with *empressement*, fluttered about the tea-tray like a butterfly, wasted her bonmots and the sugar recklessly, and was as full of pretty animation as her cousin Bethune was of elegant repose.

"I am glad you are come, Mr. Smith," said Mrs. Bethune. "Alice has been trying to spur me into a fight. I don't want to throw a lance in. Now you can be my substitute."

"Mr. Smith," said Alice impetuously, "don't you think that women ought to have the same rights as men?"

"Really, Miss Alice, I—I don't know. When women have got what they call their 'rights,' do they expect to keep what they call their 'privileges' also?"

"Certainly they do. When they have driven the men to emigrate, to scrub floors, and to jump into the East River, they will still expect the corner seat, the clean side of the road, the front place, and the pick of everything."

"Ah, indeed! And when all the public and private business of the country is in their hands, will they still expect to find time for five-o'clock teas?"

"Yes, sir. They will conduct the affairs of this regenerated country, and not neglect either their music or their pets, their dress or their drawing-room. They will be perfectly able to do the one, and not leave the other undone."

"Glorious creatures! Then they will accomplish what men have been trying to do ever since the world began. They will get two days' work out of one day."

"Of course they will."

"But how?"

"Oh, machines and management. It will be done."

"But your answer is illogical, Miss Alice."

"Of course. Men always take refuge in their logic; and yet, with all their boasted skill, they have never mastered the useful and elementary proposition, 'It will be, because it will be.'"

Mr. Smith was very much annoyed at the tone Alice was giving to the conversation. She was treating him as a joke, and he felt how impossible it was going to be to get Mrs. Bethune to treat him seriously. Indeed, before he could restore the usual placid, tender tone of their *tête-à-tête* tea,

two or three ladies joined the party, and
the hour was up, and the opportunity
lost.

However, he was not without consolation: Eleanor's hand had rested a moment
very tenderly in his; he had seen her white
cheek flush and her eyelids droop, and he
felt almost sure that he was beloved. And
as he had determined that night to test his
fortune, he was not inclined to let himself
be disappointed. Consequently he decided
on writing to her, for he was rather proud
of his letters; and, indeed, it must be confessed that he had an elegant and eloquent
way of putting any case in which he was
personally interested.

Eleanor Bethune thought so. She received his proposal on her return from a
very stupid party, and as soon as she saw
his writing she began to consider how much
more delightful the evening would have
been if Mr. Smith had been present. His
glowing eulogies on her beauty, and his
passionate descriptions of his own affection,
his hopes and his despairs, chimed in with
her mood exactly. Already his fine person
and manners had made a great impression
on her; she had been very near loving
him; nothing, indeed, had been needed but
that touch of electricity conveyed in the
knowledge that she was beloved.

Such proposals seldom or never take

women unawares. Eleanor had been expecting it, and had already decided on her answer. So, after a short, happy reflection, she opened her desk and wrote Mr. Smith a few lines which she believed would make him supremely happy.

Then she went to Alice's room and woke her out of her first sleep. "Oh, you lazy girl; why did you not crimp your hair? Get up again, Alice dear; I have a secret to tell you. I am—going—to—marry—Mr. —Smith."

"I knew some catastrophe was impending, Eleanor; I have felt it all day. Poor Eleanor!"

"Now, Alice, be reasonable. What do you think of him—honestly, you know?"

"The man has excellent qualities; for instance, a perfect taste in cravats and an irreproachable propriety. Nobody ever saw him in any position out of the proper centre of gravity. Now, there is Carrol, always sitting round on tables or easels, or if on a chair, on the back or arms, or any way but as other Christians sit. Then Mr. Smith is handsome; very much so."

"Oh, you do admit that?"

"Yes; but I don't myself like men of the hairdresser style of beauty."

"Alice, what makes you dislike him so much?"

"Indeed, I don't, Eleanor. I think he

is very 'nice,' and very respectable. Every
one will say, 'What a suitable match!' and
I dare say you will be very happy. He
will do everything you tell him to do,
Eleanor; and—oh dear me!—how I should
hate a husband of that kind!''

"You little hypocrite!—with your talk
of woman's 'rights' and woman's 'su-
premacy.' ''

"No, Eleanor love, don't call it hypo-
crisy, please; say *many-sidedness*—it is a
more womanly definition. But if it is
really to be so, then I wish you joy, cousin.
And what are you going to wear?''

This subject proved sufficiently attractive
to keep Alice awake a couple of hours.
She even crimped her hair in honor of the
bridal shopping; and before matters had
been satisfactorily arranged she was so full
of anticipated pleasures that she felt really
grateful to the author of them, and permitted herself to speak with enthusiasm of
the bridegroom.

"He'll be a sight to see, Eleanor, on his
marriage day. There won't be a handsomer man, nor a better dressed man, in
America, and his clothes will all come from
Paris, I dare say.''

"I think we will go to Paris first.''
Then Eleanor went into a graphic descrip-
tion of the glories and pleasures of Paris,
as she had experienced them during her

first bridal tour. "It is the most fascinating city in the world, Alice."

"I dare say, but it is a ridiculous shame having it in such an out-of-the-way place. What is the use of having a Paris, when one has to sail three thousand miles to get at it? Eleanor, I feel that I shall have to go."

"So you shall, dear; I won't go without you."

"Oh, no, darling; not with Mr. Smith: I really could not. I shall have to try and manage matters with Mr. Carrol. We shall quarrel all the way across, of course, but then—"

"Why don't you adopt his opinions, Alice?"

"I intend to—for a little while; but it is impossible to go on with the same set of opinions forever. Just think how dull conversation would become!"

"Well, dear, you may go to sleep now, for mind, I shall want you down to breakfast before eleven. I have given 'Somebody' permission to call at five o'clock tomorrow—or rather to-day—and we shall have a *tête-à-tête* tea."

Alice determined that it should be strictly *tête-à-tête*. She went to spend the afternoon with Carrol's sisters, and stayed until she thought the lovers had had ample time to make their vows and arrange their wedding.

There was a little pout on her lips as she left Carrol outside the door, and slowly bent her steps to Eleanor's private parlor. She was trying to make up her mind to be civil to her cousin's new husband-elect, and the temptation to be anything else was very strong.

"I shall be dreadfully in the way—*his way*, I mean—and he will want to send me out of the room, and I shall not go—no, not if I fall asleep on a chair looking at him."

With this decision, the most amiable she could reach, Alice entered the parlor. Eleanor was alone, and there was a pale, angry look on her face Alice could not understand.

"Shut the door, dear."

"Alone?"

"I have been so all evening."

"Have you quarreled with Mr. Smith?"

"Mr. Smith did not call."

"Not come!"

"Nor yet sent any apology."

The two women sat looking into each other's faces a few moments, both white and silent.

"What will you do, Eleanor?"

"Nothing."

"But he may be sick, or he may not have got your letter. Such queer mistakes do happen."

"Parker took it to his hotel; the clerk said he was still in his room; it was sent to him in Parker's sight and hearing. There is not any doubt but that he received it."

"Well, suppose he did not. Still, if he really cares for you, he is hardly likely to take your supposed silence for an absolute refusal. I have said 'No' to Carrol a dozen times, and he won't stay 'noed.' Mr. Smith will be sure to ask for a personal interview."

Eleanor answered drearily: "I suppose he will pay me that respect;" but through this little effort at assertion it was easy to detect the white feather of mistrust. She half suspected the touchy self-esteem of Mr. Smith. If she had merely been guilty of a breach of good manners toward him, she knew that he would deeply resent it; how, then, when she had—however innocently—given him the keenest personal slight?

Still she wished to accept Alice's cheerful view of the affair, and what is heartily wished is half accomplished. Ere she fell asleep she had quite decided that her lover would call the following day, and her thoughts were busy with the pleasant amends she would make him for any anxiety he might have suffered.

But Mr. Smith did not call the following day, nor on many following ones, and a casual lady visitor destroyed Eleanor's last hope that he would ever call again, for, after a little desultory gossip, she said, "You will miss Mr. Smith very much at your receptions, and brother Sam says he is to be away two years."

"So long?" asked Eleanor, with perfect calmness.

"I believe so. I thought the move very sudden, but Sam says he has been talking about the trip for six months."

"Really!—Alice, dear, won't you bring that piece of Burslem pottery for Mrs. Hollis to look at?"

So the wonderful cup and saucer were brought, and they caused a diversion so complete that Mr. Smith and his eccentric move were not named again during the visit. Nor, indeed, much after it. "What is the use of discussing a hopelessly disagreeable subject?" said Eleanor to Alice's first offer of sympathy. To tell the truth, the mere mention of the subject made her cross, for young women of the finest fortunes do not necessarily possess the finest tempers.

Carrol's next visit was looked for with a good deal of interest. Naturally it was thought that he would know all about his friend's singular conduct. But he professed to be as much puzzled as Alice. "He supposed it was something about Mrs. Bethune; he had always told Smith not to take a pretty, rich woman like her into his calculations. For his part, if he had been desirous of marrying an heiress, and felt that he had a gift that way, he should have looked out a rich German girl; they had less nonsense about them,'' etc.

That was how the affair ended as far as Eleanor was concerned. Of course she suffered, but she was not of that generation of women who parade their suffering. Beautiful and self-respecting, she was, above all, endowed with physical self-control. Even Alice was spared the hysterical sobbings and faintings and other signs of pathological distress common to weak women.

Perhaps she was more silent and more irritable than usual, but Eleanor Bethune's heartache for love never led her to the smallest social impropriety. Whatever she suffered, she did not refuse the proper mixture of colors in her hat, or neglect her tithe of the mint, anise and cummin due to her position.

Eleanor's reticence, however, had this good effect—it compelled Alice to talk Smith's singular behavior over with Carrol; and somehow, in discussing Smith, they got to understand each other; so that, after all, it was Alice's and not Eleanor's bridal shopping that was to do. And there is something very assuaging to grief in this occupation. Before it was completed, Eleanor had quite recovered her placid, sunshiny temper.

"Consolation, thy name is satin and lace!" said Alice, thankfully, to herself, as she saw Eleanor so tired and happy about the wedding finery.

At first Alice had been quite sure that she would go to Paris, and nowhere else; but Eleanor noticed that in less than a week Carrol's influence was paramount. "We have got a better idea, Eleanor—quite a novel one," she said, one morning. "We are going to make our bridal trip in Carrol's yacht!"

"Whose idea is that?"

"Carrol's and *mine too*, of course. Carrol says it is the jolliest life. You leave all your cares and bills on shore behind you. You issue your own sailing orders, and sail away into space with an easy conscience."

"But I thought you were bent on a European trip?"

"The yacht will be ever so much nicer. Think of the nuisance of ticket-offices and waiting-rooms and second-class hotels and troublesome letters waiting for you at your banker's, and disagreeable paragraphs in the newspapers. I think Carrol's idea is splendid."

So the marriage took place at the end of

the season, and Alice and Carrol sailed happily away into the unknown. Eleanor was at a loss what to do with herself. She wanted to go to Europe; but Mr. Smith had gone there, and she felt sure that some unlucky accident would throw them together. It was not her nature to court embarrassments; so Europe was out of the question.

While she was hesitating she called one day on Celeste Reid—a beautiful girl who had been a great belle, but was now a confirmed invalid. "I am going to try the air of Colorado, Mrs. Bethune," she said. "Papa has heard wonderful stories about it. Come with our party. We shall have a special car, and the trip will at least have the charm of novelty."

"And I love the mountains, Celeste. I will join you with pleasure. I was dreading the old routine in the old places; but this will be delightful."

Thus it happened that one evening in the following August Mrs. Bethune found herself slowly strolling down the principal street in Denver. It was a splendid sunset, and in its glory the Rocky Mountains rose like Titanic palaces built of amethyst, gold and silver. Suddenly the look of intense pleasure on her face was changed for one of wonder and annoyance. It had become her duty in a moment to do a very disagreeable thing; but duty was a kind of religion to Eleanor Bethune; she never thought of shirking it.

So she immediately inquired her way to the telegraph office, and even quickened her steps into as fast a walk as she ever permitted herself. The message she had to send was a peculiar and not a pleasant one. At first she thought it would hardly be possible for her to frame it in such words as she would care to dictate to strangers; but she firmly settled on the following form:

"*Messrs. Locke & Lord:*

"Tell brother Edward that Bloom is in Denver. No delay. The matter is of the greatest importance."

When she had dictated the message, the clerk said, "Two dollars, madam." But greatly to Eleanor's annoyance her purse was not in her pocket, and she could not remember whether she had put it there or not. The man stood looking at her in an expectant way; she felt that any delay about the message might be fatal to its worth; perplexity and uncertainty ruled her absolutely. She was about to explain her dilemma, and return to her hotel for money, when a gentleman, who had heard and watched the whole proceeding, said:

"Madam, I perceive that time is of great importance to you, and that you have lost your purse; allow me to pay for the message. You can return the money if you wish. My name is William Smith. I am staying at the 'American.'"

"Thank you, sir. The message is of the gravest importance to my brother. I gratefully accept your offer."

Further knowledge proved Mr. William Smith to be a New York capitalist who was slightly known to three of the gentlemen in Eleanor's party; so that the acquaintance began so informally was very speedily afterward inaugurated with all the forms and ceremonies good society demands. It was soon possible, too, for Eleanor to explain the circumstances which, even in her code of strict etiquette, made a stranger's offer of money for the hour a thing to be gratefully accepted. She had seen in the door of the post-office a runaway cashier of her brother's, and his speedy arrest involved a matter of at least forty thousand dollars.

This Mr. William Smith was a totally different man to Eleanor's last lover—a bright, energetic, alert business man, decidedly handsome and gentlemanly. Though his name was greatly against him in Eleanor's prejudices, she found herself quite unable to resist the cheery, pleasant influence he carried with him. And it was evident from the very first day of their acquaintance that Mr. William Smith had but one thought—the winning of Eleanor Bethune.

When she returned to New York in the autumn she ventured to cast up her accounts with life, and she was rather amazed at the result. For she was quite aware that she was in love with this William Smith in a way that she had never been with the other. The first had been a sentimental ideal; the second was a genuine case of sincere and passionate affection. She felt that the desertion of this lover would be a grief far beyond the power of satin and lace to cure.

But her new lover had never a disloyal thought to his mistress, and his love transplanted to the pleasant places of New York life, seemed to find its native air. It enveloped Eleanor now like a glad and heavenly atmosphere; she was so happy that she dreaded any change; it seemed to her that no change could make her happier.

But if good is good, still better carries the day, and Mr. Smith thought marriage would be a great deal better than love-making. Eleanor and he were sitting in the fire-lit parlor, very still and very happy, when he whispered this opinion to her.

"It is only four months since we met, dear."

"Only four months, darling; but I had been dreaming about you four months

before that. Let me hold your hands, sweet,
while I tell you. On the 20th of last April
I was on the point of leaving for Colorado
to look after the Silver Cliff Mine. My
carriage was ordered, and I was waiting at
my hotel for it. A servant brought me a
letter—the dearest, sweetest little letter—
see, here it is!'' and this William Smith
absolutely laid before Eleanor her own
pretty, loving reply to the first William
Smith's offer.

Eleanor looked queerly at it, and smiled.

''What did you think, dear?''

''That it was just the pleasantest thing
that had ever happened to me. It was
directed to Mr. W. Smith, and had been
given into my hands. I was not going to
seek up any other W. Smith.''

''But you must have been sure that it
was not intended for you, and you did not
know 'Eleanor Bethune.' ''

''Oh, I beg your pardon, sweetheart; it
was intended for me. I can imagine destiny standing sarcastically by your side,
and watching you send the letter to one W.
Smith when she intended it for another W.
Smith. Eleanor Bethune I meant to know
just as soon as possible. I was coming back
to New York to look for you.''

''And, instead, she went to you in Colorado.''

''Only think of that! Why, love, when

that blessed telegraph clerk said, 'Who sends this message?' and you said, 'Mrs. Eleanor Bethune,' I wanted to fling my hat to the sky. I did not lose my head as badly when they found that new lead in the Silver Cliff.''

''Won't you give me that letter, and let me destroy it, William? It was written to the wrong Smith.''

''It was written to the wrong Smith, but it was given to the right Smith. Still, Eleanor, if you will say one little word to me, you may do what you like with the letter.''

Then Eleanor whispered the word, and the blaze of the burning letter made a little illumination in honor of their betrothal kiss.

THE STORY OF MARY NEIL.

Poverty has not only many learned disciples, but also many hidden saints and martyrs. There are humble tenements that are tabernacles, and desolate, wretched rooms that are the quarries of the Almighty —where with toil and weariness and suffering the souls He loves are being prepared for the heavenly temple.

This is the light that relieves the deep shadow of that awful cloud of poverty which ever hangs over this rich and prosperous city. I have been within that cloud, wet with its rain of tears, chilled with its gloomy darkness, "made free" of its innermost recesses; therefore I speak with authority when I say that even here a little child may walk and not stumble, if Jesus lead the way or hold the hand.

Nay, but children walk where strong men fall down, and young maidens enter the kingdom while yet their parents are stumbling where no light from the Golden City and "the Land very far off" reaches them. Last winter I became very much interested in such a case. I was going to write "Poor Mary Neil!" but that would have been the strangest misnomer. Happy Mary

Neil! rises impetuously from my heart to contradict my pen.

And yet when I first became acquainted with her condition, she was "poor" in every bitter sense of the word.

A drunkard's eldest daughter, "the child of misery baptized with tears," what had her seventeen years been but sad and evil ones? Cold and hunger, cares and labors far beyond her strength sowed the seeds of early death. For two years she struggled amid such suffering as dying lungs entail to help her mother and younger brothers and sisters, but at last she was compelled to make her bed amid sorrow and suffering which she could no longer assuage by her helpful hands and gentle words.

Her religious education had not been quite neglected, and she dimly comprehended that through the narrow valley which lay between Time and Eternity she would need a surer and more infallible guide than her own sadly precocious intellect. Then God sent her just the help she needed—a tender, pitiful, hopeful woman full of the love of Jesus.

Souls ripen quickly in the atmosphere of the Border Land, and very soon Mary had learned how to walk without fearing any evil. Certain passages of Scripture burned with a supernatural glory, and made the darkness light; and there were also a few hymns which struck the finest chords in her heart, and

> " 'Mid days of keenest anguish
> And nights devoid of ease,
> Filled all her soul with music
> Of wondrous melodies."

As she neared the deeper darkness of death, this was especially remarkable of that extraordinary hymn called "The Light of Death," by Dr. Faber. From the first it had fascinated her. "Has he been *here* that he knows just how it feels?" she asked, wonderingly, and then solemnly repeated:

> "Saviour, what means this breadth of death,
> This space before me lying;
> These deeps where life so lingereth,
> This difficulty of dying?
> So many turns abrupt and rude,
> Such ever-shifting grounds,
> Such strangely peopled solitudes,
> Such strangely silent sounds?"

Her sufferings were very great, and sometimes the physical depression exerted a definable influence on her spiritual state. Still she never lost her consciousness of the presence of her Guide and Saviour, and once, in the exhaustion of a severe paroxysm, she murmured two lines from the same grand hymn:

> "Deeper! dark, dark, but yet I follow:
> Tighten, dear Lord, thy clasp."

Ah! there was something touching and noble beyond all words, in this complete reliance and perfect trust; and it never again wavered.

"Is it *very* dark, Mary dear?" her friend said one morning, the *last* for her on earth.

"Too dark to see," she whispered, "but I can go on if Christ will hold my hand."

After this a great solemnity shaded her face; she lost all consciousness of this world. The frail, shadowy little body lay gray and passive, while that greatest of all struggles was going on—the struggle of the Eternal out of Time; but her lips moved incessantly, and occasionally some speech of earth told the anxious watchers how hard the conflict was. For instance, toward sundown she said in a voice strangely solemn and anxious:

" Whom are we trying to avoid?
    From whom, Lord, must we hide?
Oh! can the dying be decoyed,
    With the Saviour by his side?"

"Loose sands and all things sinking!" "Are we near eternity?" "Can I fall from Thee even now?" and ejaculations of similar kind, showed that the spiritual struggle was a very palpable one to her; but it ended in a great calm. For two hours she lay in a peace that passeth understanding, and you would have said that she was dead but for a vague look of expectancy in the happy, restful face. Then suddenly there was a lightening of the whole countenance; she stretched out her arms to meet the messenger of the King, and entered heaven with this prayer on her lips:

"*Both hands*, dear Lord, *both hands.*"

Don't doubt but she got them; their mighty strength lifted her over the dark river almost dry shod.

"Rests she not well whose pilgrim staff and shoon
  Lie in her tent—for on the golden street
She walks and stumbles not on roads star strewn
  With her unsandalled feet?"

THE HEIRESS OF KURSTON CHACE.

Into the usual stillness of Kurston Chace a strange bustle and excitement had come— the master was returning with a young bride, whom report spoke of as "bewitchingly beautiful." It was easy to believe report in this case, for there must have been some strong inducement to make Frederick Kurston wed in his sixtieth year a woman barely twenty. It was not money; Mr. Kurston had plenty of money, and he was neither ambitious nor avaricious; besides, the woman he had chosen was both poor and extravagant.

For once report was correct. Clementina Gray, in tarlatans and flowers, had been a great beauty; and Clementina Kurston, in silks and diamonds, was a woman dedicated by Nature for conquest.

It was Clementina's beauty that had prevailed over the love-hardened heart of the gay old gallant, who had escaped the dangers of forty seasons of flirtation. He was entangled in the meshes of her golden hair, fascinated by the spell of her love-languid eyes, her mouth like a sad, heavy rose, her faultless form and her superb manners. He was blind to all her faults; deaf to all

his friends—in the glamour of her enchant-
ments he submitted to her implicitly, even
while both his reason and his sense of other
obligations pleaded for recognition.

Clementina had not won him very easily;
the summer was quite over, nearly all the
visitors at the stylish little watering-place
had departed, the mornings and evenings
were chilly, every day Mr. Kurston spoke
of his departure, and she herself was watching her maid pack her trunks, and in no
very amiable temper contemplating defeat,
when the reward of her seductive attentions
came.

"Mr. Kurston entreated the favor of an
interview."

She gladly accorded it; she robed herself
with subtle skill; she made herself marvelous.

"Mother," she said, as she left her dress-
ing-room, "you will have a headache. I
shall excuse you. I can manage this business best alone."

In an hour she came back triumphant.
She put her feet on the fender, and sat
down before the cheerful blaze to "talk it
over."

"It is all right, mother. Good-by to our
miserable shifts and shabby-genteel lodgings and turned dresses. He will settle
Kurston Chace and all he has upon me, and
we are to be married next month."

"Impossible, Tina! No *modiste* in the world could get the things that are absolutely necessary ready in that time."

"Everything is possible in New York—if you have money—and Uncle Gray will be ready enough to buy my marriage clothes. Besides, I am going to run no risks. If he should die, nothing on earth could console me for the trouble I have had with him, but the fact of being his widow. There is no sentiment in the affair, and the sooner one gets to ordering dinners and running up bills, the better."

"Poor Philip Lee!"

"Mother, why did you mention him? Of course he will be angry, and call me all kinds of unpleasant names; but if he has a particle of common sense he must see that it was impossible for me to marry a poor lawyer—especially when I had such a much better offer. I suppose he will be here to-night. You must see him, mother, and explain things as pleasantly as possible. It would scarcely be proper for me, as Mr. Kurston's affianced wife, to listen to all the ravings and protestations he is sure to indulge in."

In this supposition Clementina was mistaken. Philip Lee took the news of her engagement to his wealthy rival with blank calmness and a civil wish for her happiness. He made a stay of conventional

18

propriety, and said all the usual polite platitudes, and then went away without any evidence of the deep suffering and mortification he felt.

This was Clementina's first drop of bitterness in her cup of success. She questioned her mother closely as to how he looked, and what he said. It did not please her that, instead of bemoaning his own loss, he should be feeling a contempt for her duplicity—that he should use her to cure his passion, when she meant to wound him still deeper. She felt at moments as if she could give up for Philip Lee the wealth and position she had so hardly won, only she knew him well enough to understand that henceforward she could not easily deceive him again.

It was pleasant to return to New York this fall; the news of the engagement opened everyone's heart and home. Congratulations came from every quarter; even Uncle Gray praised the girl who had done so well for herself, and signified his approval by a handsome check.

The course of this love ran smooth enough, and one fine morning in October, Grace Church saw a splendid wedding. Henceforward Clementina Kurston was a woman to be courted instead of patronized, and many a woman who had spoken lightly of her beauty and qualities, was made to acknowledge with an envious pang that she had distanced them.

This was her first reward, and she did not stint herself in extorting it. To tell the truth, Clementina had many a bitter score of this kind to pay off; for, as she said in extenuation, it was impossible for her to allow herself to be in debt to her self-respect.

Well, the wedding was over. She had abundantly gratified her taste for splendor; she had smiled on those on whom she willed to smile; she had treated herself extravagantly to the dangerous pleasure of social revenge; she was now anxious to go and take possession of her home, which had the reputation of being one of the oldest and handsomest in the country.

Mr. Kurston, hitherto, had been intoxicated with love, and not a little flattered by the brilliant position which his wife had at once claimed. Now that she was his wife, it amused him to see her order and patronize and dispense with all that royal prerogative which belongs to beauty, supported by wealth and position.

Into his great happiness he had suffered no doubt, no fear of the future, to come; but, as the day approached for their departure for Kurston Chace, he grew singularly restless and uneasy.

For, much as he loved and obeyed the

woman whom he called "wife," there was another woman at Kurston whom he called "daughter," that he loved quite as dearly, in a different way. In fact, of his daughter, Athel Kurston, he stood just a little bit in fear, and she had ruled the household at the Chace for many years as absolute mistress.

No one knew anything of her mother; he had brought her to her present home when only five years old, after a long stay on the Continent. A strange woman, wearing the dress of a Sclavonic peasant, came with the child as nurse; but she had never learnt to speak English, and had now been many years dead.

Athel knew nothing of her mother, and her early attempts to question her father concerning her had been so peremptorily rebuffed that she had long ago ceased to indulge in any curiosity regarding her. However—though she knew it not—no one regarded her as Mr. Kurston's heir; indeed, nothing in her father's conduct sanctioned such a conclusion. True, he loved her dearly, and had spared no pains in her education; but he never took her with him into the world, and, except in the neighborhood of the Chace, her very existence was not known of.

She was as old as his new wife, willful, proud, accustomed to rule, not likely to obey. He had said nothing to Clementina of her existence; he had said nothing to his daughter of his marriage; and now both facts could no longer be concealed.

But Frederick Kurston had all his life trusted to circumstances, and he was rather disposed, in this matter, to let the women settle affairs between them without troubling himself to enter into explanations with either of them. So, to Athel he wrote a tender little note, assuming that she would be delighted to hear of his marriage, as it promised her a pleasant companion, and directing her to have all possible arrangements made to add to the beauty and comfort of the house.

To Mrs. Kurston he said nothing. The elegantly dressed young lady who met her with a curious and rather constrained welcome was to her a genuine surprise. Her air of authority and rich dress precluded the idea of a dependent; Mr. Kurston had kissed her lovingly, the servants obeyed her. But she was far too prudent to make inquiries on unknown ground; she disappeared, with her maid, on the plea of weariness, and from the vantage-ground of her retirement sent Félicité to take observations.

The little French maid found no difficulty in arriving at the truth, and Mrs. Kurston, not unjustly angry, entered the drawing-room fully prepared to defend her rights.

"Who was that young person, Frederick, dear, that I saw when we arrived?"

This question in the very sweetest tone, and with that caressing manner she had always found omnipotent.

"That young person is Miss Athel Kurston, Clementina."

This answer in the very decided, and yet nervous, manner people on the defensive generally assume.

"Miss Kurston? Your sister, Frederick?"

"No; my daughter, Clementina."

"But you were never married before?"

"So people say."

"Then, do you really expect me to live in the same house with a person of—"

"I see no reason why you should not—that is, if you live in the same house with me."

A passionate burst of tears, an utter abandonment of distress, and the infatuated husband was willing to promise anything—everything—that his charmer demanded—that is, for the time; for Athel Kurston's influence was really stronger than her stepmother's, and the promises extorted from his lower passions were indefinitely postponed by his nobler feelings.

A divided household is always a miserable one; but the chief sufferer here was

Mr. Kurston, and Athel, who loved him with a sincere and profound affection, determined to submit to circumstances for his sake.

One morning, he found on his table a letter from her stating that, to procure him peace, she had left a home that would be ever dear to her, assuring him that she had secured a comfortable and respectable asylum; but earnestly entreating that he would make no inquiries about her, as she had changed her name, and would not be discovered without causing a degree of gossip and evil-speaking injurious to both himself and her.

This letter completely broke the power of Clementina over her husband. He asserted at once his authority, and insisted on returning immediately to New York, where he thought it likely Athel had gone, and where, at any rate, he could find suitable persons to aid him in his search for her—a search which was henceforth the chief object of his life.

A splendid house was taken, and Mrs. Kurston at once assumed the position of a leader in the world of fashion. Greatly to her satisfaction, Philip Lee was a favorite in the exclusive circle in which she moved, and she speedily began the pretty, penitent, dejected rôle which she judged would be most effective with him. But, though she would

not see it, Philip Lee was proof against all
her blandishments. He was not the man to be
deluded twice by the same false woman; he
was a man of honor, and detested the social
ethics which scoffed at humanity's holiest
tie; and he was deeply in love with a
woman who was the very antipodes of the
married siren.

Yet he visited frequently at the Kurston
mansion, and became a great favorite, and
finally the friend and confidant of its master. Gradually, as month after month
passed, the business of the Kurston estate
came into his hands, and he could have
told, to the fraction of a dollar, the exact
sum for which Clementina Gray sold herself.

Two years passed away. There was no
longer on Clementina's part, any pretence
of affection for her husband; she went her
own way, and devoted herself to her own
interests and amusements. He wearied
with a hopeless search and anxiety that
found no relief, aged very rapidly, and became subject to serious attacks of illness,
any one of which might deprive him of life.

His wife now regretted that she had
married so hastily; the settlements promised
had been delayed; she had trusted to her
influence to obtain more as his wife than
as his betrothed. She had not known of
a counter-influence, and she had not

calculated that the effort of a life-long decep-
tion might be too much for her. Quarrels
had arisen in the very beginning of their life
at Kurston, the disappearance of Athel had
never been forgiven, and now Mrs. Kurston
became violently angry if the settlement
and disposing of his property was named.

One night, in the middle of the third
winter after Athel's disappearance, Philip
Lee called with an important lease for Mr.
Kurston to sign. He found him alone, and
strangely moved and sorrowful. He signed
the papers as Philip directed him, and then
requested him to lock the door and sit
down.

"I am going," he said, "to confide to
you, Philip Lee, a sacred trust. I do not
think I shall live long, and I leave a duty
unfulfilled that makes to me the bitterness
of death. I have a daughter—the lawful
heiress of the Kurston lands—whom my
wife drove, by subtle and persistent
cruelty, from her home. By no means
have I been able to discover her; but you
must continue the search, and see her put
in possession of her rights."

"But what proofs, sir, can you give me
in order to establish them?"

"They are all in this box—everything
that is necessary. Take it with you to
your office to-night. Her mother—ah, me,
how I loved her—was a Polish lady of good

family; but I have neither time nor inclination now to explain to you, or to excuse myself for the paltry vanities which induced me to conceal my marriage. In those days I cared so much for what society said that I never listened to the voice of my heart or my conscience. I hope, I trust, I may still right both the dead and the living!"

Mr. Kurston's presentiment of death was no delusive one; he sank gradually during the following week, and died—his last word, "Remember!" being addressed, with all the strong beseeching of a dying injunction, to Philip Lee.

A free woman, and a rich one, Mrs. Kurston turned with all the ardor of a sentimental woman to her first and—as she chose to consider it—her only true affection. She was now in a position to woo the poor lawyer, dependent in a great measure on her continuing to him the management of the Kurston property.

Business brought them continually together, and it was neither possible nor prudent for him to always reject the attentions she offered. The world began to freely connect their names, and it was with much difficulty that he could convince even his most intimate friends of his indifference to the rich and beautiful widow.

He found himself, indeed, becoming

gradually entangled in a net of circumstances it would soon be difficult to get honorably out of.

The widow received him at every visit more like a lover, and less like a lawyer; men congratulated or envied him, women tacitly assumed his engagement. There was but one way to free himself from the toils the artful widow was encompassing him with—he must marry some one else.

But whom? The only girl he loved was poor, and had already refused him; yet he was sure she loved him, and something bid him try again. He had half a mind to do so, and "half a mind" in love is quite enough to begin with.

So he put on his hat and went to his sister's house. He knew she was out driving—had seen her pass five minutes before on her way to the park. Then what did he go there for? Because he judged from experience, that at this hour lovely Pauline Alexes, governess to his sister's daughters, was at home and alone.

He was not wrong; she came into the parlor by one door as he entered it by the other. The coincidence was auspicious, and he warmly pressed his suit, pouring into Pauline's ears such a confused account of his feelings and his affairs as only love could disentangle and understand.

"But, Philip," said Pauline, "do you

mean to say that this Mrs. Kurston makes love to you? Is she not a married woman, and her husband your best friend and patron?''

''Mr. Kurston, Pauline darling, is dead!''

''Dead! dead! Oh, Philip! Oh, my father! my father!'' And the poor girl threw herself, with passionate sobbings, among the cushions of the sofa.

This was a revelation. Here, in Pauline Alexes, the girl he had fondly loved for nearly three years, Philip found the long-sought heiress of Kurston Chace!

Bitter, indeed, was her grief when she learned how sorrowfully her father had sought her; but she was scarcely to be blamed for not knowing of, and responding to, his late repentance of the life-long wrong he had done her. For Philip's sister moved far outside the narrow and supreme circle of the Kurstons.

She had hidden her identity in her mother's maiden name—the only thing she knew of her mother. She had never seen her father since her flight from her home but in public, accompanied by his wife; she had no reason to suppose the influence of that wife any weaker; she had been made, by cruel innuendoes, to doubt both the right and the inclination of her father to protect her.

It now became Philip's duty to acquaint

the second Mrs. Kurston with her true position, and to take the necessary steps to reinstate Athel Kurston in her rights.

Of course, he had to bear many unkind suspicions—even his friends believed him to have been cognizant all the time of the identity of Pauline Alexes with Athel Kurston—and he was complimented on his cleverness in securing the property, with the daughter, instead of the widow, for an incumbrance. But those may laugh who win, and these things scarcely touched the happiness of Philip and Athel.

As for Mrs. Kurston she made a still more brilliant marriage, and gave up the Kurston estate with an ostentatious indifference. ''She was glad to get rid of it; it had brought her nothing but sorrow and disappointment,'' etc.

But from the heights of her social autocracy, clothed in Worth's greatest inspirations, wearing priceless lace and jewels, dwelling in unrivalled splendor, she looked with regret on the man whom she had rejected for his poverty.

She saw him grow to be the pride of his State and the honor of his country. Loveless and childless, she saw his boys and girls cling to the woman she hated as their ''mother,'' and knew that they filled with light and love the grand old home for which she had first of all sacrificed her affection and her womanhood.

"ONLY THIS ONCE."

Over the solemn mountains and the misty moorlands the chill spring night was falling. David Scott, master shepherd for MacAllister, of Allister, thought of his ewes and lambs, pulled his Scotch bonnet over his brows, and taking his staff in his hand, turned his face to the hills.

David Scott was a mystic in his own way; the mountains were to him "temples not made with hands," and in them he had seen and heard wonderful things. Years of silent communion with nature had made him love her in all her moods, and he passionately believed in God.

The fold was far up the mountains, but the sheep knew the shepherd's voice, and the peculiar bark of his dog; they answered them gladly, and were soon safely and warmly housed. Then David and Keeper slowly took their way homeward, for the steep, rocky hills were not easy walking for an old man in the late gloaming.

Passing a wild cairn of immense stones, Keeper suddenly began to bark furiously, and a tall, slight figure leaped from their shelter, raised a stick, and would have struck the dog if David had not called out,

"Never strie a sheep-dog, mon! The bestie willna harm ye."

The stranger then came forward; asked David if there was any cottage near where he could rest all night, said that he had come out for a day's fishing, had got separated from his companions, lost his way and was hungry and worn out.

David looked him steadily in the face and read aright the nervous manner and assumed indifference. However, hospitality is a sacred tradition among Scotch mountaineers; whoever, or whatever the young man was, David acknowledged his weariness and hunger as sufficient claim upon his oaten cake and his embers.

It was evident in a few moments that Mr. Semple was not used to the hills. David's long, firm walk was beyond the young man's efforts; he stumbled frequently in the descent, the springy step necessary when they came to the heather distressed him; he was almost afraid of the gullies David took without a thought. These things the old man noted, and they weighed far more with him than all the boastful tongue could say.

The cottage was soon reached—a very humble one—only "a but and a ben," with small windows, and a thatched roof; but Scotland has reared great men in such cottages, and no one could say that it was not

clean and cheerful. The fire burnt brightly
upon the white hearthstone, and a little
round deal table stood before it. Upon this
table were oaten cakes and Ayreshire cheese
and new milk, and by its side sat a young
man reading.

"Archie, here is a strange *gentleman* I
found up at Donald's cairn."

The two youths exchanged looks and
disliked each other. Yet Archie Scott
rose, laid aside his book, and courteously
offered his seat by the fire. The stranger
took it, eat heartily of the simple meal,
joined decently in their solemn worship,
and was soon fast asleep in Archie's bed.
Then the old man and his son sat down and
curtly exchanged their opinions.

"I don't like yon lad, fayther, and I more
than distrust his being aught o' a gentleman."

David smoked steadily a few minutes ere
he replied:

"He's eat and drank and knelt wi' us,
Archie, and it's nane o' our duty to judge
him."

When Archie spoke again it was of other
matters.

"Fayther, I'm sore troubled wi' Mac-
Allister's accounts; what wi' the sheep
bills and the timber and the kelp, things
look in a mess like. There is a right way
and a wrong way to keep tally of them and
I can't find it out."

"The right way is to keep the facts all correct and honest to a straw's worth—then the figures are bound to come right, I should say."

It was an old trouble that Archie complained about. He was MacAllister's steward, appointed by virtue of his sterling character and known worth; but struggling constantly with ignorance of the methods by which even the most honest business can alone satisfactorily prove its honest condition.

When Mr. Semple awoke next morning, Archie had disappeared, and David was standing in the door, alone. David liked his guest less in the morning than he had done at night.

"Ye dinna seem to relish your parritch, sir," said David rather grimly.

Mr. Semple said he really had never been accustomed to anything but strong tea and hot rolls, with a little kippered salmon or marmalade; he had never tasted porridge before.

"More's the pity, my lad. Maybe if you had been brought up on decent oatmeal you would hae thankit God for your food;" for Mr. Semple's omission of grace, either before or after his meat, greatly displeased the old man.

The youth yawned, sauntered to the door, and looked out. There was a fresh wind,

19

bringing with it flying showers and damp, chilling mists—wet heather under foot, and no sunshine above. David saw something in the anxious, wretched face that aroused keen suspicion. He looked steadily into Mr. Semple's pale, blue eyes, and said:

"Wha are you rinnin awa from, my lad?"

"Sir!"

There was a moment's angry silence. Suddenly David raised his hand, shaded his eyes and peered keenly down the hills. Mr. Semple followed this movement with great interest.

"What are you looking at, Mr. Scott? Oh! I see. Two men coming up this way. Do you know who they are?"

"They may be gaugers or they may be strangers, or they may be policemen—I dinna ken them mysel'."

"Mr. Scott! For God's sake, Mr. Scott! Don't give me up, and I will tell you the whole truth."

"I thought so!" said David, sternly. "Well, come up the hills wi' me; yon men will be here in ten minutes, whoever they are."

There were numerous places of partial shelter known to the shepherd, and he soon led the way to a kind of cave, pretty well concealed by overhanging rocks and trailing, briery stems

The two sat down on a rude granite powlder, and the elder having waited until his companion had regained his breath, said:

"You'll fare best wi' me, lad, if you tell the truth in as few words as may be; I dinna like fine speeches."

"Mr. Scott, I am Duncan Nevin's book-keeper and cashier. He's a tea dealer in the Gallowgate of Glasgow. I'm short in my cash, and he's a hard man, so I run away."

"Sortie, lad! Your cash dinna gang wrang o' itself. If you werna ashamed to steal it, ye needna be ashamed to confess it. Begin at the beginning."

The young man told his shameful story. He had got into gay, dissipated ways, and to meet a sudden demand had taken three pounds from his employer *for just once*. But the three pounds had swollen into sixteen, and finding it impossible to replace it, he had taken ten more and fled, hoping to hide in the hills till he could get rowed off to some passing ship and escape to America. He had no friends, and neither father nor mother. At mention of this fact, David's face relaxed.

"Puir lad!" he muttered. "Nae father, and nae mother, 'specially; that's a awfu' drawback."

"You may give me up if you like, Mr.

Scott. I don't care much; I've been a wretched fellow for many a week; I am most broken-hearted to-day."

"It's not David Scott that will make himself hard to a broken heart, when God in heaven has promised to listen to it. I'll tell you what I will do. You sall gie me all the money you have, every shilling; it's nane o' yours, ye ken that weel; and I'll take it to your master, and get him to pass by the ither till you can earn it. I've got a son, a decent, hard-working lad, who's daft to learn your trade—bookkeeping. Ye sall stay wi' me till he kens a' the ins and outs o' it, then I'll gie ye twenty pounds. I ken weel this is a big sum, and it will make a big hole in my little book at the Ayr Bank, but it will set Archie up.

"Then when ye have earned it, ye can pay back all you have stolen, forbye having four pounds left for a nest-egg to start again wi'. I dinna often treat mysel' to such a bit o' charity as this, and, 'deed, if I get na mair thanks fra heaven, than I seem like to get fra you, there 'ud be meikle use in it," for Alexander Semple had heard the proposal with a dour and thankless face, far from encouraging to the good man who made it. It did not suit that youth to work all summer in order to pay back what he had come to regard as "off his mind;" to denude himself of every shilling, and be

entirely dependent on the sternly just man
before him. Yet what could he do? He
was fully in David's power; so he signified his assent, and sullenly enough gave
up the £9 14s. 2d. in his possession.

"I'm a good bookkeeper, Mr. Scott," he
said; "the bargain is fair enough for you."

"I ken Donald Nevin; he's a Cample-
town man, and I ken you wouldna hae
keepit his books if you hadna had your
business at your finger-ends."

The next day David went to Glasgow,
and saw Mr. Semple's master. The £9 odd
was lost money found, and predisposed him
to the arrangement proposed. David got
little encouragement from Mr. Nevin, however; he acknowledged the clerk's skill in
accounts, but he was conceited of his appearance, ambitious of being a fashionable
man, had weak principles and was intensely
selfish. David almost repented him of his
kindness, and counted grudgingly the shillings that the journey and the carriage of
Mr. Semple's trunks cost him.

Indeed it was a week or two before
things settled pleasantly in the hill cottage;
the plain living, pious habits and early
hours of the shepherd and his son did not
at all suit the city youth. But Archie,
though ignorant of the reasons which kept
such a dandy in their humble home, soon
perceived clearly the benefit he could derive

from him. And once Archie got an ink-
ling of the meaning of "double entry" he
was never weary of applying it to his own
particular business; so that in a few weeks
Alexander Semple was perfectly familiar
with MacAllister's affairs.

Still, Archie cordially disliked his
teacher, and about the middle of summer it
became evident that a very serious cause of
quarrel was complicating the offence.
Coming up from MacAllister's one lovely
summer gloaming Archie met Semple with
Katie Morrison, the little girl whom he had
loved and courted since ever he carried her
dinner and slate to school for her. How
they had come to know each other he could
not tell; he had exercised all his tact and
prudence to prevent it, evidently without
avail. He passed the couple with ill-con-
cealed anger; Katie looked down, Semple
nodded in what Archie believed to be an
insolent manner.

That night David Scott heard from his
son such an outburst of anger as the lad
had never before exhibited. In a few days
Mr. Semple went to Greenock for a day or
two. Soon it was discovered that Katie
had been in Greenock two days at her married sister's. Then they heard that the
couple had married and were to sail for
America. They then discovered that
Archie's desk had been opened and £46 in

notes and gold taken. Neither of the men had any doubt as to the thief; and therefore Archie was angry and astonished to find his father doubt and waver and seem averse to pursue him. At last he acknowledged all, told Archie that if he made known his loss, *he also* must confess that he had knowingly harbored an acknowledged thief, and tacitly given him the opportunity of wronging his employer. He doubted very much whether anyone would give him credit for the better feelings which had led him to this course of conduct.

Archie's anger cooled at once; he saw the dilemma; to these simple people a good name was better than gold. It took nearly half the savings of a long life, but the old man went to Ayr and drew sufficient to replace the stolen money. He needed to make no inquiries about Semple. On Tuesday it was known by everyone in the village that Katie Morrison and Alexander Semple had been married the previous Friday, and sailed for America the next day. After this certainty father and son never named the subject but once more. It was on one calm, spring evening, some ten years after, and David lay within an hour of the grave.

"Archie!" he said, suddenly, "I don't regret to-night what I did ten years ago. Virtuous actions sometimes fail, but virtuous lives—never! Perhaps I had a thought o' self in my good intent, and that spoiled all. If thou hast ever a chance, do better than I did."

"I will, father."

During these ten years there had been occasional news from the exiles. Mrs. Morrison stopped Archie at intervals, as he passed her door, and said there had been a letter from Katie. At first they came frequently, and were tinged with brightest hopes. Alexander had a fine place, and their baby was the most beautiful in the world. The next news was that Alexander was in business for himself and making money rapidly. Handsome presents, that were the wonder of the village, then came occasionally, and also remittances of money that made the poor mother hold her head proudly about "our Katie" and her "splendid house and carriage."

But suddenly all letters stopped, and the mother thought for long they must be coming to see her, but this hope and many another faded, and the fair morning of Katie's marriage was shrouded in impenetrable gloom and mystery.

Archie got bravely over his trouble, and a while after his father's death married a good little woman, not quite without "the bit of siller." Soon after he took his savings to Edinburgh and joined his wife's

brother in business there. Things prospered with him, slowly but surely, and he
became known for a steady, prosperous
merchant, and a douce pious householder,
the father of a fine lot of sons and
daughters.

One night, twenty years after the beginning of my story, he was passing through
the old town of Edinburgh, when a wild
cry of "Fire! Fire! Fire!" arose on every
side of him.

"Where?" he asked of the shrieking
women pouring from all the filthy, narrow
wynds around.

"In Gordon's Wynd."

He was there almost the first of any
efficient aid, striving to make his way up
the smoke-filled stairs, but this was impossible. The house was one of those ancient
ones, piled story upon story; so old that it
was almost tinder. But those on the opposite side were so close that not unfre-
quently a plank or two flung across from
opposite windows made a bridge for the
benefit of those seeking to elude justice.

By means of such a bridge all the in-
habitants of the burning house were removed, and no one was more energetic in
carrying the women and children across the
dangerous planks than Archie Scott; for
his mountain training had made such a feat
one of no extraordinary danger to him.

Satisfied at length that all life was out of
risk, he was turning to go home, when a
white, terrible face looked out of the top-
most floor, showing itself amid the gusts of
smoke like the dream of a corpse, and
screaming for help in agonizing tones.
Archie knew that face only too well. But
he remembered, in the same instant, what
his father had said in dying, and, swift as
a mountain deer, he was quickly on the top
floor of the opposite house again.

In a few moments the planks bridged the
distance between death and safety; but no
entreaties could make the man risk the
dangerous passage. Setting tight his lips,
Archie went for the shrieking coward, and
carried him into the opposite house. Then
the saved man recognized his preserver.

"Oh, Mr. Scott!" he said, "for God's
sake, my wife and my child! The last of
seven!"

"You scoundrel! Do you mean to say
you saved yourself before Katie and your
child!"

Archie did not wait for the answer; again
he was at the window of the burning room.
Too late! The flames were already devour-
ing what the smoke had smothered; their
wretched pallet was a funeral pyre. He
had hardly time to save his own life.

"They are dead, Semple!"

Then the poor creature burst into a

paroxysm of grief, moaned and cried, and begged a few shillings, and vowed he was the most miserable creature on earth.

After this Archie Scott strove for two years to do without taint of selfishness what his father had begun twenty years before. But there was not much now left to work upon—health, honor, self-respect were all gone. Poor Semple was content to eat the bread of dependence, and then make boastful speeches of his former wealth and position. To tell of his wonderful schemes, and to abuse his luck and his false friends, and everything and everybody, but the real cause of his misfortune.

Archie gave him some trifling post, with a salary sufficient for every decent want, and never heeded, though he knew Semple constantly spoke ill of him behind his back.

However the trial of Archie's patience and promise did not last very long. It was a cold, snowy night in mid-winter that Archie was called upon to exercise for the last time his charity and forbearance toward him; and the parting scene paid for all. For, in the shadow of the grave, the poor, struggling soul dropped all pretences, acknowledged all its shortcomings, thanked the forbearance and charity which had been extended so many years, and humbly repented of its lost and wasted opportunities.

"Draw close to me, Archie Scott," he

said, "and tell your four brave boys what my dying words to them were: Never to yield to temptation for *only this once*. To be quite sure that all the gear and gold that *comes with sin* will *go with sorrow*. And never to doubt that to every *evil doer* will certainly come his *evil day*."

PETRALTO'S LOVE STORY.

I am addicted to making strange friendships, to liking people whom I have no conventional authority to like—people out of "my set," and not always of my own nationality. I do not say that I have always been fortunate in these ventures; but I have had sufficient splendid exceptions to excuse the social aberration, and make me think that all of us might oftener trust our own instincts, oftener accept the friends that circumstance and opportunity offer us, with advantage. At any rate, the peradventure in chance associations has always been very attractive to me.

In some irregular way I became acquainted with Petralto Garcia. I believe I owed the introduction to my beautiful hound, Lutha; but, at any rate, our first conversation was quite as sensible as if we had gone through the legitimate initiation. I know it was in the mountains, and that within an hour our tastes and sympathies had touched each other at twenty different points.

Lutha walked beside us, showing in his mien something of the proud satisfaction which follows a conviction of having done a good thing. He looked first at me and then at Petralto, elevating and depressing his ears at our argument, as if he understood all about it. Perhaps he did; human beings don't know everything.

People have so much time in the country that it is little wonder that our acquaintance ripened into friendship during the holidays, and that one of my first visits when I had got settled for the winter was to Petralto's rooms. Their locality might have cooled some people, but not me. It does not take much of an education in New York life to find out that the pleasantest, loftiest, handsomest rooms are to be found in the streets not very far "up town;" comfortably contiguous to the best hotels, stores, libraries, picture galleries, and all the other necessaries of a pleasant existence.

He was just leaving the door for a ride in the park, and we went together. I had refused the park twice within an hour, and had told myself that nothing should induce me to follow that treadmill procession again, yet when he said, in his quiet way, "You had better take half an hour's ride, Jack," I felt like going, and I went.

Now just as we got to the Fifth Avenue entrance, a singular thing happened. Petralto's pale olive face flushed a bright crimson, his eyes flashed and dropped; he whipped the horse into a furious gallop, as if he would escape something; then became preternaturally calm, drew suddenly up, and stood waiting for a handsome equipage which was approaching. Its occupants were bending forward to speak to him. I had no eyes for the gentleman, the girl at his side was so radiantly beautiful.

I heard Petralto promise to call on them, and we passed on; but there was a look on his face which bespoke both sympathy and silence. He soon complained of the cold, said the park pace irritated him, but still passed and repassed the couple who had caused him such evident suffering, as if he was determined to inure himself to the pain of meeting them. During this interval I had time to notice the caressing, lover-like attitude of the beauty's companion, and I said, as they entered a stately house together, ''Are they married?''

''Yes.''

''He seems devotedly in love with her.''

''He loved her two years before he saw her.''

''Impossible.''

''Not at all. I have a mind to tell you the story.''

''Do. Come home with me, and we will have a quiet dinner together.''

''No. I need to be alone an hour or two. Call on me about nine o'clock.''

Petralto's rooms were a little astonishment to me. They were luxurious in the extreme, with just that excess of ornament which suggests under-civilization; and yet I found him smoking in a studio destitute of everything but a sleepy-looking sofa, two or three capacious lounging chairs, and the ordinary furniture of an artist's atelier. There was a bright fire in the grate, a flood of light from the numerous gas jets, and an atmosphere heavy with the seductive, fragrant vapor of Havana.

I lit my own cigar, made myself comfortable, and waited until it was Petralto's pleasure to begin. After a while he said, "Jack, turn that easel so that you can see the picture on it."

I did so.

"Now, look at it well, and tell me what you see; first, the locality—describe it."

" A dim old wood, with sunlight sifting through thick foliage, and long streamers of weird grey moss. The ground is covered with soft short grass of an intense green, and there are wonderful flowers of wonderful colors."

"Right. It is an opening in the forest of the Upper Guadalupe. Now, what else do you see?"

"A small pony, saddled and bridled, feeding quietly, and a young girl standing on tip-toe, pulling down a vine loaded with golden-colored flowers."

"Describe the girl to me."

I turned and looked at my querist. He was smoking, with shut eyes, and waiting calmly for my answer. "Well, she has— Petralto, what makes you ask me? You might paint, but it is impossible to describe *light;* and the girl is nothing else. If I had met her in such a wood, I should have thought she was an angel, and been afraid of her."

"No angel, Jack, but a most exquisite, perfect flower of maidenhood. When I first saw her, she stood just so, with her open palms full of yellow jasmine. I laid my heart into them, too, my whole heart, my whole life, and every joy and hope it contained."

"What were you doing in Texas?"

"What are you doing in New York? I was born in Texas. My family, an old Spanish one, have been settled there since they helped to build San Antonio in 1730. I grew up pretty much as Texan youths do—half my time in the saddle, familiar with the worst side of life and the best side of nature. I should have been a thorough Ishmaelite if I had not been an artist; but the artistic instinct conquered the nomadic and in my twentieth year I went to Rome to study.

"I can pass the next five years. I do not pretend to regret them, though, perhaps, you would say I simply wasted time and opportunity. I enjoyed them, and it seems to me I was the person most concerned in the matter. I had a fresh, full capacity then for enjoyment of every kind. I loved nature and I loved art. I warmed both hands at the glowing fire of life. Time may do his worst. I have been happy, and I can throw those five careless, jovial years in his face to my last hour.

"But one must awake out of every pleasant dream, and one day I got a letter urging my immediate return home. My father had got himself involved in a lawsuit, and was failing rapidly in health. My younger brother was away with a ranger company, and the affairs of the ranch needed authoritative overlooking. I was never so fond of art as to be indifferent to our family prosperity, and I lost no time in hurrying West.

"Still, when I arrived at home, there was no one to welcome me! The noble, gracious Garcia slept with his ancestors in the old Alamo Church; somewhere on the llano my brother was ranging, still with his wild company; and the house, in spite of the family servants and Mexican peons, was sufficiently lonely. Yet I was astonished to find how easily I went back to my old life, and spent whole days in the saddle investigating the affairs of the Garcia ranch.

"I had been riding one day for ten hours, and was so fatigued that I determined to spend the night with one of my herdsmen. He had a little shelter under some fine pecan trees on the Guadalupe, and after a cup of coffee and a meal of dried beef, I sauntered with my cigar down the river bank. Then the cool, dusky shadows of the wood tempted me. I entered it. It was an enchanted wood, for there stood Jessy Lorimer, just as I had painted her.

"I did not move nor speak. I watched her, spell-bound. I had not even the power, when she had mounted her pony and was coming toward me, to assume another attitude. She saw that I had been watching her, and a look, half reproachful and half angry, came for a moment into her face. But she inclined her head to me as she passed, and then went off at a rapid gallop before I could collect my senses.

"Some people, Jack, walk into love with their eyes open, calculating every step. I tumbled in over head, lost my feet, lost my senses, narrowed in one moment the whole world down to one bewitching woman. I did not know her, of course; but I soon should. I was well aware she could not live very far away, and that my herd must

be able to give me some information.   I
was so deeply in love that this poor ignorant fellow, knowing something about this
girl, seemed to me to be a person to be
respected, and even envied.

"I gave him immediately a plentiful
supply of cigars, and sitting down beside
him opened the conversation with horses,
but drifted speedily into the subject of new
settlers.

" 'Were there any since I had left?'

" 'Two or three, no 'count travelers, one
likely family.'

" 'Much of a family?'

" 'You may bet on that, sir.'

" 'Any pleasant young men?'

" 'Reckon so.   Mighty likely young
gal.'

"So, bit by bit, I found that Mr. Lorimer, my beauty's father, was a Scotchman,
who had bought the ranch which had for-
merly belonged to the old Spanish family
of the Yturris.   Then I remembered pretty
Inez and Dolores Yturri, with their black
eyes, olive skins and soft, lazy *embonpoint ;*
and thought of golden-haired Jessy Lorimer
in their dark, latticed rooms.

"Jack, turn the picture to me.   Beautiful
Jessy!   How I loved her in those happy
days that followed.   How I humored her
grave, stern father and courted her brothers
for her sake!   I was a slave to the whole

family, so that I might gain an hour with or a smile from Jessy. Do I regret it now? Not one moment. Such delicious hours as we had together were worth any price. I would throw all my future to old Time, Jack, only to live them over again.''

''That is a great deal to say, Petralto.''

''Perhaps; and yet I will not recall it. In those few months everything that was good in me prospered and grew. Jessy brought out nothing but the best part of my character. I was always at my best with her. No thought of selfish pleasure mingled in my love for her. If it delighted me to touch her hand, to feel her soft hair against my cheek, to meet her earnest, subduing gaze, it also made me careful by no word or look to soil the dainty purity of my white lily.

''I feared to tell her that I loved her. But I did do it, I scarcely know how. The softest whisper seemed too loud against her glowing cheek. She trembled from head to foot. I was faint and silent with rapture when she first put her little hand in mine, and suffered me to draw her to my heart. Ah! I am sick with joy yet when I think of it. I—I first, I alone, woke that sweet young heart to life. She is lost, lost to me, but no one else can ever be to her what I have been.''

And here Petralto, giving full sway to his

impassioned Southern nature, covered his
face with his hands and wept hot, regretful
tears.

Tears come like blood from men of cold,
strong temperaments, but they were the
natural relief of Petralto's.   I let him
weep.   In a few minutes he leaped up,
and began pacing the room rapidly as he
went on:

"Mr. Lorimer received my proposal with
a dour, stiff refusal that left me no hope of
any relenting.   'He had reasons, more
than one,' he said; 'he was not saying
anything against either my Spanish blood or
my religion; but it was no fault in a Scots-
man to mate his daughter with people of her
own kith.'

"There was no quarrel, and no dis-
courtesy; but I saw I could bend an iron
bar with my pleadings just as soon as his
determination.   Jessy received orders not
to meet me or speak to me alone; and the
possibility of disobeying her father's command never suggested itself to her.   Even
I struggled long with my misery before I
dared to ask her to practice her first deceit.

"She would not meet me alone, but she
persuaded her mother to come once with
her to our usual tryst in the wood.   Mrs.
Lorimer spoke kindly but hopelessly, and
covered her own face to weep while Jessy
and I took of each other a passionate

farewell. I promised her then never to marry anyone else; and she!—I thought her heart would break as I laid her almost fainting in her mother's arms.

"Yet I did not know how much Jessy really was to me until I suddenly found out that her father had sent her back to Scotland, under the pretence of finishing her education. I had been so honorably considerate of Jessy's Puritan principles that I felt this hasty, secret movement exceedingly unkind and unjust. Guadalupe became hateful to me, the duties of the ranch distracting; and my brother Felix returning about this time, we made a division of the estate. He remained at the Garcia mansion, I rented out my possessions, and went, first to New Orleans, and afterward to New York.

"In New York I opened a studio, and one day a young gentleman called and asked me to draw a picture from some crude, imperfect sketch which a friend had made. During the progress of the picture he frequently called in. For some reason or other—probably because we were each other's antipodes in tastes and temperament—he became my enthusiastic admirer, and interested himself greatly to secure me a lucrative patronage.

"Yet some subtle instinct, which I cannot pretend to divine or explain, constantly warned me to beware of this man. But I was ashamed and angry at myself for linking even imaginary evil with so frank and generous a nature. I defied destiny, turned a deaf ear to the whisperings of my good genius, and continued the one-sided friendship—for I never even pretended to myself that I had any genuine liking for the man.

"One day, when we had become very familiar, he ran up to see me about something, I forget what, and not finding me in the outer apartments, penetrated to my private room. There, upon that easel, Will Lennox first saw the woman you saw with him to-night—the picture which you are now looking at—and he fell as desperately in love with it, in his way, as I had done in the Guadalupe woods with the reality. I cannot tell you how much it cost me to restrain my anger. He, however, never noticed I was angry. He had but one object now—to gain from me the name and residence of the original.

"It was no use to tell him it was a fancy picture, that he was sighing for an imagination. He never believed it for a moment. I would not sell it, I would not copy it, I would not say where I had painted it; I kept it to my most sacred privacy. He was sure that the girl existed, and that I knew where she lived. He was very rich, without an occupation or an object, and Jessy's pure, lovely face haunted him day and night, and supplied him with a purpose.

"He came to me one day and offering me a large sum of money, asked me finally to reveal at least the locality of which I had painted the picture. His free, frank unembarrassed manner compels me to believe that he had no idea of the intolerable insult he was perpetrating. He had always been accustomed to consider more or less money an equivalent for all things under the sun. But you, Jack, will easily understand that the offer was followed by some very angry words, and that his threat to hunt the world over to find my beauty was not without fear to me.

"I heard soon after that Will Lennox had gone to the South. I had neither hidden nor talked about my former life and I was ignorant of how much he knew or did not know of it. He could trace me easily to New Orleans; how much further would depend upon his tact and perseverance. Whether he reached Guadalupe or no, I am uncertain, but my heart fell with a strange presentiment of sorrow when I saw his name, a few weeks afterward, among the European departures.

"The next thing I knew of Will Lennox was his marriage to some famous Scotch beauty. Jack, do you not perceive the rest? The Scotch beauty was Jessy Lorimer. I feared it at the first. I knew it this afternoon."

"Will you call there?"

"I have no power to resist it. Did you not notice how eagerly she pressed the invitation?"

"Do not accept it, Petralto."

He shook his head, and remained silent. The next afternoon I was astonished on going up to his rooms to find Will Lennox sitting there. He was talking in that loud, happy, demonstrative way so natural to men accustomed to have the whole world minister unto them.

He did not see how nervous and angry Petralto was under his easy, boastful conversation. He did not notice the ashy face, the blazing eyes, the set lips, the trembling hands, of the passionate Spanish nature, until Petralto blazed out in a torrent of unreasonable words and taunts, and ordered Lennox out of his presence.

Even then the stupid, good-natured, purse-proud man could not see his danger. He began to apologize to me for Petralto's rudeness, and excuse "anything in a fellow whom he had cut out so badly."

"Liar!" Petralto retorted. "She loved me first; you can never have her whole heart. Begone! If I had you on the Guadalupe, where Jessy and I lived and loved, I would—"

The sentence was not finished. Lennox struck Petralto to the ground, and before I raised him, I persuaded the angry bridegroom to retire. I stayed with Petralto that night, although I was not altogether pleased with him. He was sulky and silent at first, but after a quiet rest and a few consoling Havanas he was willing to talk the affair over.

"Lennox tortured me," he said, passionately. "How could he be so unfeeling, so mad, as to suppose I should care to learn what chain of circumstances led him to find out my love and then steal her? Everything he said tortured me but one fact—Jessy was alone and thoroughly miserable. Poor little pet! She thought I had forgotten her, and so she married him—not for love; I won't believe it."

"But," I said, "Petralto, you have no right to hug such a delusion; and seeing that you had made no attempt to follow Jessy and marry her, she had every right to suppose you really had forgotten her. Besides, I think it very likely that she should love a young, rich, good-looking fellow like Will Lennox."

"In not pursuing her I was following Jessy's own request and obeying my own plighted promise. It was understood between us that I should wait patiently until Jessy was twenty-one. Even Scotch customs would then have regarded her as her own mistress and acknowledged her right to marry as she desired; and if I did not write, she has not wanted constant tokens of my remembrance. I have trusted her," he said, mournfully, "without a sign from her."

That winter the beauty of Mrs. Lennox and the devotion of her hubsand were on every tongue. But married is not mated, and the best part of Jessy Lorimer's beauty had never touched Will Lennox. Her pure, simple, poetic temperament he had never understood, and he felt in a dim, uncertain way that the noblest part of his wife escaped him.

He could not enter into her feelings, and her spiritual superiority unconsciously irritated him. Jessy had set her love's first music to the broad, artistic heart of Petralto; she could not, without wronging herself, decline to a lower range of feelings and a narrower heart. This reserve of herself was not a conscious one. She was not one of those self-involved women always studying their own emotions; she was simply true to the light within her. But her way was not Will Lennox's way, her finer fancies and lighter thoughts were mysteries to his grosser nature.

So the thing happened which always has and always will happen in such cases; when the magic and the enchantment of Jessy's great personal beauty had lost their first novelty and power, she gradually became to her husband—"Something better than his dog, a little dearer than his horse."

I did not much blame Will Lennox. It is very hard to love what we do not comprehend. A wife who could have sympathized in his pursuits, talked over the chances of his "Favorite," or gone to sea with him in his yacht, would always have found Will an indulgent and attentive husband. But fast horses did not interest Jessy, and going to sea made her ill; so gradually these two fell much further apart than they ought to have done.

Now, if Petralto had been wicked and Jessy weak, he might have revenged himself on the man and woman who had wrought him so much suffering. But he had set his love far too high to sully her white name; and Jessy, in that serenity which comes of lofty and assured principles, had no idea of the possibility of her injuring her husband by a wrong thought. Yet instinctively they both sought to keep apart; and if by chance they met, the grave courtesy of the one and the sweet dignity of the other left nothing for evil hopes or thoughts to feed upon. One morning, two years after Jessy's marriage, I received a note from Petralto, asking me to call upon him immediately. To my amazement, his rooms were dismantled, his effects packed up, and he was on the point of leaving New York.

"Whither bound?" I asked. "To Rome?"

"No; to the Guadalupe. I want to try what nature can do for me. Art, society, even friendship, fail at times to comfort me for my lost love. I will go back to nature, the great, sweet mother and lover of men."

So Petralto went out of New York; and the world that had known him forgot him—forgot even to wonder about, much less to regret, him.

I was no more faithful than others. I fell in with a wonderful German philosopher, and got into the "entities" and "non-entities," forgot Petralto in Hegel, and felt rather ashamed of the days when I lounged and trifled in the artist's pleasant rooms. I was "enamored of divine philosophy," took no more interest in polite gossip, and did not waste my time reading newspapers. In fact, with Kant and Fichte before me, I did not feel that I had the time lawfully to spare.

Therefore, anyone may imagine my astonishment when, about three years after Petralto's departure from New York, he one morning suddenly entered my study, handsome as Apollo and happy as a bridegroom. I have used the word "groom" very happily, for I found out in a few minutes that Petralto's radiant condition was, in fact, the condition of a bridegroom.

Of course, under the circumstances, I could not avoid feeling congratulatory; and my affection for the handsome, loving fellow came back so strongly that I resolved to break my late habits of seclusion, and go to the Brevoort House and see his bride.

I acknowledge that in this decision there was some curiosity. I wondered what rare woman had taken the beautiful Jessy Lorimer's place; and I rather enjoyed the prospect of twitting him with his protestations of eternal fidelity to his first love.

I did not do it. I had no opportunity. Madame Petralto Garcia was, in fact, Jessy Lorimer Lennox. Of course I understood at once that Will must be dead; but I did not learn the particulars until the next day, when Petralto dropped in for a quiet smoke and chat. Not unwillingly I shut my book and lit my cigar.

"'All's well that ends well,' my dear fellow," I said, when we had both smoked silently for a few moments; "but I never heard of Will Lennox's death. I hope he did not come to the Guadalupeand get shot."

Petralto shook his head and replied: "I was always sorry for that threat. Will never meant to injure me. No. He was drowned at sea two years ago. His yacht was caught in a storm, he ventured too near the shore, and all on board perished.''

''I did not hear of it at the time.''

''Nor I either. I will tell you how I heard. About a year ago I went, as was my frequent custom, to the little open glade in the forest where I had first seen Jessy. As I lay dreaming on the warm soft grass I saw a beautiful woman, clothed in black, walk slowly toward the very same jasmine vine, and standing as of old on tip-toe, pull down a loaded branch. Can you guess how my heart beat, how I leaped to my feet and cried out before I knew what I was doing, 'Jessy! darling Jessy!' She stood quite still, looking toward me. Oh, how beautiful she was! And when at length we clasped hands, and I gazed into her eyes, I knew without a word that my love had come to me.''

''She had waited a whole year?''

''True; I liked her the better for that. After Will's death she went to Scotland— put both herself and me out of temptation. She owed this much to the memory of a man who had loved her as well as he was capable of doing. But I know how happy were the steps that brought her back to the Guadalupe, and that warm spring afternoon under the jasmine vine paid for all. I am the happiest man in all the wide world.''